BLOOD
OF
KINGS

BY

STEPHANIE HUDSON

Blood of Kings
The Transfusion Saga #3
Copyright © 2020 Stephanie Hudson
Published by Hudson Indie Ink
www.hudsonindieink.com

Blood of Kings/Stephanie Hudson – 2nd ed.
ISBN-13 - 978-1-913769-38-3

This book is dedicated to the all the people affected in the terrible Australian bushfires, that so far has taken lives, destroyed homes, burned millions of hectares and decimated hundreds of millions of animals. It goes out to the thousands upon thousands of volunteers that banded together to try and stop the flames and help those in need.

Your kindness, selflessness and strength, is what makes the world a better place.

You will forever be in my heart.

WARNING

This book contains explicit sexual content, some graphic language and a highly additive dominate Vampire King.

This book has been written by an UK Author with a mad sense of humour. Which means the following story contains a mixture of Northern English slang, dialect, regional colloquialisms and other quirky spellings that have been intentionally included to make the story and dialogue more realistic for modern day characters.

Thanks for reading x

PROLOGUE

'My *Šemšā'... my Šemšā... Še...mšā'*

I heard these words playing over and over in my mind, like a whispered chant. A desperate prayer, spoken from a desperate man, who I knew was currently on his knees speaking directly to the Gods asking them to save my soul.

His first one spoken in over two thousand years...

'Save my Šemšā, that's all I fucking ask!' he growled, shouting this last part as he hammered his fist down on the floor, and in that single moment, the image of him on his knees disappeared and a blinding light replaced it. It erupted all around me, with me at its centre, as if something in me had just exploded!

My eyes snapped open just to find branches of light penetrating the water like the sun had just breached the clouds. I didn't know what was happening or if it wasn't just in my mind, but something made me realise I needed to move. It felt as though I had just died and was being jolted back to life, being given a second chance. Which meant it was now my job not to blow it and drown as I was still floating in the water. So, pushing my mind into action, I forced my pained limbs to move until desperate action was taking over and I started dragging myself up towards the surface.

Finally, I burst up out of the water and dragged in great lung filling gasps that hurt my chest and I knew if I hadn't been desperate for the air, I would have forced myself to stop already. I was also freezing and knew that if I didn't get out the water soon, then something else would take my life other than drowning. But of course, that's what happens when you fall half naked from a helicopter into a river in the middle of winter!

And speaking of which, the second I heard a thundering crash I spun in the water in time to see an explosion in the distance amongst the trees, with flames and smoke now bellowing above the tree line. And even as my teeth chattered and I was barely still able to tread water, I still found myself smiling and with only one satisfying thought in my mind...

They were right...*they couldn't fly.*

CHAPTER ONE

AMELIA

THIS MEANS WAR

'*T*o *line up to the ring, for a battle that you can't win, swing as hard as you can swing, it will still mean nothing. Should've seen it coming, it had to happen sometime. But you went and brought a knife, to an all-out gunfight*'. These were the lyrics I was currently listening to just as I punched one guy, knocking him out with an instant break to his nose. The next, I dodged his swing by side stepping before delivering a gut punch, seeing him fall to his knees gasping for air.

Thank you, Nickleback.

But wait, I am getting way ahead of myself. So, rewinding ten minutes and that took me right back to swimming my freezing ass to the riverbank, after just witnessing the helicopter crashing into a nearby woodland area at the side of the river.

After dragging myself up a riverbank, clawing my way up a fallen tree like some damn wet cat, I found a dirt track that didn't look overly used by the public. I pulled my now loose hair to one side and arched my neck to the side so I could ring it out with my hands, taking care that the freezing cold drips didn't hit my skin. Because really, even saving my already freezing skin from further discomfort was worth the pain it caused my stomach.

But feeling this pain made me take time to go over my injuries. I pressed a hand to my stomach and hissed in pain, knowing that the kick I had received had been hard enough to bruise. So, I took in a big breath and was at least rewarded with the knowledge it hadn't broken any ribs, so joy for small mercies. I also looked down and saw the bruise to my elbow and also one down my thigh on the left side where I had fallen when taking down the second guy in the bedroom. Along with those I also had lacerations on my hands from where the wire had cut into my palms. And as for my face, well I wasn't even going there, but hey, at least I hadn't lost my contact lenses, or this would have been the shit fest to beat all shit fests.

Well, I think it was safe to refer to this as hitting rock bottom, so I gathered there was only one way up to go from here. Besides, I had survived, I was no longer a pawn to use by the bad guys and although bruised, I was at least in one piece, minus the shoes and dress.

And with a glance to the smoke bellowing from the tops of the trees in the distance, I was definitely classing this one as a win, especially when I looked up to see a massive highway bridge above me. This instantly gave me hope that I might have a chance in getting back to the city without too much of a problem. Well, that was if I didn't die of hyperthermia first. Because I had to say, as much as I had been a fan of Liessa's choice of underwear for me, I wasn't exactly loving it right now! No, now I wished I had opted for full body long johns, as I was basically wearing a strapless swimming costume. But, considering where I had just crawled out from, then maybe it was better than just a bra and panties. Either way, I was fucking cold!

Oh, and did I mention I was also killing mad! Like seriously furious, just thinking about the entire night and basically how my first date with Lucius had been ruined! So, walking barefoot, freezing my ass off and nearly naked on a dirt track wasn't exactly my idea of fun. But what made it even less so was the gang of assholes I could see gathered under a walkway bridge.

There were four of them all with dirt bikes parked, music pumping from some palm sized speaker and two of them were spray painting the wall with graffiti. Oh, and they were passing around a spliff longer than my middle finger. Great, that's all I needed, a gang of stoners whose favorite pastime was painting the streets of Munich with their own shit brand of art. I mean what did that say, 'pussy' in German, perfect...

Just. Fucking. Perfect!

Just to top off my perfect fucking day!

The one whose turn it was with the spliff saw me coming first, a skinny guy dressed in leather pants and a ripped, long sleeved Rammstein shirt. He smacked the guy nearest to him on the shoulder before nodding in my direction. Now, what were the chances of these four not being assholes and this not ending up in a fight...umm, the weed and whisky bottle didn't give me much hope. Oh well, I was itching to break something anyway...or should I say, *someone.*

But hey, it's not like I just walked up to the first guy and punched him...well, not until he said,

"Schau, wir haben eine Schlampe zum Ficken gefunden" Which I knew translated into, 'Look, we found a bitch to fuck'.

Then I did, but not until I replied,

"Not tonight, asshole, you just found a bitch!" This before walking straight up to him and punching him in the face. Which brought me back to Nickleback singing about war.

The first guy dropped to the floor holding his now blood streaming nose, mumbling something in German I couldn't be bothered to try and translate. Then, after putting the second guy down, who was soon like his friend, cradling a part of his anatomy, the other two watched on looking panicked.

"Now, let us try this another way, I have had the mother of bad fucking days and really feel like murdering someone, and really, at this point anyone will do, so unless you leather clad string beans fancy your chances, then here is what is going to happen..." the next part came in German, because really, it was the bit I really needed them to understand right now. Of course, it was just a shame that when I finally did get to say one of the coolest movie lines in history, one that every Arnie fan dreams of saying in real life, it was a shame I had no choice but to first say it in German.

But translated it sounded a little something like this...

'I need your clothes, your boots and your motorcycle.'

So, two minutes later, and I found myself wearing skinny guy's leather pants, (rolled up at the ankles) biker boots (three sizes too big), a Led Zeppelin T shirt (that I knotted at the side to make it fit me) and skinny man's leather jacket, that actually fit me pretty well, thanks to the boobs that managed to fill it out.

I had also grabbed the smallest helmet, a rucksack in case it had anything useful in it, and the best looking bike. Well, this was after twisting the keys out of the owners hand, which meant breaking his wrist first. Because, well I wasn't in the mood to be bitch slapped like he tried to do first.

I also stole the guy's phone who, after hearing his buddy's wrist bone crack, was willing to give me anything I wanted. But seeing as I wasn't in the market for first borns or kidneys, I told him the phone would do.

Then I picked up the spliff, and because I was embracing my inner bad ass, I inhaled a drag, thinking it would look cool. Unfortunately, this was me we were talking about, so my cool, inner bad ass only extending to kicking ass, meaning I just ended up coughing as though I was choking, before telling them,

"Now this shit will kill ya!" Then I unlocked the guy's phone, found his Spotify account that was linked to the speaker, and tapped in the only song that had to be heard right in that moment.

Then I twisted up my hair and winced as I pushed on my helmet, thanks to my bruised face and lump on the back of my head. Once ready, I kicked up the stand to the shitty dirt bike I had no choice but to ride. And I did this all to the sound of no other than…

'Bad to the Bone' by George Thorogood and the Destroyers.

I started up the Kawasaki KLX250, kicking up the dirt around me as I headed in the direction of where I had seen the helicopter go down, unable to resist the urge to say aloud,

"It's been fun guys, but now it's time to...*Get to the chopper!*" Then I giggled to myself which was lost over the sound of the shitty old two stroke engine. Gods, but I was going to stink of bike fumes by the time I got to where I was going, but then again, I was on my way to a crash site, so really if anything I was simply going to blend with the stench.

Now why wasn't I on my way back to Transfusion you might ask? Well, it was simple, as I gathered by now they had informed Lucius they had me and would simply hold me to ransom until he handed over the box...*the real one this time.* Which meant that by the time I made it back to the club, I would most likely already be too late to stop him from falling for whatever contingency plan they had conjured up. One they would have had no choice to do seeing as I hadn't yet shown up.

Meaning that my only hope left was to find the wreck and hide whilst I waited for the bad guys to show up. That way I could hopefully discover their plan, follow them to wherever their hide-out was and get to Lucius before he had chance to make what he thought was an exchange. Who knows, maybe if I was really lucky, then I would get a chance at intercepting him before he got there.

Well, this was my plan anyway, and despite Lucius' stern belief that I couldn't be trusted to make these kind of decisions, I knew that this was the best one we had.

Besides, my decision to switch the boxes had been pretty spot on.

So, with this decision already made, I travelled along the dirt road that ran alongside the river, one I remembered was named Isar, from what I had overheard being said in the helicopter. Of course, it helped enormously having a great bellowing plume of smoke to follow and even though the bike was old and crappy, it did the job quite well in getting there in between all the dirt tracks that weaved throughout the thicket of trees.

I was just thankful I knew how to ride and unlike firing a gun earlier, doing what I was doing now wasn't my first rodeo. Of course, this was thanks to my Uncle Vincent who was as into bikes as my dad was into cars. Meaning that after much convincing and admittedly when my parents were out of town, my uncle Vince taught me how to ride. And thank the shiny happy chrome Gods that he did, as otherwise, this bad ass biker chick look I had going on would have looked similar to Ragnar wearing a pink tutu and doing ballet.

But instead of swerving all over the place before crashing into some tree, I actually made it there in one piece. But then I also knew it was probably wise not to get too close. As I stopped my bike, skidding side-on the second I saw that the bad guys had already beaten me to the crash site. Which meant I was now faced with a convoy of blacked out off roaders, and even more mercenaries. I mean jeez, where did they keep getting these guys, 'Ebay for ex-military'? Was there like some app for your phone out there for bad guys, like dating with profiles, list of accomplishments, hobbies, pictures and shit?

I could see it now…

'Likes to take long walks on the beach after a long day of kidnapping, murdering and blowing up shit. Hobbies include reading about evil dictators, fertilizing the garden with dead bodies and sharpening blades by a warm fire whilst watching Rambo with that special person.'

"Hey, move along asshole, this isn't a fucking show!" I jumped the second I heard someone behind me and then felt the back of my helmet being smacked, causing me to wince in pain. This was thanks to the lump there from where that bitch had shot me with a tranquilizer and I had fallen backwards. And well this, along with a bruised face that was currently being smushed into a fucking helmet, wasn't exactly what I would have called a fun time.

But then again, at least it was all black and currently hid the fact that the person they would have been looking for was staring them right in the face. So, it was a little more than satisfying when I heard him say into a radio,

"Nah, just some punk kid that's gonna get his ass kicked if he doesn't fuck off." I actually smiled at this before starting back up the bike and making my way past the wreckage going as slow as I could. There must have been about twenty guys, all stationed around it, making me wonder why the cops hadn't arrived yet? It wasn't as if a helicopter crash would have been missed, not being so close to the city.

However, my question was soon answered, but first I drove off in the opposite direction and into the tree line. Then, once I knew I was out of site, I ditched the bike and started backtracking through the cover of the trees. It also helped that it was dark and I had the movements of their flashlights to follow.

So, thankfully, I managed to stay hidden and thanks to the smoke that clogged the air near the crash site, well then, I managed to get close enough to see what was going on. The helicopter was a crumpled mess of twisted and burnt metal and I couldn't help but suck in a shuddered breath, just thinking how risky my actions had been just to escape. Gods, but just knowing that I could have ended up in that wreck was enough to make me suddenly want to be sick, and in the end, I could barely get my helmet off quick enough before I did in fact hurl.

Thankfully, I wasn't heard as there was too much going on with the wreckage to hear, which included the bent and twisted propeller that came crashing to the ground making everyone shift further back. I watched as an older man emerged from one of the many vehicles and despite being dressed the same as the others, he held an air of importance like armour. This told me even before he spoke that he was about to start issuing orders. And I was right.

"Right, ten minutes people and the authorities will be here, as they can't be delayed any longer, so start moving out. Echo team, you know what to do, erase all evidence. Carter, get him on the phone, he will want to plan our next…"

"Sarge! We've got something!" This came from a man who barely even let the car he had been in come to a complete stop before he was out of it and running to who I assumed was his Sergeant. He cut the guy off, who was obviously put in charge of this shit show and when I saw what he now held in his hand I gasped, knowing why he thought it so important…

They had found my dress.

"Oh shit," I whispered knowing that having any evidence of me right now was only going be a bad thing. Because yes, they could have told Lucius that they had me, but any smart person would have demanded proof of life. And well, the words, 'trust me' wouldn't have exactly cut it here.

Besides, Lucius would hear of the crash before long, so even I knew they had to act quickly here. Because it wouldn't take him long to put two and two together and no doubt the equation would equal my charred broken remains somewhere in the centre of all that broken burning metal. Oh Gods, but that thought was enough to make me want to heave up even more river water, because I couldn't imagine the suffering he would endure thinking I was dead.

"Where was it found?" the one in charge asked, taking hold of my torn and bloody dress and fisting it in his hand, as if he had just found a lifeline. Of course, not that they would know, but the blood wasn't mine. No, it had been from when Lucius had held me to him, seeing as at the time he himself had been covered in the blood of his victims.

"Not too far from here, less than half a klick, Sir…one of my men found it hanging in a tree." This was when the Sergeant frowned as if thinking now how the hell that had happened…oh, if only he knew, ha the asshole wouldn't have believed it!

"Do you think the hostage is dead?" The merc asked, making the one in charge look down at the dress in his hand now deep in thought.

"It would stand to reason, as I couldn't see her surviving that," he answered looking up at the wreckage, no doubt thinking that I had somehow been thrown from the helicopter as it was crashing.

"And the dress?"

"I take it your men did a throughout sweep of the perimeter?"

"Yes, Sarge," the merc replied making me wonder if they'd found the robbed punks under the bridge yet?

"Then it's a fucking mystery but at least this is something we can use until we find a body…better keep looking, we may need a few of those body parts later on as proof, should this not be enough," he said before pulling out his phone and making a call. Man, I didn't think I could have hated them anymore than I did, but then they started talking about my body parts and well, I was once again killing mad!

"We have your little bitch." The Sarge said before quickly pulling the phone away from his ear, as even from this distance and I could hear the roar of rage. One that obviously was coming from Lucius who was on the other end of the phone.

"You can make all the threats you want but it won't change the fact we have her and in exchange for getting her back in one piece, my client wants the box and the real one this time," he said in an authoritative tone that would have meant diddly squat to Lucius. It also made me wonder whether or not 'sergeant pepper' here would have sounded quite so convincing in his demands had he played witness to what Lucius had been able to do to over twenty of his men. And this was all in the time that it had taken me to tear out an all-important testicle…ouch, even my eyes watered at the memory and I wasn't even a dude!

"You want proof, fine, I will send you proof but mark my words Vampire, the next time you demand evidence of her capture, then I will be sending you a far bloodier picture, in the form of a piece of her mailed to your fucking door, assuming you still have one!" Then he hung up to the sound of another giant, supernatural man paddy that was coming from my boyfriend in the form of another demonic roar.

"That sounded like it went as expected," Soldier boy said, making his superior sigh before handing him the dress.

"Indeed. Now hold this up," he demanded and before long, my dress was being held up as he snapped a picture with his phone. And well, unless he was considering one just like it for his private collection when playing Sergeant Sally at the weekends, then it didn't take much brain power to guess what he planned to do with this snapshot.

"There, let the blood sucking bastard stew over that," he said after sending the picture and I could only imagine the destruction that followed that particular message. Considering that by them sending him a picture of my dress meant that they most likely would have had to remove it from me first.

It seriously made me start to question whether it was possible for a Vampire to suffer an aneurism or not. Because let's face it, I very much doubted the first thing to come to mind was that your girlfriend woke up in a helicopter, shot the pilot with a tranquilizer, before purposely throwing herself into a river from a crashing helicopter, something only accomplished by losing her dress. Yeah, that was a stretch even for me, I thought with a shake of my head. An action that only managed my headache to strengthen in its power, making me now want to swear like a sailor waking up with a hangover and finding 'I love Mom' tattooed on his ass!

"Your orders, Sarge?"

"Layla will lead him to Luitpoldkaserne. Have our men ready to intercept as he heads northwest on Föhringer Ring, that way we can barricade him in and escort him to the compound. The witch will take care of the rest as soon as he gets there. Now go, make it so!" I couldn't help but laugh at this last bit, I mean who did this jackass think he was, Captain of the Enterprise!

But then with this thought I couldn't help but smile. As it made me think back to what Lucius had said this morning, shocking me enough to turn high pitch 'only dogs can hear me' levels when I found out he had googled the name.

Well, at least now I knew their plan and all I needed to do was think of a way to get to him before they did. But, other than waving a great big flag in the air with a picture of the box circled in red with a great big line through it, then how I was going to achieve this I didn't know. Because it also wasn't as though I could just find that road he spoke about and start doing jumping jacks in hopes he would see me, and the bad guys wouldn't! Damn it, but why didn't I memorize his phone number! Gods, at this rate, then I was thinking about getting the damn thing tattooed on the back of my hand, labelled 'for when the shit hits the supernatural fan!'

Oh, how I remembered when my life used to be simple and what I wouldn't give right now for a fluffy robe, a tub of Ben and Jerry's and an overly complicated Lego set to complete. Now, that sounded like a Friday night to me! Not a night sneaking around in some bloody German woodland, squeaking as I walked thanks to the most impractical pants in existence…no matter how Arnie'esque bad ass they looked!

So, on that note, as I watched the GI Josephine and Picard wannabe depart, I stuffed back on my helmet and made my way back to the bike I had hidden behind a fallen dead tree.

"Now what?" I asked myself after slumping down with my back to the deadwood, trying to think of a viable plan of action that wouldn't get me killed for real this time. Or one that meant possibly getting Lucius killed when he handed over that box.

I spotted the rucksack I had stolen along with the bike and well, everything else I was wearing, and dragged it over to me before unzipping it, hoping that German stoners also carried flare guns these days. Then, just as I was about to rummage inside, I heard a twig snap behind me.

"You again! I thought I told you to piss off!" I turned around and quickly got to my feet to see the same merc that had caught me earlier. So, I raised my hands the second I saw him start to raise his weapon and started shaking my head, mumbling all the fruit I knew in German, because for some reason in that moment it was the only shit that came to mind.

"What the fuck you saying!?" The guy snapped as he came closer, which was exactly what I needed. I mumbled again, so he fell for it, taking that last step needed. Then I acted,

"I said Strawberries are in season, dickhead!" Then I grabbed him by the tactical vest and yanked him to me at the same time headbutting him with my helmet. Something that ended up jarring my bruised face painfully but it was worth it, for the guy dropped to the floor unconscious half a second later.

Then I smirked down at him and said,

"Oh look, wouldn't you know, I just made it so." Then I reached for my bag, knowing my time here was up but then I as I caught sight of something in there an idea suddenly hit me.

And well, there was only one way to describe it...

It was...out of this world!

CHAPTER TWO

LUCIUS

UNDERESTIMATED

T*hey had her.*

They had my Chosen One.

I swear to the fucking Gods the wrath I would inflict on the world should anything happen to her was something no God would be able to prevent! The end of days had fucking nothing on me and neither did the wrath of a fucking Titan!

I was beyond murderous. I was reaching a limit named 'close to tearing this fucking city apart and burning it to the fucking ground' furious! That's where my head was at, which was why my already crumbling club was a single wrong word away from becoming swallowed up by Hell. So naturally, it was of little wonder why my people continued to give me a wide berth as I stormed back inside the building only seconds after knocking the bitch Layla unconscious. Only sparing her life thanks to Liessa's interference. Something that forced me to see sense enough to stop from ripping her head from her shoulders...*for now.*

I had no patience to wait for anything, needing now to get to the bottom of what happened to my girl, starting with the last place I knew she had been before being taken. By the Gods, but if I found evidence of her being hurt, then Hell was going to know about it, for even the lowest levels would quake in fear of my wrath!

So, I ignored the lift and opted instead for the way I had got down here so quickly, doing so now by releasing my wings and launching myself straight up in the centre of the staircase, at least being thankful that it had been built larger than it had needed to be. But then, the second I took my first step into the lobby, I felt something so powerful it rocked me back on my heels. I would have thought it something else the Rogues had planted, as the force felt far too powerful for it to be anything other than that of a witch.

But I had been wrong.

It had been the force of the Gods.

I found the wall behind me just so the strength of it wouldn't land me on my ass, and then I was forced to close my eyes as a sense of dread washed over me. It felt as though I had just been plunged into an icy abyss, now drowning from my greatest fears.

It was my Amelia.

"My Šemšā'... my Šemšā... Še...mšā" I whispered this over and over again, shaking my head, trying to tell myself it couldn't be true...*it couldn't be fucking true!*

I roared out and this time it wasn't only in anger, it was

in pure undiluted agony! The feeling that something had just happened where I was quite literally seconds away from losing her to the Heaven the Gods believed her destined for! This was when blind panic set in and in my desperation, I didn't know what else to do but pray to the only entity that had given me anything other than my second life. Because he only had the power to take life, not grant it back like I wished he did have right now.

As the Gods only knew how much he fucking owed me!

So, instead, I ran into my apartment with a speed even I didn't know I possessed until then. Then, the second I was inside, I was at the doors of my vault in another heartbeat knowing time was critical. So, I simply twisted the metal door with so much power that my hands transformed into that of my demon. Meaning that soon the metal wasn't simply a warped and distorted version of its former self, but now it was dripping molten steel, from where my hands had brought forth the eternal flames of Phlegethon, one of the five rivers in Hell.

It was one that branched off into Tartarus itself and right now, I could feel its pull trying to drag me further down into being consumed with its power. But my will was beyond all strength of others, and nothing could control me, not even the Devil himself as he soon discovered, when he demanded I take a life I would not grant him.

But that was the past, and since then my power over Hell had only grown in strength. Meaning it was a war which Lucifer dared not risk for fear of losing his crown...a crown I most certainly didn't fucking want! That was unless the Gods took what was mine in these very seconds and I needed an army big enough to storm into the gates of Heaven in order to claim her soul back. One that belonged to me and only me.

But right now, I simply prayed it didn't come to that, so instead I destroyed the vault doors in seconds, making sure to use my will to bend the metal outwards enough to let me enter before coming to the gift once bestowed to me from the Gods.

"Caliburnus," I said kneeling down in front of it and then, once placing my hand upon the blade itself, I lowered my head. I bowed to its power before slicing my hand down it so as when I made this vow, I did so by honouring it with my blood.

"My Šemšā .... 'Save my Šemšā, my Electus born. Save her and my blood is yours... *that's all I fucking ask!"* I shouted hammering my fist down next to the sword, feeling the floor give way as it cracked around my hand.

"SAVE HER!" I roared down at the floor and after this the sword, the chooser of Kings, started to glow as if powered by the blood I'd just offered. A second later, the whole room erupted into a blinding flash of light, the force of which nearly blew me backwards. However, my sacrifice still needed to be made so I held on as my blood was drawn up through my flesh and into the blade. I ignored the pain, as to me it was simply a state of mind. Now the pain of losing Amelia, however, was one that had the power to tear me to pieces and completely destroy me!

So, I held on, despite the blood it took, drawing it out of me as though it was feeding from my very life that Lucifer had granted me. It ran along the gleaming blade in rivulets of crimson streams feeding down into an ocean of blood. It coated the hand that held it, one that mimicked the Lady of the Lake who had been the blade's bearer, charged with gifting it to its next chosen King.

One it deemed worthy.

One worthy of owning her.

I only let go of the blade when the glowing steel started to simmer down, knowing that I had done all in my power to save her in that moment. But even then, it still didn't feel like enough. So, all that was left for me to do was to hold onto hope that whatever it was that had suddenly befallen my girl, my vow had at least kept her alive long enough until I *could* save her. And speaking of saving her, I rose to my feet and grabbed the only thing left that had the power to do that...

My one and only bargaining chip.

The Gods be damned box was one I simply wished I could have destroyed and have done with it, but unfortunately it wasn't that easy...*as I had tried!*

I had even had my own witch, Nesteemia, try and overpower the protective barrier which was held over it. But it was no use, as there was only one way to beat it and that was to actually open it. And by all accounts, doing so would lead to my destruction, so that wasn't exactly my idea of a fucking solution either.

In truth, even my own people studying it hadn't discovered as much as my girl had. Amelia's intelligence and cunning wasn't just something that impressed me, it was something that utterly astounded me! It was also something that I was beyond proud of.

Now, if she could just stop using that cunning against me in trying to leave, then I would revel in her skills instead of silently dread them. As right now, and knowing what she was like, well all I could hope for was that pretty little head of hers was smart enough not to try anything that would end up getting her killed. For I swear the first thing I would do when kidnapping her from Heaven would be to spank that ass hard enough she wouldn't be sitting on her vessel's behind for a fucking week!

After this I walked back into the lobby with the box and cause of my current cluster fuck situation, before entering Amelia's apartment. All my council were here already and the second I started growling, Clay spoke,

"Nothing was touched, as I knew you would wish to see for yourself." This appeased me enough to nod, thankful at least that my people knew me and knew me well enough to act under orders I hadn't yet needed to voice.

I scanned the room, first taking in the state of my people, and for the moment, purposely ignoring the dead bodies. Ruto was on the sofa looking slightly less worse off than I had seen him last when being pulled from the wreckage by Clay.

Clay himself still had the metal imbedded in his side as if this was a mere annoyance that came secondary to all else. Liessa was being cradled in her husband's arms trying to soothe him, for he looked nearly as murderous as I did. Especially seeing as he was still plucking out spent tranq darts from her body, then I could understand why. It also told me how they had managed to overpower her, for it looked as if she had been shot with enough to take down a herd of African Game.

Hakan was taking in the scene, as if seeing it all playing out in front of him and Percy was doing what Percy did best, trying to care for others. He was currently dabbing at one of the many cuts on Ruto's torso, one that ran the full length of his face and torn shoulder.

"So it's easy to say that we got our asses handed to us," Clay commented drily making me growl before swiftly grabbing hold of the metal shard about the size of his forearm and yanking it out of his side in anger. He winced, gritting his teeth from pain but remained strong enough not to make a sound other than a clenched,

"Point taken."

"Good, now explain to me what happened?" This was aimed at Liessa.

"She was fucking shot, that's what!" Caspian snapped clearly struggling with this and with only a stern look from me, did he back the fuck down and yield. This was also helped by Liessa muttering something in his ear before feeding him her wrist so he could suckle on the siphons on her skin that let her secrete the deadly ink. One her husband was not only immune to but mainly addicted to. To say that they were meant to be together was more than just a romanticized statement, but more of destiny throwing these two into each other's paths.

Although, if I recall I do believe his original mission had been to eliminate her and the threat she possessed to my people. This being because it was a substance that could kill a weak Vampire while putting one of greater strength on his ass for a considerable time.

But seeing as Caspian had the unique gift of immunity to all poisons, natural or unnaturally made, then he became the obvious man for the job. One that didn't exactly go the way anyone expected, especially when he returned with who he now deemed as his personal prisoner, instead of the dead body I had ordered.

And technically speaking, she had remained his prisoner ever since and one he even married near a hundred years ago. If memory serves me right, then it was the only order he refused and fought me on. So, in the end his solution to this was to shackle her physically to him for the next decade, just so he could prove that she was going nowhere, and her every move would be under his command. Of course, his obsession with her morphed into one of love and it was soon clear to all around him that he wasn't just pussy whipped, as Ruto would say, but she ruled his heart. Doing so with her own sacrificed in return for the obsession most definitely went both ways.

A sentiment I was only now coming to fully understand. I almost shook my head at my once naive belief. A foolish belief that my own obsession with the girl had reached its peak seven years ago when I started having the entirety of her life monitored. Oh, but how wrong I had been, for since having her here with me at Transfusion, only then had the full depth of my obsession come to light.

And now that she had been taken from me, it seemed that my ability to deal with that knowledge was a hairsbreadth away from giving way to my demon entirely. Meaning that a simple look at Caspian and I was remembering all those times my second in command, Adam, had been fearful for his wife. Even the rash and desperate actions from Dom were all now no longer believed as foolish as they once had been out of fear for his Keira. For I too was close to bursting out of my fucking skin with worry and I had to say the sight in the room wasn't fucking helping.

"Liessa?" I said her name in a way this time that silenced her husband and demanded answers. She lowered her head in shame and told me,

"They shot me like Caspian said."

"Was this after you attacked them?" I asked nodding to the two dead humans that looked to have met a gruesome end. The moment her eyes widened was when the reality of the situation really hit home.

My girl had once again been underestimated.

"I didn't do this, I had little chance to do anything as they burst in and shot me before I even had chance to fire a single drop."

"Fuck me, so this was all Birdy girl?" Clay asked, his surprise evident. Liessa nodded before looking to me with pain in her eyes before telling me,

"I am so sorry Sire, I failed you." And had this been anything other than my girl's life on the line, then I would have been in a mind to make this easier on her. However, it wasn't and therefore *I would not.*

"Yes, you did. You failed me and *you failed her."* Caspian was about to speak, no doubt arguing in his wife's defence, but I was having none of it.

"ENOUGH!" I roared letting a wave of dominant power to roll over them and making them visibly flinch before showing me their submission with lowered heads. Then I walked closer to Percy and said in a somewhat calmer tone,

"Percy, if you please." I then handed him the box to hold whilst I was on my mission to discover what had happened. He nodded and his scarred little hands took it from me, no doubt happy to help in any way he could. Only then did I turn back to Hakan.

"Now, walk me through what happened!" I shouted making him nod his head before speaking, something he only ever reserved for times it was most needed. After Clay got in there first of course,

"Oh, I just have to see this shit!" My head of security commented like an excited child, obviously intrigued to know what else 'my little human' was capable of. I rolled my eyes in sight of his exuberance and then nodded for Hakan to continue.

"This way, my Chieftain," he said, long ago granting me this name as was the old ways of his people. His voice was hoarse but not from disuse, it was this way from what had been done to him at the hands of Westerners intent on stealing his father's lands many years ago. Since then, his vessel had been healed the moment he had been destined to become the fallen, doing so in the name of revenge.

For the moment he discovered his own life after death, he ripped the wings from his vessel the second he tried to break free of the bonds still wrapped around his reincarnated body and tamed the very manner in which he had died.

Tortured and wrapped in thorned wire before being thrown into the river to drown.

Needless to say, after this two things happened. The first was that when I heard of his history, I felt inclined to offer him a position at my table. The second was happily aiding him in executing that revenge.

But as it turned out, he was the best damn tracker in existence. Which meant the second he took in the scene around him now, he started to piece together what had happened and played it out in his own mind as if it had been recorded and put on rewind. It was a tracker's way and a skill used to retrace a person's steps or past movements. The gifts were those similar to a seeker, but instead of being gifted the sight of the past and the future, a tracker could only see into the past.

It was due to their talents in picking up a lingering energy left by a person's soul. He could tap into the unique signature left behind and watch the person's aura act out the past like the ghost of a vessel was actually still there. Unfortunately, for most trackers there was a fairly small window for this to be achieved before that person's steps were lost over time. Or that they were simply overwhelmed by the presence of far too many others. Hakan, however, well he was one of the only trackers who could eradicate all other auras in his way and pinpoint the one he wanted. Doing so even as far back as six months in a crowded space.

It was this strength that made him the best there was. A talent I had been gifted the option to exploit many times over in the past and if truth be told, one even exercised on Keira when the occasion was needed to find her.

Which was why I trusted his account implicitly, no matter how strange it first started, something that began in the bathroom.

"Well, it's got to be said, Sire, that girl of yours certainly has a unique way of killing people," Clay commented as we stepped around one dead body that looked to have been killed with an electrical cord. This was from a broken lamp, a piece of which was still embedded in his cheek, telling me she had first hit him with it. Gods, but just the sight of her kills had me worried, proud and fucking hard all at the same time. I could only hope that when I witnessed this account of past actions, that by the end of it I was satisfied that she had done all this unscathed.

"It started in here, my Chief..."

"Let's forgo the formalities for the time being, yes." I said holding up a hand knowing I didn't have the fucking patience for all that Chieftain, my Lord, Sire shit right now. He nodded before disappearing inside the bathroom where there was a man lay on the floor, strangely covered in white foam and blood.

"You were saying?" I remarked with a raised brow at Clay's earlier comment about Amelia's unique way of dissipating her enemies.

"Yeah, well she left this shithead alive," Clay scoffed as if disappointed. On the other hand, I thought differently.

"And lucky for us, for now we have someone to torture," I said unable to stop myself from cracking my fingers when they turned into fists by my sides. But that would have to wait,

"Hakan, if you please," I said nodding for him to proceed, something I knew had started when his eyes turned as black as the strip of ink across his eyes. Then they started to flicker from white to black, looking now as if he had an old black and white film flickering out the scene in his mind and we were getting a mere glimpse at it.

Then it stopped and his eyes snapped back to his usual dark shade.

"I...um...well." This was all Hakan said and for once, his opting for few words said wasn't through choice.

"What is it!?" I snapped as I didn't have the fucking patience for it either!

"I think it best I show you my…Sir," he said stopping himself with just a cautionary look sent his way.

"Proceed," I said through gritted teeth.

"Oh, this ought to be good," Clay commented just before Hakan started to bring forth the ghosts of their auras for us to watch. It was as if an invisible body had been surrounded by smoke, allowing its shell to be seen.

I swear just the sight of her aura taking shape had me tensing and having to resist the irrational action to reach out and try and touch her. Then I was forced to watch as she attacked the other smoked figure after it first rose up from the unconscious piece of shit still breathing on the floor. Hers was white, and his black, which I could see started off holding a gun to her. Then she disarmed him, with the aid of…

"Is that shaving cream?!" Clay took the thoughts right out of my head as he watched what I did when the smoked ghost of her raised an arm as if spraying something in his face. Clay had at this point walked over to the star patten left on the counter and brought a fingertip to his nose as his curiosity got the better of him.

"I wonder how this…oh, never mind." Clay was cut off when we all saw that after swiftly breaking his arm, she then slammed his head face first into the counter, creating a burst of cream and blood splatter to decorate the stone top. Then, as another aura burst into the room, from what I perceived was to be the man that now lay dead in the bedroom, she opened her mouth and spoke to him. Now I found myself intrigued to know exactly what it was she said to him before she let go of the now unconscious man whose aura quickly slid back down to the floor. Floating down like a wave, it disappeared on top of where her victim still lay slumped to the side and indeed, still breathing.

Well, not for long, I thought with some satisfaction.

After this she retrieved what I can only assume was a gun and started firing. I looked to the doorway, to see the new aura move out of the way of the flying bullets. But I could see for myself that none had been on target, not if the wide array of bullet holes in the walls were anything to go by. So, instead, she used the weapon to her advantage and decided to throw it at the mercs head, knowing she had a better chance, seeing as her aim with a gun was shocking.

Fuck me, but after tonight then I was considering our second date to be at a fucking gun range, just to be sure she could use one, for I hoped never again!

The aura stumbled back on impact and then unbelievably I watched as her own aura charged the man, taking him down to the ground.

"Whoa, look at her go!" Clay commented enthusiastically as we both followed Hakan into the bedroom. He had halted the re-enactment until we were positioned in the room so we could continue to follow the fight. This was where things got more difficult for my girl, and even I could see the added texture of features the ghost of her showed. The strain in the shadow as it vibrated, humming with tension. Especially when she started to reach whatever was closest to her in desperation to beat her opponent.

I swear but it felt as if I was watching it in real time and found myself trying to anchor myself to the spot, so I wouldn't step forward and try to intervene. This was by far one of the hardest things I had ever forced myself to experience, as unlike all others, this I did so willingly. Because I needed to know. I had to know just what she had endured at the hands of these fuckers!

Gods, but the one left alive was going to die and fucking slowly! Hell, at this point I considering carving out his fucking heart and having the fucking thing gift wrapped as a welcome home present for when I finally got my girl home!

In fact, I was that worked up, that Clay had to get my attention to make me aware of the damage I was doing to the walls behind me as plaster started to crack and rain with powder. It was coming from the force of my fisted gloved hand, one that I could feel humming with unleashed pent-up power. One that only relaxed when I saw the moment she finally wrapped the cord around his neck. Then she placed a foot to his shoulder and arched her back, using his own body against him as she used him as leverage to strangle the life from his body.

In the end, he had died suffering like I hoped he had, for there was a bloody gash on his forehead and large shards of ceramic embedded in his face. There was also yet again another broken arm, multiple kicks to the face and an electrical wire cutting into his flesh. One deep enough that if he hadn't died of asphyxiation, he would have from blood loss. Not that all of this had been enough, for at my hands it would have been far more bloody and violent. But more importantly, it wouldn't have been so quick.

Yet, all in all, my girl had done well and to the point I couldn't help my lips from twitching when Clay had remarked,

"Fuck, but what is it with your girl and breaking arms?" I didn't reply, but then again I didn't need to. As it was obvious, my ferocious little princess was a force to be reckoned with and I very much doubted that even Dom knew the extent of this.

A thought that both pleased and amused me greatly.

In fact, I had a feeling as though Amelia had been underestimated her whole life and I was starting to understand her annoyance at the common mistake of most.

I nodded to Hakan when I saw him look to the door. But he paused in a strange manner, as if this next part was something he didn't want to show me. So, I prompted,

"You may continue, Hakan."

"My Ch…"

"Just fucking spit it out!" I snapped making him bow his head and tell me,

"She struggled in this next room…*greatly,*" he confessed, and the last word uttered make me grit my teeth so hard I thought the fuckers would crumble!

"Just fucking show me!" I barked knowing there was no other way I could speak in that moment. Not now knowing that if I had found this last one difficult to watch, then this next fight would be fucking agonizing.

And I wasn't wrong, for in my heart, it was nothing short of…

Torturous.

CHAPTER THREE

DAVID AND GOLIATH

I walked into the living space, following the ghost of Amelia's past footsteps as she ran into the room and crouched down to nothing. I then looked to Liessa, who just nodded shamefully at my unspoken question. Which meant my girl had been worried about one of my council members. And from the look of things, the significance of the scene was not lost on a certain enforcer of mine. A clear show of concern that now gave Liessa's husband something to think about, especially seeing as it came from a human.

After this, I then watched as the auras of the two dead men were sucked from where they now lay dead and were swept backwards to the entrance. Now with the auras in place, the scene started to play out once again, and as soon as the men took one look at Amelia, they decided to each take a side. Both of them did this with their mouths silently moving, no doubt spewing their threats.

Then Amelia looked down at what I presumed was a knife in her hand before she looked back up at the last to speak and I didn't need to hear her words to make out her next line,

'Oh, you mean this one...oh, okay then.' Then she moved her arm back and let the invisible blade fly and I looked down just in time to see the aura fall backwards and land in the body. One now with a very visible blade sticking out of his heart. This made me proud to see that she hadn't been foolish enough to let the guy live, as she once had. But this time there was no mistake, not like before back at the museum. No, now she was fighting to kill, that much was clear from that single action alone.

But this was when I knew things were going to get difficult, as one look at the aura still standing and just from the sheer size of him I knew that this was the difficult fight Hakan had spoken of. Well, at the very least I could see from his body, that he had been beaten to a very bloody pulp, and for that, I was more than thankful for. Now, all I could hope for was that her own injuries weren't half as bad.

Again, Hakan looked to me as if silently asking me if I was sure I wished to continue and for just a single moment I found myself torn. For one, I needed my people safe and not buried under a hundred tons of rubble. But then after the feeling of dread that had hit me when stepping from the stairwell, I knew I had to fucking know!

So, I nodded for him to continue and once more, myself and the whole of my council watched as nothing short of a battle between David and Goliath ensued. A fight starting when he ran at her in clear rage after just seeing her kill his comrade. She sidestepped and blocked what must have been a knife in his hand, making me fucking curse, knowing she had no weapon of her own. Damn it, but she shouldn't have been so hasty in giving up her weapon so soon!

She brought her knee up and hit him in the gut but seeing the way he was dressed from the dead body, then that move would have little effect for he looked to be wearing a bullet proof vest.

"FUCKER!" I suddenly roared the second I saw him pick her up by the waist and throw her against the wall! Gods, but I could feel myself losing my shit and fucking quickly!

"Gods, but she is one tough little…"

"Don't you fucking dare finish that Gods be damned sentence!" I snapped at Clay not needing his fucking opinion right now, even if the big bastard was right!

I watched her stagger from it but then she soon recovered and just in time to as he swiped out at her with what must have been his blade. I was just happy to see that she managed to dodge the blow but then the male's aura started to motion with his hands, waving them back and to in front of him. He did this about a foot apart and it took me a moment to figure out what he was doing. That was until I could just make out her words, thanks to the distinct moving of the mouth,

'Seriously, just pick a fucking hand would you!' she told him making Ruto this time unable to resist commenting,

"Dickhead, what does he think he is doing, like that would fucking scare her!" I decided to let him have this one, for if watching this play out would make him respect her more, then at least one fucking thing arose from this torturous sight!

She side stepped and continued to block his advances,

managing to get a kick to the knee before delivering a bruising blow to his back with her elbow. The move I knew was one that she was hoping would have brought him down, but despite jumping up and putting all her weight into the hit, he was big enough that he stayed on his feet. Instead he swiped out haphazardly behind himself, very nearly catching her once more with his weapon.

She managed to dodge it again, *thankfully,* but wasn't quick enough to completely come out unscathed as she received a hard kick to the stomach, sending her backwards into the piano. Again, I found myself trying to contain my rage at the sight, but unable to stop myself from stepping forward this time, as even some of my council visibly shifted as if they too felt the need to jump in and protect her. This at the very least pleased me to see. However, I just wished it hadn't come on the back of her getting hurt.

I watched her curse before she then decided to turn around in what I assumed was to pick up the piano stool.

"Stop!" I shouted and Hakan paused the smoked figures long enough for me to ask,

"Can you bring through the stool and his weapon," as I was curious to see how she intended to use it, as I knew it was most likely a means to protect herself against the oncoming blade. But I wanted to see how she managed it, and after a little extra energy on Hakan's side, he nodded making it materialize into a thick shadow.

Of course, it had never been intended for this when I had insisted the instrument had been purchased for her room. For I knew that she played. This had been something I had learned from one of the few trips to Afterlife I'd had no choice but to make. But each time, I had found myself drawn to where inside the large mansion she had been hiding. Then once located, I had spent some time observing her from afar.

It had been strange watching her in her own domain, as I found myself irrationally jealous that she had been there and not situated safely behind my own walls instead.

However, I was no fool and knew this was my own doing, as like I said, it was an irrational irritation due to my own past decisions. But this didn't help, as I then usually forced myself to leave and took my seat at the table of the Kings in a fucking foul mood. And who was there watching me with a curious fucking eye like she knew the exact reasons why…Her mother!

Of course, after that my mind was never on the meeting, one usually about the Sons of Afterlife and their own prophecy as it was being lived at the time. But soon, even the lost children of our world, the ones each of the Kings had been charged with mentoring had grown and left. Gone after first being shaped by our hand into what destiny had in store for them and were now all currently forging the path for a new future.

But Amelia had never been included in this, and I knew just from the sight of melancholy on her face as she played the large instrument so beautifully, that she felt the exclusion cut to the core.

She simply wanted to belong.

The guilt of this had always plagued me and she would never know why…*no one would.*

Which is why later on I would reflect on my time there and quickly made a promise to myself that after this particular visit, that when the time finally came, then I would get her a piano to play on. Just in case she wished to indulge in the pastime and share with me the clear talent she had. Because it had to be said, she was most certainly a natural and very few things until that point had captivated me so intently.

But, looking back on that day then I would have said the shy, sweet young girl of eighteen, one sat getting lost in the music, was a far cry from the ghost of a girl that faced me now. Especially when I watched her brutally run at him with the legs of the piano stool facing his chest. Legs she meant to stab into him and managing it as one struck him in the shoulder, effectively pinning him to the wall for a short time.

"Fuck, Yeah!" This time it was Caspian who shouted at her victory but unfortunately it was short lived as her foe roared in pain as he started bringing himself closer to her. Doing so despite the narrow leg that traveled further into his flesh. This way he could wield his blade at her once more but with a knowing grin she suddenly twisted the seat and finally forced the blade from his hand. His head followed the motion of both shadowed blade and stool flying off to one side before they hit the wall above the sofa.

I had to admit, I found myself breathing slightly easier now that blade was out of the equation. Especially when his smokey aura kept his head turned long enough after watching the blade's trajectory, giving Amelia the chance to uppercut him in the chin. It hit hard enough that he went back a few steps. My council all cheered her on in a subtle way, no doubt not to set me off into another rage, but I had to say, the sight was encouraging. Not only to see her knocking back a much larger opponent, but also that my council were all naturally rooting for her.

It also looked to have caused damage too, as he even raised a hand to his face before looking down at his palm, which I easily guessed meant that he was awarded the sight of his own blood. I watched her mouth something at him and given her cocky grin, I could imagine it was something witty and in the moment. He spit off to one side and looked to have screamed something at her in rage. She responded back and then kind of stopped, cocked her head slightly to the side and started smiling before speaking again.

"There was music playing when I gained consciousness," Liessa informed me, telling me that Amelia must have actually been commenting on the song playing. I swear I would have shaken my head at her if in that moment he wasn't swinging a right hook at her, one she thankfully managed to block. Then there were two more after this in quick succession that again she blocked. But then my biggest fear played out as I watched the heavy bastard take her off guard and getting in a blinding punch to the face, one strong enough it knocked her to the floor.

"FUCK!" I roared as she landed hard on the coffee table before rolling to the floor next to the sofa.

"Gods!" Liessa hissed through her teeth and even Clay, Percy Caspian and Ruto now looked concerned for her.

"FUCKING STOP!" I bellowed just as the figure crouched over her and grabbed what looked like a handful of her hair yanking her head back. The scene paused and I raked a furious hand through my hair before turning away from the fucking nightmare playing out the past like some sick twisted Greek tragedy!

"My Lord I…"

"Sire…"

"Luc I…"

"Shut the fuck up, all of you!" I roared again the second my council all started to speak. Gods be fucking damned! I wanted to kill so badly I nearly dragged the unconscious one in here just for someone to feel the same pain my Amelia had. Only by my hand it would be felt tenfold!

But then I knew I might be killing an asset and that would have been foolish and rash. I swear I just couldn't watch anymore, as it was fucking torture of the worst kind! But then I also knew that I couldn't not see this through to the end. She deserved that and my devotion in all forms was hers.

But most of all, I needed to know if she was alright and what type of injuries she had sustained. I also wanted to know what had been done to her so when the time came for making all responsible pay, then I wanted this memory in my mind fueling my demon's wrath to ensure that I inflicted the right amount of torture in return. And well, so far, their crimes were weighty enough to drown them in their own fucking blood!

Even hung, strung and quartered was too quick for them. I would tear them piece by little Gods be damned piece until they had been begging me for hours to end their suffering! One I would never grant, for where I intended to send them, would make their torture an hourly occurrence.

"Continue!" I snapped making Hakan look to the others in an unsure manner.

"My Chieftain, I could…"

"I said fucking continue!" This time the order came from

my demon, one that each of them knew was far too close to the surface than he had ever been before. At least without control or allowance to do so. But seeing as I was currently one of the most dangerous and powerful beings on the planet, and one on the fucking edge of losing my shit at that, well it meant a very real Hell breaking loose was on the horizon. And the only thing that would calm me now was watching my girl kill this mother fucker in the most painful of ways!

"Yes, but of course," Hakan said bowing, and with a wave of his hand the figures once more continued, starting with the agonizing reality of watching as my Chosen One's head was slammed down into the floor. Which meant painfully watching as my mind conjured up all the blood that now gushed from her nose from the jarring blow. I thought this was the worst of it, but unfortunately, I was about to find out that it could in fact, get so much worse.

"Oh shit." This came from Ruto.

"Fuck no." This from Clay.

"Oh Gods!" This from Liessa and lastly, a horrified gasp from Percy. The other two kept their composure, I on the other hand, the second I saw him lifting her torn skirt and then lean back to undo his pants…well…

I. FUCKING. LOST. IT!

I felt my other form bursting through without restraint, and long gone were the wings of a phoenix, or the eyes of the sun. This time it was all my former demon and more now being mixed with the Venom of God! My once damaged wings of skin stretched over fingers of bone like some demonic bat, were now back to ones untortured.

These I felt spanning the length of the two horns that had

43

grown from the inferno on my back, harnessed straight from Hell's fiery rivers. My hands burned away any leather that covered the one I kept concealed, allowing my people to see the hand of a Titan left behind for the first time. One that was black and charred with the power of Tartarus flowing beneath the cracked skin, glowing and pulsating as it begged me to deliver the destruction upon the Earth it was always pressing me to do.

A destruction it was capable of.

I felt my size increase to a size even Caspian would fear, as I literally became more powerful than Lucifer himself. The reason being why now even he feared me, if ever I was back in the realm in which I had been reborn into.

Because like this, I was quite literally,

The end of fucking days, with power of Gods fueling my veins!

My people all quickly gave me a wide berth, moving back to the other side of the room with Caspian, rightly so, putting himself between me and his woman. I would have done the same thing if Amelia had been in the room but as it turned out, I couldn't even save her from being...

"FUCKING RAPED BY A MORTAL BASTARD!" The last of this dark thought was bellowed out by my demon that had enough power to crack the walls and floor where I stood, shaking the already unsteady foundations of Transfusion. And somewhere deep down inside me, I knew that my club wouldn't be able to take much more and that I needed to calm the fuck down. Especially if I was to be any good, for not only to my people, but more importantly to my Chosen One. My girl who was still out there somewhere and fucking needed me!

Which included keeping my shit together, something Hakan was trying to achieve. As it was only he who braved close proximity with me and I was soon to understand why.

"Look, My Sire, my Chieftain, look now, for you will miss her wrath if you do not calm enough to look," he implored,

"LOOK AT WHAT, MY WOMAN GETTING…"

"No, but her revenge! Watch now and you will see!" he beseeched again, stopping me before my rage could consume my senses once and for all. So, I did as he said and forced myself and my fucking demon to look at her and what we saw astounded us all. For I could see that she was faking submission, lying still and waiting for when he let his guard down and get close enough for whatever it was in her hand to do its job.

I wondered if it was the knife that might have travelled behind the sofa and within her reach. One by one everyone inched forward so as not to miss what happened next and I had to say, it was thank the Gods, worth waiting for!

His aura leaned over her, getting close to whisper something vulgar in her ear and something no doubt that would have been more than enough for me to rip his still beating heart out of his chest. Then she suddenly reached across herself and hammered something into his head, making him fall back from her before gaining his feet as clear panic set in. You could then see the way his mouth opened as he no doubt started screaming.

But I wasn't watching the vile mortal, I was watching my girl and I swear the pride I felt was beyond compare to anything else in this world. Especially now when watching her get swiftly to her feet, seemingly unphased as she merely made a gesture as if to wipe the blood from her face on the back of her arm.

Then she focused back on her enemy and it clearly wasn't enough that she had stabbed him in the face. For her next crowning glory came in the form of her yanking the weapon from what looked to be his eye, before then kicking out his knees and making him go down this time. Then she grabbed a smoky handful of what I assumed to be his hair and said something to him just before she yanked his head back and rammed the weapon then into his neck.

Then she closed her eyes as she held on until what time I didn't know, my guessing was until the sound of his death. After this she yanked her weapon free and let go, where the aura fell forward and like the others, landed face forward into the real bloodied vessel.

But soon after this point, I was forced to watch her capture, as she dropped her weapon when she was shot. This was with what I assumed was a tranquilizer, as she was too important to them to risk killing. But still knowing the fact did nothing to ease the pain at seeing it, especially when I could easily make out it was by Layla's hand.

Gods but that bitch was going to die soon!

I took a deep breath, now calming myself in the knowledge that she had won, despite how it ended. As, all in all, she had been fucking spectacular and if she had been here right now, then nothing in this world or the next would have stopped me from fucking her raw! Doing so as I uttered the three words I had still yet to say, but by the Gods was now unashamed in my fucking desperation to say them!

In fact, I didn't even realise that during this whole climax, I was back to my usual self with my demon fully sated enough now that we knew that our girl hadn't sustained too great an injury.

"Fuck me, but are we sure this girl of yours is human?" Clay asked in astonishment and I had to try not to react to that particular question.

"Wow, that was just...wow," Percy said in a dreamy tone and Ruto simply said,

"Now that was kick ass...for a human of course."

"The little one did well," Caspian said begrudgingly, which for him was a major compliment but then it all stopped when Clay suddenly shouted,

"No fucking way!" I turned quickly and snapped,

"What is it this time?!" This was when I found him now holding up a long blood soaked stick before then rolling over the dead body of the big bastard, I wanted to bring back to life just to kill all over again. Starting with taking his other eye...or better yet, I would leave that so he could witness the horror of seeing his own body being torn apart!

"It's a fucking pencil!"

"What?!" I snapped yet again.

"Holy shit, she did all that with a fucking pencil!?" Clay said now getting closer to the body and seeing for himself the carnage she had inflicted with an item only a few days ago she had been using so innocently. Gods, but if I had known at the time that something so small would end up saving her from such violation and possible deadly fate, then I would have stored a fucking arsenal under there. Gods, how I thanked the urge to run my fingers through her beautiful hair at the time, first needing to rid her of the pencils she had stuffed in there to keep handy.

"Wow, she even pierced the jugular...I have to say, Sire,

I am liking this badass chick of yours…in fact, what are we waiting for, let's go get your girl, so you can just fucking marry her already!" Clay commented making me close my eyes and take a deep breath as I let that information wash over me…

Marry her?

CHAPTER FOUR

RUDE PUNK

Marry her!

Gods, but why would I fucking need to do something like that! She was already mine and I didn't need some preaching prick in a robe and a room full of flowers and shit to declare it so! If anything, Clay's words surprised me and even more so when I looked around the room to see the rest seemed to be in agreement.

I was fucking dumbfounded!

Which was why I snapped,

"Hardly the fucking…." This, however, was cut short as the sound of a phone ringing which thankfully brought me from this mortal notion of marriage and just how ridiculous an idea it seemed. Clay on the other hand was trying in vain to hide his smirk, knowing that he had gotten a rise out of me in the way I suspected he had meant to.

"It's the phone I took off the bitch," Liessa said coming

forward and handing it to me, despite the hold Caspian had on her, something she squirmed right out of.

"Speak!" I demanded the second I accepted the call.

"We have your little bitch," a male said making me roar in anger before giving him a little insight as to what his future held,

"By all the Gods in Hell, I swear you will fucking beg me to kill you by the time I am through pealing skin from your worthless flesh!" I said, with my demon snarling at the end.

"You can make threats all you want, it won't change the fact we have her and in exchange my client wants the box and the real one this time." But of course, they fucking did! I looked to the table where Percy had placed the box when prompted to do so, finding myself willing the fucking thing to burn to ash just to have done with the fucking Hex it had brought on my life!

I closed my eyes and tried for even a shred of calm, one I felt myself losing like the Devil himself was pulling on the thread.

"I want proof of life!" I snapped, hating the fucking words that I had no choice but to force through my lips.

"You want proof, fine, I will send you proof but mark my words Vampire, the next time you demand evidence of her capture then I will be sending you a far bloodier picture, in the form of a piece of her mailed to your fucking door, assuming you still have one!" The human said and just before ending the call I threw my head back and couldn't stop my demon from erupting once more, as he roared up at the ceiling, making the building shake. Luckily Ruto had the foresight to at least rush to my side and grab the phone, before spinning out of me and my demon's reach. And all before I hammered the hand that once held the phone into the wall. I swear there would be nothing left of this building before long and right in that moment I didn't give a fucking shit if it fell into the fucking ground and became a ruin at the gates of Hell!

All I wanted was my fucking Chosen One back!

"Sire, he sent a picture." Ruto's voice was enough to bring me back to a simmer of anger and I snapped my gaze to his, knowing my eyes didn't hold a single pinprick of grey steel they usually did. The term of a person seeing red with rage was a very real statement for me right in that moment, for it was as if the world around me had been painted a darker shade of crimson. Fuck, but I just hoped it was a sign of things to come because all I wanted right in that fucking moment was to bathe in the blood of my enemies and paint the Gods be damned walls of Transfusion with it!

"Show me!" I barked in between my heavy breathing as I tried further still to bring myself down from my rage. My people had seen more emotion and uncontrollable wrath in me during these last few days than the entire time they had been one of my turned. So, it was little surprise that everyone around me was beyond wary.

Ruto came forward and showed me the phone, purposely not giving it to me in fear no doubt of what I may do to it and seeing it was our only way to communicate with the bastards, then I was more than thankful for his caution. Especially when I saw the picture of her torn, bloody dress being held up. Well, it wasn't surprising when I took my anger out on the nearest thing, and before I knew it my demon tore the head from the already dead piece of shit

Amelia had killed. Killed with a fucking pencil! Seconds later I had his spine hanging from my hand like a knotted bloody rope after first ripping it from his body as easily as if I was opening a fucking package!

"When?!" I snarled like some wild Hell Beast that could barely get out the single word.

"They just sent through the details now…"

"WHEN!?" I roared making Ruto flinch.

"Layla is to lead us to their base where we will make the exchange." I growled low before slapping down the spine like a whip until it landed on top of the body it once had been a part of, feeling slightly better for the sight.

"Well, that's shit, I was hoping we would get to kill the bitch this time!" Liessa said with a pout.

"Oh, don't worry, I have plans for that demon and that special place in Hell will be what she fucking begs me for by the end of it! But until then, get the bitch some blood, she's not much good to me with a broken neck and the inability to speak!" After issuing this order I walked from the apartment as the evidence of the attack on my girl was fucking with my head, no matter how proud I was of her for killing these men. But then I paused and snarled at the door leading into her bedroom as I detected the heartbeat, telling me of the one still alive. Then I felt my crimson soaked hand fist, relishing the blood I felt pool between my fingers before looking over my shoulder and issuing one last order,

"And someone torture the fuck out of that piece of shit and get me what you can before the Hex takes his life…I want to see a pool of human waste on the floor by the time I get back!" Then I left, going back to my own apartment before I ended up losing my shit completely and for good this time.

Besides, healing that bitch would take at least twenty minutes and when I got my girl back, then I didn't want her seeing me covered in blood and thanks to my vessel growing, now wearing fucking rags! And get her back I most certainly would do, for nothing else mattered.

So, with this in mind I tore the rest of my clothes from my body, material that was barely still holding together thanks to erupting fully into my demon form only moments ago. A form that was considerably bigger, as were most when allowing their demons to fully take hold when in Hell. But doing so topside, well most didn't have enough power for it to happen and for those that did, that power came at a price. Because the strength of will it then took to overpower and master your demon back into submission was easier said that fucking done!

I showered quickly, then walked into my closet, grabbed the first fucking thing that would clothe me, forgoing the suit for dark grey denim and a black Tee, just so if blood were spilled, then it wouldn't show as much for when I finally got Amelia back in my arms. I had no idea what she was currently enduring at the hands of my enemies and wanted to take her state of mind into consideration. She was all that mattered right now and not knowing what was happening to her was fucking with my head!

Half of me wanted to know and the other half was fucking terrified of finding out! The thought of what they could be doing to her, Gods, but I very nearly found my demon facing me in the mirror rather than the face of rage that did. One that blood lust made my irises crimson and framed by infected black veins that overshadowed my eyes. Well, I could at least be thankful my horns hadn't emerged I thought with a distasteful shake of my head.

After then grabbing a thick leather glove to hide my demonic abomination, I walked straight into the vault. One look at what I had done to the door in my haste to beg the fucking Gods to save my girl and keep her safe, and I knew I would now need my collection sent to Königssee. There was, however, one piece that was staying with me, so I picked up Caliburnus, the sword of Kings and walked back out with purpose, testing its weight once more with one swing.

It was the moment to get this shit done and this time, death would come from much more than a fucking pencil!

"No fucking way, I am not getting in the car with you!" Layla shouted and I swear I just wanted to break her fucking neck again! We were outside where most of the cars were parked and I was very aware that the police minds could only be controlled for so long and I didn't want to fucking have to deal with that shit too.

So far authorities had been led to believe the building was too much of a risk to enter after there had been a gas explosion. One that the sprinkler system had managed to contain in preventing the flames from consuming the building entirely but the building itself was still too unsafe to enter.

I had therefore put Clay in charge of sorting out the shit with the humans, which had not been to his liking. In fact, after I ordered all my men to back down and sort out the clusterfuck that was my club, it had been Ruto who had stepped up, backing up my order. Of course, he also knew why I did this, as he had read the instructions that followed the picture of Amelia's dress. Meaning he also knew that if I was seen heading to this base of theirs with a fucking convoy of my people, then the likelihood of getting Amelia back would be none-fucking existent, and an all-out war would be the only outcome.

But then war was inevitable, for no-one took what was mine and lived. Oh, they might have been blessed enough to see the coming sunrise, but pretty soon that sunrise would be their last. For I didn't care how long it took me, I would see every single fucker pay for their crimes against me and my Chosen! A vow made to the Gods and paid for by my blood down a length of steel.

"The instructions are clear, they are sending a car for me, once it gets here you will follow us, and we will take you to where the exchange will be made," Layla said, now surprisingly less cocky and confident since I had come but a mere second away from killing her. I released a low growl at this but knew that I also had to play this their way for now, because I couldn't afford to lose my shit so close to getting her back.

"Fine, then I suggest you make a call and get that fucking car here now!" I snapped before throwing her the phone, for her to do just that. She caught it and instead of giving me shit, she did as she was told, eyeing the box in my hand as she did. Gods, but even then, I tried to crush the fucking thing in my grasp, but it didn't give, not even an inch. It was Gods be damned indestructible and other than burying the thing inside a fucking volcano, then I didn't see this thorn in my side being yanked out anytime soon!

"They are here and need the space clearing," she said nodding to the destruction I had left to prevent what I thought at the time was my girl from being kidnapped. Something that turned out to be a fucking decoy!

I saw the headlights bathe the now twisted metal in a yellow glow and with a flick of my wrist pulled what remained of the gates back inside the open space, with little care about what cars they hit when doing so. Time was of the essence here and taking the seconds needed to manoeuvre around parked cars wasn't something I was wasting what little patience I had on. So, they crashed into anything in their way, now giving enough room for the main objective.

"Good, now give me the box," Layla said making me snap back,

"If you think I am that fucking stupid, then I will first ask for you to donate your severed head in return…or I could just ask those assholes in the car and let's see just how fucking loyal they are to you!" At this she paled considerably before shaking her head.

"No, I didn't fucking think so! Now get your bony ass in the car and let's go, before I just lose my fucking patience all together and just slaughter the fucking lot of you!" I snapped out this threat without knowing if it was idle or not, because I was that close to the edge here and just the sight of this traitorous bitch was making my gloved hand clench.

"Fine! Just be sure to keep up!" she snapped back, and I looked behind me to the sound of my car being brought to me from my private underground parking and said,

"Oh, don't worry, that won't be a fucking problem." Then I watched as my customised black and blood red Lamborghini Centenario was stopped in front of me. Gods almighty but I loved this fucking car. It's very meaning meant a hundred years in celebrating its ancestry and was made as a tribute to the 100th anniversary of the birth of Mr. Ferruccio Lamborghini, the man who managed to create the world-class brand.

It was black carbon fibre all over with the hint of crimson accents, which included it side skirts, calipers, a red line over the door and matching line on the wingmirrors. The whole design was created with aerodynamics in mind like most supercars, but with the extended front air splitter it meant it gave the car a mean and intimidating presence that looked as if I was driving a beast on the road.

Of course, the fact that it could do 217 miles an hour and get to speeds of 62 miles an hour in 2.8 seconds meant it could practically fly without wings. So, when Layla warned me to keep up, it was a fucking joke when getting into this car.

Ruto got out and handed me the keys, before looking to my left to see Layla getting into a blacked-out Mercedes G wagon.

"Are you sure about this?" he asked when he deemed it safe to do so.

"I can't risk anyone being seen," I told him.

"And the box?" he asked, and it was one I couldn't help but look down at, seeing as it had been in my hand all this time.

"First comes the girl, then we will wage war for the box." Now this made him grin and out of habit his thumb circled the top of what I knew was his favourite knife.

"About fucking time," he agreed as I knew he would.

"In the meantime, you're in charge, I want this place cleared out, the vault, the cars, even all of Amelia's belongings, I want everything in Königssee by tomorrow," I informed him, making him nod and hand me my phone so I could keep in contact with my council.

"And our people?" he asked referring not only to those that played nightly at the club, but also those that lived far beyond Germany.

"Bring them all home," I said as I lowered myself into the sinking dip of the bucket seat and reached up for the red leather strap ready to pull down the door, but before doing so I told him,

"And tell them, *that their King is about to go to war.*"

Thankfully at this time of night the roads were clear and would have been ideal for punishing my car and getting my frustration out in the form of a fucking good engine roaring its way through the city. However, with the car in front that I was being forced to follow, then my speeds were considered conservative at best. But then it made me think back to Amelia and how she had reacted when I had driven the stolen Aventador out of the mansion's grounds. Doing so like what she wanted to say was a bat out of hell. I would have laughed had I not been killing mad at the time. To be honest I had been surprised she had even known of the car, seeing that now it was of considerable age, just like the Centenario was now. But it was also her father's obvious love for Ferraris which made me question now, was it solely a rebellious thing or did she like Lamborghinis because she knew of my personal preference for the car brand?

She certainly would have learned common facts of my life had she wanted to, more easily through Pip who had stayed at Afterlife throughout her life. Now, as for her mother, she could fool herself into believing Pip being there was down to something she wanted and in some ways she would be right. However, Adam was my more permanent second in command and had been for hundreds of years, since I turned him.

Meaning that if I deemed it so, he would be back by my side and aiding me in ruling my world after a single phone call. But then by him being there, he was also a secret guardian to my Chosen One, which was why I hadn't yet called them back home. And even if for the last seven years Amelia hadn't lived there, she still went back on occasion, holidays and such, so it was still a natural base for them to be.

As for now though, well that was a different matter, which meant that particular phone call wasn't long in coming. As in the next few weeks ahead, I knew that I would need my most loyal and powerful beings that I had sired standing where they belonged...*by their King's side.*

I couldn't help but look to the seat next to me where I had placed that damn box and just wished that I had learnt more about it before now. The markings on the outside spoke of a great weapon used against Vampires, about the shift of power in Hell's greatest leaders and something of sacrifice. It spoke of the secrets it held inside its core as something that had the power to destroy a King's entire race. But it was as cryptic as these fucking things came!

However, one thing was as clear as fucking day, whoever had created the box knew of me and knew me well enough to know how to destroy me and with it, my people. And now I was about to hand it over to a fucking cult fully intent on making that happen!

But really, what was the alternative, for I couldn't let

them have her. I couldn't let them hurt her! Even if with my death that same outcome would become inevitable.

Gods be damned, but this was like having that fucking gun pointed to the back of her head all over again! Well, this time there was no calling their bluff and getting the box back would be something I would have to plan for, but only once I knew I had her back safely in my arms. Back to where she belonged and fucking locked away in my mountain fortress, something admittedly now, I should have done the very first second I knew her life was potentially in danger. However, my arrogance and belief that I could protect her at Transfusion had been my failing…something that wouldn't happen again, that was a fucking vow to the Gods!

I continued to follow them and was forced to cut through the lights, tapping on the large carbon fibre shift panels at the side of the steering wheel so as to speed through before traffic could prevent me from keeping on their tail. I then continued on past the Westin Grand Munich hotel and on to the Effnerstraße road, now being able to reach greater speeds on the duel carriageway. However, I was still restricted due to the car I unfortunately couldn't overtake as I would have liked. Fuck, but I hated driving at these speeds when I had a vehicle like this to play with!

I continued on heading towards the Föhringer Ring and was soon on the bridge crossing the Isar river which was when I noticed another Mercedes G wagon now coming up behind me. Well, fucking peachy, it was now a convoy. What were they expecting, a one man battle on the side of the road?

Well, the road had now turned back into a single lane so there was little they *or I* could do at this point other than all follow the Mercedes 4x4 in front. But I obviously spoke too soon, as I heard a shitty dirt bike coming up and weaving in between the cars, trying to overtake everyone and making me frown at the punk with an obvious death wish. Really, with the maneuvers he was pulling you would have thought him riding a better bike, not a shitty two stroke engine. One that I could now see cut dangerously in front of the Mercedes behind me making them beep their horn angrily. I could even see the smoke from here bellowing behind it as it was obviously burning too much oil.

But then its rider waited for the traffic to clear on the opposite side before unbelievably the brazen little fucker decided to be brave enough to overtake a fucking Lamborghini! Something I would never have allowed had I not had a car in front I was supposed to be following.

Then it got stranger still, as when overtaking me, the rider purposely stuck up his middle finger at me, making me frown in question. But then if I thought that surprising, what I saw next had me cursing in utter fucking disbelief!

"You have got to be shitting me!" I said a second after the rider pulled in front of me having only just enough room to do so, clearly having adequate skills with a bike. However, this was an insignificant thought in sight of what I could now read had been hastily spray painted on the back of a leather jacket. Three little words that I could barely believe I was fucking seeing sprayed down the rider's back, words I couldn't now ever ignore…

'Make

It

So'

And then underneath was an arrow pointing off to the right which I soon understood the second I could see the slip road, that the rider was veering off towards. So, the second I saw this I let fucking hope cloud all judgement and doubt and went with my gut. Deciding to follow the rider and doing so at the last second. The car behind me didn't react in time and other than being forced into driving into the barrier, it continued on, now running parallel to us. But I didn't care, as all I was focused on was that rider and praying like I never had before that beneath that helmet was the face I was beyond fucking desperate to see.

"Come on, fucking pull over already!" And as if hearing me, the rider pulled over onto a grass verge on the left hand side, giving me enough room to do also. Then, before I had chance to get out of the car, I watched utterly dumb-fucking-founded as the rider kicked out the stand, got off the bike and removed the helmet like some Gods be damned sex kitten all dressed in leather. Then she shook out all that black hair of hers and I swear my fucking mouth went dry and my cock threatened to split my damn denim!

Oh, but now I was out of the car, doing so with enough strength it broke the fucking door! A little factor I didn't give a shit about, as there was only her!

Only my Amelia.

But then, as if needing to confirm that this wasn't a damn dream, I was at her before she could blink, taking her face in my hands and tilting it up to me. At least I did so in a gentle way, for I could see the bruises to her skin, ones I would have been furious about had I not been too busy being in total fucking awe at seeing her again.

And this was why I ended up saying the first fucking

thing that came to my mind. And it was two words I would have never believed would have ever come from my lips.

But they did.

And I meant every fucking syllable…

"Marry me!"

CHAPTER FIVE

AMELIA

MISSING YOU

Okay, so it had to be said, when I formulated this plan, I never expected it to go as perfectly as it did. Especially being on the crappy bike I had been on. But then, when I had seen his Lambo speeding past and doing so at a forced speed I would actually have a chance at keeping up with, then I sent a thank you up to the Gods that must have been looking out for me. I also couldn't help but flip him the bird as I was overtaking him, just to be sure he would take it as another signal that it was me.

After all, it had been what I had done when locked in his safe and thinking he would likely put two and two together, the other two being in the form of my main plan. Because if that didn't work, then I knew the words of Picard would certainly do the trick, especially after what he had said this morning. And well, other than writing 'this is your girlfriend, so please follow me' on my back, then I didn't know what else was safe to do without the assholes seeing it first and taking me out.

Which brought us to now and being unable to resist getting off the bike and removing my helmet in a way all cool chicks did in the movies, with a sexy shake of my hair of course. Well, from the look of things it worked for other than a second of clear astonishment from him inside the car, the next heartbeat and he was in front of me, framing my face in his hands and asking me to bloody marry him!

Okay, so I know he was only joking but let's just say it hadn't been my first guess on what he would say to me when we were finally reunited. But then again, it was probably at the very bottom of a list of five hundred things, with 'hello Jedi master butt muncher' being about a hundred before bloody 'marry me'!

"Erm," was the only response I could give in that moment and it was thankfully one he ignored as instead, he focused on kissing me. Doing so now as though I had been gone a year, or if I was looking into this with the depth it fully deserved, then it was more like he didn't know if I had still been alive or not. And that thought broke my heart just as his kiss bound it quickly back together again.

His kiss was one of desperation, relief, love and salvation all rolled into one. To the point that I didn't know if he was ever going to let me go and it was only when I heard a vehicle reversing and now crossing the grass verge we were parked at the side of, did I think kissing me was probably something that should wait...like, I don't know, maybe until we had made our speedy getaway or something equally as smart.

So I pulled back, ignoring the way his hands were now at my back and fisted in my stolen leather jacket as if he didn't want to let me go. So, I thought it best to point out the obvious,

"Erm, shouldn't we deal with that first?" I then nodded to the car that had now only just come to a stop and Lucius in his total bad ass way, grinned down at me before looking to the side, with eyes glowing red and dangerous.

"Oh, don't worry, my sweetheart, *I intend to,*" he said and before even a door had chance to open, Lucius narrowed his eyes and after turning to face it, he raised his hands giving me that inner 'oh shit' moment. The car began vibrating as if the energy around it was humming to Lucius' commanding tune and I could hear the screaming begin even from where I stood.

Then, when one tried to brave opening a door, in what was obviously a desperate attempt at escaping a Vampire King's mighty and Hellish wrath, Lucius made a quick fist. This caused the metal around the doors to groan in an angry, twisted sound before the roof actually started boiling. The paint started to form large black bubbles that slid down the sides and onto the windows, popping and causing a strange reaction with the glass. Then, the now molten roof started to slide down the sides of the car and seem to fuse the doors shut as if they had been welded.

After this Lucius seemed to be satisfied enough that none of his victims could escape which meant he was now free to lift the car and send it hurtling in the air, flipping it so it was now making its way overhead where we stood. It was suddenly as if time had slowed down to the point where I actually had time to lift my head and watch open mouthed as the vehicle travelled over us.

However, Lucius obviously now finished with needing his hands, reached out and grabbed the front of my jacket. Then with a fisted hand, I was suddenly tugged into him, where he caught my head with his other hand. His fingers threaded through my hair where he then roughly forced my head back so he could continue where he left off, now drawing my attention away from the fact there was a flying car overhead.

The kiss was heated and all-consuming and other than the sound of the car now crashing into the woodland at the side of the road, I would most definitely have placed it in my top three. But then, with a man like Lucius, I guess it stood to reason that at least some point in our relationship, him kissing me to the sound of murder would be the norm for him. And as for me, well as long as they were in the bastards category who had tried to, attack, kidnap, rape or murder me, then I was okay with that.

"Are you alright?" he asked me once he allowed the kiss to end. Something, had we not been on the side of the road next to where he had just flipped a car like a bloody superhero, I doubted would have ended without us getting naked. But with his forehead to mine and the deep sigh he released as he asked me this question, then I could just tell that he had been going crazy with worry.

So, I raised a hand to his cheek and told him in a breathy way,

"Yeah, I'm okay." After this he raised my face to his and ran the back of his fingers over what I guessed was my

very bruised cheek. He looked as though he wanted to say something else but decided against it, so instead he took my hand and led me to his masterpiece of a supercar. He then fixed the door, one he had obviously broken in his haste to get out, then lifted it up for me like a wing on a bird. But then before letting me sit down, he reached inside and took hold of the box that had been on the seat. One I was more than a little relieved to see was still safely in his possession.

Then, whilst still holding my hand this whole time, I was lowered into the car. It was almost as if he didn't want to lose our connection, as I don't know, maybe as if he was afraid to.

The second he pulled down the door, he was around to his side and seated next to me with a speed that blurred my eyes. Then he tucked the box in the small space behind my side, telling me that by it being here, he had been ready to hand it over for what he believed was my ransom. Thank the Gods for foolish rash actions, tranquilizer guns, idiot mercenaries that don't consider them a threat and my ability to swim.

But then, when seeing for myself where he had now stowed the box, I noticed that it shared the space with something else…Lucius' sword, better known as Excalibur. I wanted to ask what exactly his plans were when bringing that kind of weapon but seeing how Lucius was focused on getting out of here, I thought it could wait.

So, after this, he flipped up a red fighter jet style switch and pressed the start button, making the impressive car sound like a beast had just been awakened from hibernation in some demonic cave somewhere in Hell. Gods, but I don't think I had heard a car so loud before or where it actually sounded as if it roared.

"Put your seatbelt on sweetheart, because this is one ride, where I am afraid, the speed limit just isn't an option." Then he pressed a button on the centre console that said corsa, flipped the overly large paddles at the side of the steering wheel, and we were hitting over 60 miles an hour in what felt like two seconds flat! It threw me back into the curve of the deep bucket seat and made me find the side of the door to hang on to. Then, doing what I deemed was crazy speeds, he continued on, weaving in and out of cars now that it was back to being two lanes. He did this until we came alongside oncoming traffic, where the second there was break in the centre, he said,

"Hold on." Then he pulled an illegal U turn using his handbrake to aid him and the car wheels screamed against the tarmac road. I had even closed my eyes for this only to open them soon after and find that unsurprisingly, we were now heading back towards the city. Of course, I screamed during this near collision, but it had to be said, Lucius could most certainly handle a car!

Then he took it up a gear and sped on, taking advantage of the light traffic and overtaking most of the time, obviously being averse to whenever there was a car in front of us. Now normally I would have tried to at least try and prevent him from driving killing speeds but considering this was about to turn into a high speed chase, I didn't think that was a bad thing.

"We are being followed," I said the second I saw the blacked out Mercedes now on our tail.

"I know," was Lucius' calm tone as if this was nothing

but a leisurely Sunday drive. Hell, I almost expected to tap on the media icon on the large centre screen and Easy by the Commodores to start playing!

We quickly approached the bridge and I instantly recognised it as not far from where I had escaped so said without thinking,

"That's where I jumped from the helicopter." At this I heard a low, rumble of a growl before Lucius said in a dangerous tone,

"You did what!?"

Ooops, in the words of my aunty Pip, 'My bad'.

"Erm…I mean stepped safely from it?" I said in a questioning tone that asked if this sounded better for him. This time when he growled it was followed swiftly by a,

"We will be discussing this! Now hold the fucking wheel," he told me making me reach across and at an awkward angle trying my best to steady the wheel. And before I could ask why I noticed another Mercedes coming towards us on the other side of the road and I knew that with the one behind also, that they would try and block us in. But then, just as we were in the centre of the bridge and the two G Wagons were close enough to create a barricade Lucius' eyes started to glow an intense fiery amber. It was as if this time he called forth his Angel side, one that I had only heard rumors about.

His whole body started to glow also, coating his skin in a luminous hue, and just as the two cars started to turn their wheels towards us, Lucius crossed his hands over his chest. Then holding his fingers curled as if he was holding something in his hands I couldn't see, he roared out and at exactly the right moment before we could hit the one in front, he threw his hands out with fingers extended. This strange action caused the two vehicles to go flying through the air and over the edge of the bridge at exactly the same time creating a mirror image of destruction.

Then Lucius calmly retook the wheel and I leaned into my side window so I could get a better look at the car that had been behind us now sinking into the water with its occupants now trying to get out before it was consumed entirely by water. One of which of these was none other than...*Layla.* I just caught her kicking out the side window before snaking her body through the gap.

"Well, that's annoying," I commented as we reached the other side of the bridge.

"What is?" Lucius asked now looking as he once did.

"Bitch face survived." He scoffed at this and promised,

"Not for long." I decided not to ask, not because I didn't want to know, as yeah, I totally did. But I just figured with him driving like he was already on the Autobahn, I didn't think it wise to piss him off any more than he clearly was. Especially seeing as I had a feeling it would have been the accelerator that would have got the brunt of his frustrations.

"Are we heading back to Transfusion?" I asked thinking this was the safest question right now.

"No," was his simple answer and one I didn't find enough to satisfy me.

"No?"

"Transfusion is compromised," he stated and I could tell with the tense line in his jaw that just the thought of what they did to the place pissed him off.

"Okay, so where to then?" I asked next, with the sinking feeling I already knew the answer.

"To where I should have taken you and the box the second you arrived in Germany," he said sternly, as it was clear he blamed himself here. So, I decided it was time to be lighthearted and say,

"The police station?" I asked as a joke, one he obvious didn't think was funny, not if the glare was anything to go by.

"Königssee." Ah, his mountain fortress, but of course that feeling had been correct.

"You weren't to know this would happen Lucius, and locking me away in some…"

"Gods be damned, Amelia, I should have fucking shackled you to me the moment you set foot in my club!" he snapped making my jaw go slack.

"Erm…that's a little caveman, don't you think, even for someone with an obviously big club," I said this time thanking the Lords in Heaven it at least got me a slight lip twitch, one that nearly made it into a small smile when I wagged my eyebrows at him.

"Big club or not, the temptation to chain you to me is increasing by the day, princess," was his equally possessive reply.

"Wow, how Jabba the Hut of you…what's next, a gold and red bikini and a chained collar around my neck, because you know, that shit didn't end so well for Jabba," I said and one look told me he had no clue what the Hell I was talking about. His next comment confirmed as much,

"Okay, so I am liking the idea of the gold and red bikini, especially the chained collar to match…however, I have no idea what a Jabba is," he told me, making me throw my hands up dramatically and say,

"Seriously, where were you in 1977, hibernating in a coffin somewhere in Transylvania?" I said making him roll his eyes and reply with a curt,

"Really?"

"And in the early eighties at least?" I asked trying to even picture him in that era.

"Probably wishing I was fucking hibernating, that's where" he said making me smirk before saying,

"What's wrong, weren't a fan of shiny shirts, white suits and big hair?" I asked giggling at just the thought. He granted me a look as if to say, 'what do you think'.

"Oh wait, I have just the thing!" I said getting excited and pressing the media button on the centre console screen. Then I found the music player and knowing the car had its own access to the internet I tapped in the song I wanted.

"This one is just for you, lover boy," I said as 80's 'Missing you' by John Waite started playing, making Lucius groan and shake his head as if he didn't know what to do with me. Then I started biting my fingers, smiling around the tips of two just before I asked in a cheeky way,

"Come on, handsome, admit it…"

"Admit what?" he asked trying to be stern but failing when his lips twitched again at my playful mood, one that I needed right now just to keep from focusing on what had happened to me in the last Gods only knew how many hours.

So, I teased,

"That you had a blonde perm." At this his face was a picture and his reaction was so funny, that I threw my head back and roared with laughter when he shouted,

"Fuck no!" Then he growled the rest of the way through the song, speeding through the streets of Munich, with what I knew was him trying to keep his face straight the whole time. Well, at least I was laughing instead of crying and I had to say, when I was falling from that helicopter to what I knew could have been to my death, I didn't think the day would end by me laughing my ass off to the idea of Lucius once having a perm!

"All that neon, I am not surprised it was my aunty Pip's favorite era," I said smiling at the thought of her back then.

"I am going to take a wild guess here and say that she made quite an impression on your childhood, giving your obvious love for old pop culture?" he asked and I wondered if he really wanted to know or just knew that I obviously needed the distraction from the reality of what we had just endured. Either way, I was grateful for both.

"That she did. Although, I can't say that my dad was grateful, seeing as he was always the one that ended up taking me to Comicons," I said making Lucius look incredulous for a moment.

"What?" I asked with a frown.

"I am shocked that he would." I frowned harder at this and asked,

"Why, because he is King? He is also a dad and seeing as he is an overprotective one at that, he wouldn't have trusted me going with anyone else…besides, I think he felt guilty because there was so much I wasn't allowed to do," I said making Lucius look thoughtful a moment.

"Your protection came first, as it should have," he commented and I released a sigh and with it, all humour left me.

"What, you didn't approve?" he asked, and I shrugged my shoulders before telling him,

"Not really, but then again, he isn't the only one to continue underestimating me, so what else was this mortal princess to expect." I think my deflated tone was easy to detect as he said my name in a soft but reprimanding tone,

"Amelia."

"It's fine, let's just drop it okay," I said looking out the window and seeing my sullen expression looking back at me, now that the bright lights of the city were behind us. I suddenly wondered how long it would take us to get to his fortress and would have asked but Lucius got there first, obviously having something to say. So, after this moment of silence Lucius cleared his throat before he told me,

"I saw what you did to those men, Amelia." I closed my eyes and swallowed hard just thinking back to that last fight and what I had to do to survive it. Meaning now I wasn't sure how I felt about him knowing what I had to do just to keep breathing, as it wasn't as if he would have been opposed to the violence. No, it was more the guilt I knew he would have felt at seeing what could have happened.

I released a sigh before turning to face him, seeing his features now only lit from the reds and blues from the illuminated display in front of him, no doubt telling him a speed that was way past the limit. Or at least it would have done had we not been on the Autobahn, which technically, didn't have one.

"Yeah," was all I had it in me to say, as like I said, not fully understanding how I felt with him knowing what I did…that was until he replied with,

"Your father would have been proud of you." I sucked in a shuddered breath, as he had no idea how much that meant to me but then I was about to find out, it wasn't quite as much as what it meant to me when he added,

"I was proud of you." This time when I closed my eyes, I did so as the emotions filled me with peace. I was just about to say something else, probably a joke or something equally inappropriate in that moment just to lighten the mood, when he beat me to it.

And when he did, I really wished that joke had made it out first, as dread now filled me,

"Now, as for jumping out of a fucking helicopter, well it's time to explain that to me and be warned, princess, it better not start with…" I quickly cut him off and finished that sentence for him with what actually happened, doing so before the echo of one pissed off demon boyfriend…

"I shot the pilot."

Jump of Faith

CHAPTER SIX

JUMP OF FAITH

"**Y**ou did what?!" he shouted making me wince and I had to ask myself why the hell I just blurted that shit out like that! Seriously, what was wrong with me, well apart from the obvious verbal diarrhea...*eww.*

"Okay, so that sounded bad," I admitted, not that this helped much.

"So, it didn't happen that way then?" Lucius said with premature relief coating his words, which I didn't think wise to let him believe for too long. Not seeing as I had already tore the band aid off, so didn't see any point in putting that sucker back on there.

"Oh no, it happened that way, but just sounded worse being blurted out like that."

"Gods give me fucking strength," Lucius uttered under his breath and closed his eyes for a moment as he rubbed the top of his forehead. I tensed the whole time, and decided it was wise to bite my lip on making a remark like, 'shouldn't you be watching the road', or 'hey honey, please don't kill us because I pissed you off'…that type of something.

"Hey, but shouldn't you be contacting your council, you know, to let them know what happ…"

"They can wait, this however, cannot!" he snapped and for the moment I allowed his little freak out, knowing it was done solely because he cared about me and most likely, he had been going out of his mind with worry. I could tell that in that single look alone when he finally saw that I was alright and also, well let's face it, saving the fucking day, thank you very much!

"Alright, I will tell you but first just for my peace of mind, is there any way I can just sugar coat this for you seeing as you are currently driving what must be a million dollars' worth of…" This was where he swiftly cut me off in his usual pissed off way.

"One point nine million and no, there is no way you can sugar coat you purposely shooting a pilot and having no other choice but to open the door and jump from a fucking helicopter into the fucking Isar river!"

"Does it help that I killed those on board too?" I asked thinking back to him being proud that I had kicked ass back at the club. He raised a brow my way and said,

"Then consider it slightly frosted and continue, whilst my patience isn't spent and therefore going to cost me that one point nine million." I rolled my lips again, trying really hard not to smile at that, making him shoot me a look and say on a growl,

"Don't you dare fucking laugh." So, I tightened my lips and tried to hold it in because really, Lucius was pretty funny with his dry wit, even when he was trying not to be. But then, when I felt it breaking free, I covered my mouth and shook my head, making him roll his eyes and scoff at me.

However, as usual I could see him trying to hide his own amusement at my childish behaviour, no doubt slightly glad that I was acting this way instead of falling to pieces. Because really, I had lost count of the amount of times I could have died tonight, therefore it was little wonder why I didn't exactly want to think too much about it. But then, how far I could get 'not thinking about it' when Lucius was expecting a minute by minute recap on what had happened, I didn't know. So, I decided to tell it in a matter fact type of way, as much as I could and wondered if it would come across as not just being downplayed like I was hoping.

"Okay, so the short version, I woke up on the floor of the helicopter, managed to grab what I thought was a gun and threatened to shoot the two soldier boys if they didn't land and let me go. Then, after they informed me it was a tranquilizer gun, I called their bluff and threatened to shoot the pilot," I told him thinking this was reasonable...*his face said otherwise.*

"Good Gods, Amelia," he said shaking his head.

"Well, I knew I had to do something because it didn't take a genius to know that they would use me to get the bloody box and we both know how that can't happen!" I snapped making him rub a hand at the back of his neck and groan before forcing out,

"Continue telling me what happened next."

"Are you sure you can handle it?" I asked in a tone that suggested I didn't think he could. However, he just shot me a look that I knew not to argue against because there was no point. He was like a dog with a bone and wanted to know everything, despite how obvious it was that this was difficult for him to hear. Which is why I said,

"Okay, so just remember that before I tell you this next part that I am here, I didn't die, I am safe, and I am in the car with you...*yeah?*"

"Yes, and by the grace of the fucking Gods so it would seem!" he snapped, making me frown before telling him,

"Err, I hate to point shit out here Lucius but shouldn't you be thanking the fucking Gods that you have a girlfriend who didn't just sit in a corner, lose her shit, and cry for someone to save her but instead actually was the one that just saved the fucking day!?" I shouted back, finally giving him enough to think on. Only instead of saying calmly, 'Yes Amelia, you're right, you're brave and courageous actions did in fact save the fucking day and I love you dearly for it!' no, this was Lucius we were talking about... *clearly,* I thought with a frown.

"Yes and I would like to remind you that your life is too

fucking important to me for you to risk, so I will kindly ask you not to do so *ever-a-fucking-gain* and instead wait for me to come and save the fucking day! *Got it?!"* he growled making me fold my arms across my chest and pout, deciding I was too pissed off right now to argue against that statement. So, instead, I looked out the window, again seeing myself instead of the world we were passing at speed. I heard him release a heavy sigh before saying my name, this time in a softer tone than 'Mr Angry, I look hot in denim pants' from seconds ago.

"Amelia."

"What!?" I snapped back.

"Sweetheart, look at me." This time I was the one to release a sigh before eventually giving in and looking at him, seeing that his gaze had finally softened.

"I *am* proud of you. You were incredibly brave and yes, I thank the Gods that it turned out the way it did. However, you must admit, that your actions could have gone very wrong and in a way you would not have come back from. So, given this fact, surely you understand why being the person who very much wants to keep you alive for a fucking eternity, would be pissed off at hearing the way his Chosen One had risked her life to… how did you put it, save the fucking day…yeah?" Okay so when he put it like that, then yeah, I guess I could see his point.

"Now please, tell me the rest."

"Alright, but please try and reserve your judgement until the end or at least try and be less growly." He raised a brow but that was it, so I continued,

"So, instead of just calling my bluff, they tried to take the gun by force which meant the gun went off, *by accident* and shot the pilot…so, not entirely my fault with that one. But then seeing as neither of them could fly, I saw we were headed for over the river and decided to take my chances," I told him and tried to ignore the way his knuckles on his one bare hand turned bone white from holding onto the steering wheel that hard.

"So, you pulled the door and jumped," he surmised and I could see that it was taking a vast amount of restraint from losing his temper again.

"Well, not exactly." I confessed quietly, wondering why I did. Jeez Fae, next time your big bad broody boyfriend asks you a question like that, you just, smile and nod. That way it's not really a lie if you don't speak.

"Okay, so I tried that but then the asshole had it in his head that if he was going down then I was going with him, seeing as he was a bit pissed off with…well, you know, the fact I'd just caused their deaths and stuff…anyway, he grabbed my dress and to get free I needed to…"

"I think I am seeing where this is going," he said cutting me off seeing as they had found my dress and sent him a picture of it as proof of life.

"And do I want to know the reason you're dressed in leather?" he asked nodding down at my rock biker chick attire.

"You like?" I asked winking at him making his lips twitch again and shake his head before informing me,

"Sweetheart, when I get to fuck you in leather, it won't be some skinny guy's worn biker gear, but something skintight that needs to be clawed off you just to free your skin from it," he said making me swallow a whopping great lump named lust! Holy mother of a moon goddess, that was quite a picture he just painted. I just hoped I wasn't visibly panting.

"Mmm, I see you like this idea…this pleases me," he informed me now adding to that secret pant with a not so secret blush.

"So, you stole some clothes, adding to the reason you smell of Marijuana," he said after voicing his sexual fantasy that had momentarily just stolen my voice. Which was why when I did finally speak, I didn't fully think about my words or the way I should have worded them.

"Oh, that, no I just stopped for a quick spliff with my new homies, only well…let's just say that they weren't as accommodating as I would have liked, so they needed a little convincing to give up the goods. But then, I didn't exactly feel bad for breaking a guy's nose and then some other guy's arm seeing as they made their intentions pretty clear when seeing a half-naked soaking wet girl, who was obviously in need of aid." I said making him growl dangerously enough to tell me it was coming more from his demon this time.

"For fuck sake, Amelia! Is there ever going to be a fucking day, just one, where you are not intent on getting fucking attacked!?" he snapped making me frown and finally I officially lost my shit and in a big way!

"Stop fucking swearing at me! And may I remind you that up until that fucking box came into my life, then the only danger to me was my own clumsiness and shit like falling off the toilet whilst painting my own damn nails was the only reason I ended up in an emergency room!"

"Amelia, sweet…" I cut him off as I wasn't finished with my freak out rant,

"So, can you at least cut me some fucking slack, as it's

not like I have a damn sticker on my forehead asking for this shit to happen and who wants to see what it feels like to be stabbed by a damn pencil! I mean don't you think that all I want is one Gods be damned night in my pajamas, on takeout Fridays, a Lego set to make, whilst spilling shit on my rug for like the millionth time whilst watching the USS Enterprise getting wrecked for the gazillionth time, instead of killing people with stationery like John fucking Wick!" After I had finished, I was now panting for a very different reason. I was that angry and didn't realise until he was out of the car that he had actually pulled over. Then, just before I had chance to get out of the car and ask what the hell he was doing, my door was opened, my seatbelt was undone, and I was being pulled out the car!

"What are you..." I was cut off the second I found myself in Lucius' arms, and this time he simply held me to him, cradling my head to his chest and I wasn't sure in that moment who needed this more, him or me. But whichever it was, the fact remained that the second he took me in his arms, the flood gates opened and I found myself with tears in my eyes, as the entirety of the night slammed back into me. Because I may have been strong and brave when it all happened but right now, well I could be vulnerable. I could be emotional. I could be...*human*. And I could be all these things because I trusted Lucius to take care of them. To accept them as being me and to know that this was all I needed right now.

And because he knew this, well it just made me love him all the more for it.

"I...I killed people, Lucius." I whispered into his chest as I felt the tears get too heavy and fall, soaking his dark T

shirt. I felt the crook of his finger under my chin and as he raised my face up, I found him looking down at me tenderly. Then he wiped my tears away and said,

"You only did what you had to do, sweetheart."

"I know but…" At this he placed a finger over my lips and said more sternly this time,

"There is no but with that one, Amelia, there is only death and suffering to those that try to take you away from me and for doing so without hesitation on your part, is what makes me proud…*you did so well, sweetheart…so well,*" he told me, whispering this last part over my lips after tipping my face up even more, so he could seal his words with a soft and gentle kiss.

"So, you're not mad at me?" I asked in what I knew was a shy voice.

"No, I'm not mad at you, I am angry at myself for not being there, for not protecting you the way I should have."

"Lucius that's not…" I tried but he cut me off.

"But that changes from this moment on, do you understand, for you will always be by my side from now on, *where you will remain,*" he told me making me visibly gulp before needing to clear my voice.

"But Lucius that's not…"

"No, Amelia! There will be no fighting me on this and that is final," he vowed and I knew in that moment it was useless even trying to get him to see sense. But the reality was clear…*he felt responsible.*

So, I just released a heavy sigh and remained silent, that way I wasn't disagreeing or agreeing to anything. But instead, I looked up at him and said the only thing in that moment that was needed, for both of us.

"Kiss me."

And thankfully...*I didn't need to ask twice.*

A little time later and we were back in the car heading towards Königssee. I had to say, the moment we left the city behind I had wished it had been daylight outside, as I just knew the views would have been incredible. You could almost see it, the vast fields, woodlands, and lakes in the distance only lit by the soft touch of the moon. And to say that after Lucius' vow to never let me leave his side, well then, I needed the solitude in that moment to try and sort out exactly what that meant in his mind.

I would have asked, but to be honest, I was actually too afraid to. Because I was rapidly losing the life I had built around me until I could barely remember what it had been like. And in my rant I had conveyed as much. Because once upon a time my life had been simple. It had been the same as most people. The route of life that consisted of getting up in the morning and going into work, whilst juggling at the time what felt like a million things.

Things that only ever mattered in that safe normal life. Things like if I had enough clean panties to last me the rest of the week? Would the rest of the milk last out just one more bowl of cereal before I have to buy another? How many toilet rolls were there in the cupboard under the sink and did I remember to pay my internet bill that month before Netflix was cut off?

These were the extent of my worries, even with who my parents were and with the knowledge of the hidden world around me. This had been *my world*. And now, in such a short space of time, my life had been turned upside down and shaken a few times at that, just for good measure. Oh, and then add a couple of bad guys, a few fights to the death, guns, and psycho ex and a ridiculously hot Vampire King who just happened to become my new boyfriend and all that safe, normal, 'the milk might have gone sour' life had unravelled the second I stepped inside Transfusion.

"That looks like a lot of heavy thoughts there, sweetheart," Lucius said breaking through the silence as he had obviously been giving me this time to sort my head out. But I didn't exactly think now was the best time to get into it.

"I am just tired," I lied, something he actually laughed at.

"What?"

"Gods, but you're a shit liar," he said calling my bluff…*annoyingly so.*

"I don't think I have done too badly, after all your stupid ex bought it."

"Yes, and emphasis on the word stupid," he remarked in a knowing tone.

"You bought it," I argued making him shrug his shoulders and say,

"Under the circumstances, then yes you're right but now, well I know when you are lying to me, so stop trying to change the subject and tell me, what is on your mind, Amelia." I released another heavy sigh and decided to be honest, telling him,

"I just don't know how any of this is going to work."

"Ah, this again," he commented. However, his tone was empathetic and non judging.

"I take it this has to do with what I said earlier?" he asked making me nod.

"Alright, sweetheart, we still have over an hour to go, so let's talk." Um, me and Lucius talking about the future of our relationship, well this should be fun, as in *not at all*. Because even though I had pretty much won the love lottery with finally getting to be with the man I had been obsessed with since I was sixteen, it still didn't mean I was ready to throw my entire, independent life away for a guy.

"I think this is the part where you start talking," Lucius said trying to prompt this awkward conversation into gear. Which is precisely why I stalled it by saying,

"I don't know where to start."

"Well, what are your biggest fears?" he asked and again, I went for the easy answer this time,

"That I wake up one morning and find out that Sci- fi never existed and Star Wars was just the name of some lame reality tv show, where famous people try to kill each other," I said making him shake his head, but at least I got out a few deep chuckles from him.

"Let's try and focus on reality right now."

"But that's just my point!" I suddenly shouted.

"Your point, sweetheart, you haven't made a point yet, *that is my point,*" he said, making me shake my head a little and ask,

"Wait, I am confused, whose point are we focusing on?"

"Mine, because you haven't made one yet!" Lucius snapped making me giggle before pointing a finger at him and saying in a cheeky tone,

"Gotchya!" He gave me an exasperated look and then

one of those 'trying to find patience from the patience tree' type of ways, he said my name…yet…again…

"Amelia, please, I am trying to have a conversation with you about this, which is increasingly difficult when two things are happening."

"Them being?" I asked in earnest this time.

"You stalling, and you being cute when stalling." At this I couldn't help but smile this time, doing so like a cat licking the cream off her paws.

"You think I'm cute?" I asked in that knowing, cocky way that was now totally teasing him, I knew this when he rolled his eyes at me.

"You fucking know I do, so stop playing with me and just tell me…"

"I miss my Lego okay!" I blurted out, then quickly frowned at myself for starting with something so lame.

"Come again?"

"Well, not just Lego, I mean that was way down the list really but somehow just ended up at the top and should have even been under Crunchy Nut Chocolate Clusters." Lucius shook his head as if trying to make sense of my craziness and his conclusion was,

"You miss playing with toys?"

"No! Okay, so for starters Lego is not a toy…I mean, well, yes it is if you're a kid, but to an adult collector, it is so much more, like a puzzle you frame and put on your wall."

"People do that?" he asked with a frown that said, 'why the fuck?' without the words.

"Yeah…wait you've never seen that?" I asked realising before he said anything my mistake in asking that question.

Because really, a Vampire King and puzzles? He confirmed this blunder of mine when he said,

"When in the Gods long list of names, would I have ever seen that Amelia, do I look like the puzzle junkie to you?"

"See, now that is called making a point," I commented with another smirk, one that had him muttering,

"Gods give me…"

"I am pretty sure you're strong enough there, honey and anyway, just because…"

"Wait, what did you just call me?" he asked me suddenly cutting me off again and I had to say that this conversation was thankfully off the rails. In fact, it was more like flying off the track and currently hurtling into space. Although now I was unsure as to whether this was a good thing or not, considering his reaction to being called honey. Which is why I tentatively said,

"Erm…honey? Or if you don't like that, you could be a babe, sugar, sweetie, but then that's too close to my own pet name and there will just be sweets all over the place and left, right, and centre… but then there are things like, hottie, sexy pants, or my personal favorite, Master of the Vampire Universe, although on reflection that might be a bit too long to shout in a supermarket when I can't find you…like when people name their cats Miss snuggle mittens…I mean, who the hell wants to be shouting that at two in the morning when you need to get the damn cat in 'cause its thundering… please by the Gods will you stop me already!" I ended up shouting at him even though it was clear he was enjoying himself far too much to do such a thing, seeing as this was when he threw his head back at laughed at me.

"Seriously, could you be any more fucking cute!" he said

through his laughter, making it hard to hold back the smile, because well one, I loved being able to make him laugh and secondly, I seriously loved it when he called me cute. But then he started shaking his head as if something had just hit him, making me ask,

"What?"

"Well, sweetheart, you are a fucking enigma." I frowned, all traces of happy 'cute endearment' glow gone.

"Why?"

"Because you can be fucking adorable and cute and fucking funny in one instance and then I think back to the four broken bodies I found in your apartment that you brutally took down, then I find myself still asking how you can be the same person?" I couldn't help but start biting my fingertip at this, both embarrassed that he had pointed this all out but liking that he was proud all the same. Which was why I commented in what I knew was a shy way,

"Well, I couldn't exactly see the Chosen One of a Vampire King being weak and scared...not like I had been when I first came to Transfusion." At this he granted me a soft and tender look and before saying anything he took my hand from near my mouth and pulled it to his lips to kiss.

"You are right, I am blessed with both the funny and cute personality I adore and the bad ass warrior woman that I can't wait to get back in my bed after first showing off her new home," he told me and this time my smile wasn't hidden behind my fingertips or suppressed by a roll of my lips.

"I am glad you think so," I commented when he released my hand, after first biting the tips for himself of course.

"Besides, I am looking forward to getting you on my mats and seeing what you've got."

"Erm…your mats?"

"In my training room," he told me making me gulp at this and before I started panicking that he might mean what I really hoped he didn't mean, I asked,

"And what would I be doing there?" At this Lucius granted me his own version of total badass, in the way of a bad boy grin, before saying,

"Isn't it obvious…"

"You will be fighting me."

CHAPTER SEVEN

MONEY FIGHTS

"*Y*ou will be fighting me,*" he said making me tense.

"Erm, yeah okay, that is so not happening!" I scoffed making him raise a brow at me.

"Oh, it's happening sweetheart, make no mistake about it, for I will have my way."

"Oh yeah and what makes you so sure…what exactly is in it for me?" I asked with a fold of my arms.

"Well, apart from learning all I can teach you and adding to what skills you already possess…"

"Yes, apart from that, what else?" I said quickly before he could make any more of those all-important 'good points' of his.

"Well, then there is also the end of our training when I get to fuck you raw on those mats but just to add to the incentive, what about if I buy you all the fucking Lego sets you want…will that be enough for my arm breaking, little

95

princess?" he asked making me burst out laughing before saying,

"Yep, that will do it!"

"Which part?" he enquired making me grin.

"Well, you will just have to wait and see, won't you? Besides, I have always wanted the Hogwarts castle...it's over six thousand pieces."

"The what now?" he asked clearly clueless on yet another geek cult masterpiece. Reason why I muttered to myself,

"But of course, he hasn't heard of Harry Potter."

"I am taking this as yet another passion of yours?" he surmised making me wonder just how long it was going to take me to bring him up to speed on all the cult classics beloved the world over.

"Well, I do have many," I said with a wink.

"Um, yes and I have a feeling one will take precedence over them all, starting from when I finally get you there." I laughed at this knowing he was talking about sex and well, I had to agree with him on that one. I was getting horny just sat in this car for over an hour and well, let's just say the leather pants weren't helping much. Still, I felt the need to enquire,

"You seem very keen on getting me there and I have a feeling it's not solely down to getting me into bed, seeing as if that were the case we would have just stopped at a nearby hotel for the night." He granted me a look and again there was enough light from the dash to show me his features had turned serious.

"It is the safest place I can keep you."

"Keep me? You make me sound like a diamond

necklace," I replied on a laugh but then he looked far too thoughtful in that moment that it compelled me to have to remind him,

"You do get that I am not a possession...*right?*"

"Well, you are mine," was his blunt response and in a way that was as if he was pointing out the obvious and simply stating facts. Something that really started to worry me.

"Lucius!" was my own shocked reply.

"Alright, but *you do get*, that you were born for me, the Gods chose you to be mine, what do you think that means?" he asked with a raise of his brow.

"That you're going to put me on a shelf and light me up so I look pretty?" I joked making him frown and groan.

"Oh, come on Lucius, you know what I mean," I complained.

"No, it's you that doesn't understand, Amelia. You. Are. Mine. Which means this is it for you. Now, I understand this maybe a lot to take in but ask yourself, when your mother met your father, did her life stay the same?" Now this thought really had me frowning because I knew for a fact that it most certainly did not. Of course, she had been at college when she met my dad and started working for him as a waitress as a side gig. Which was when she caught his eye and after that, well destiny had already set a course for them, seeing as she was his Chosen One.

However, I also knew that because of my dad and all the things surrounding how they eventually got together, that it had taken her quite a while until she finished college. This was mainly because she got pregnant with me shortly after they were married, or at least, that's the story they told. As I don't know why, but I had a feeling that my dad had knocked up his Chosen One, that being my mum, before the church bells rang. And what gave it away was my dad's face any time my mum ever told stories of the past. One time he even patted a desk in a suggestive way that totally grossed me out seeing as it was obviously to relay a secret message to my mum.

But that was my mum's life, and this was mine we were talking about here, which was why I focused back on that.

"So, what exactly are you saying here, Lucius, that I have no choices anymore?" I couldn't help but snap out the question.

"No, just that they are limited," was his tactful and pragmatic response. Needless to say, he was fooling no one.

"And what is that supposed to mean!?"

"Exactly how it sounds, sweetheart," he said still keeping his tone at an even level, unlike my own which was hitting highs only dogs could hear.

"Oh, don't you sweetheart me! Exactly how it sounds isn't my idea of how it should sound!"

"And how should it sound?" he asked, again keeping his tone calm and even, which infuriated me more.

"Like we are in a relationship, not like I am your bloody pet to be cared for and carried around like one of those poor handbag dogs that has no choice but to find themselves in Louis Vuitton staring longingly out of a net window wishing they could just be free to take a piss on the grass whenever they want!"

"What, by the Gods, are you talking about, woman!?" This was a bloody good question.

"Oh, I don't fucking know, it's not like I am saying pull

over so I can squat on the grass here, Lucius! I am just saying that I want a say in my life and just because you are my boyfriend it doesn't mean that I am handing over all of my important life making decisions to you."

"Gods Amelia, but I am not your fucking boyfriend here." Oh, now he snaps!

"Then what the hell are you!?" I asked unable to help sounding offended. He growled in frustration before snapping back,

"I am your soul mate, your eternal life partner, your King, your fucking Chosen One and who knows, maybe one day the word husband will make it in there too, but boyfriend, Gods Amelia, it sounds so...so..." Okay, so the marry me part of the night had just been confirmed as a definite joke then, although had to say...Not. Fucking. Funny.

Which was why I yelled,

"What?!"

"Juvenile," he answered in frustration, raking a hand through his hair.

"Yeah, well it may sound juvenile to you, but that's exactly what you are, because I am not going to start going around and introducing you as my 'eternal life partner' because for one, that sounds hippy and will just make me want to braid daisies in your hair, which I am pretty sure you would be opposed to?" At this he granted me a stern look and said,

"What do you fucking think?"

"Apart from you looking pretty, that you would rather shave off your eyebrows and wear comedy stick on ones from a dollar store for the month of June…" Well, at least at this point he burst out laughing, as I carried on,

"But that is beside the point here, as until we are married then I am not introducing you as anything other than my boyfriend."

"*Until* we are married?" he asked, suddenly catching me out on my words and I swear I don't think I had felt my cheeks get so hot so quickly.

"I just mean… well, I didn't…I mean of course I don't think that we will…you know… erm what was I saying…I mean really, what did I even say, 'cause I can't remember now…so this car, does it get good mileage?" At this Lucius burst out laughing again before telling me,

"Gods, but how I do love to watch you squirm." At this I shot him an 'I am not impressed look' and knew instantly with his smirk that it was one he didn't take seriously. But then again, when did he ever?

"Can we please drop this subject," I asked knowing that there was no way to dig myself out of the marriage hole, one he seemed far too happy watching me trying to scramble out of.

"As you wish," he said again fighting that knowing grin of his before he went on to say,

"So, getting back to our conversation, before it was swayed by me getting you in my training room and talk of marriage."

"Oh, you wanna talk about Lego instead?" I asked with a smirk of my own.

"Not really no, but I would like you to elaborate on why that statement was blurted out…*above your favorite cereal,*" he asked letting me know that he had most definitely been listening. It was sweet, how he wanted to talk through my fears. But seeing as the more he spoke about what my future held, the more freaked out I became, I knew this wasn't going to be a conversation in my favour. That he would probably end up railroading me into making decisions I wasn't ready to make yet.

"Okay, so it's like my job, I love my work." At this he looked thoughtful a moment and I knew he couldn't just say what I wanted him to say. Like he would move to London for me so I could continue working. Which led me on to my next biggie,

"And it's like my flat."

"Amelia, really…it's just a flat." I couldn't say that I particularly cared for the tone he used, which is why I told him,

"But that's where you are wrong, it's not just a flat, *it's my flat.*"

"So, you intend to live there your entire life and never move?" he asked making something of a point.

"I am not saying that, but you have to understand where I am coming from, that flat isn't just a place I live for the time being, it's mine."

"I know this," he stated believing in his words.

"No, you don't, and how could you, you are thousands of years old and have lived in I don't know how many places. You're also probably richer than a bloody sultan and can afford to buy whatever you want. I bet you couldn't even list all the addresses of the buildings you own."

"Yes, and if I recall I am not the only rich person in this car." I frowned at him realising that he really had no clue, which is why I stated,

"That is where you are wrong."

"And your parents, what of their fortune, for you can't tell me…"

"Exactly…*my parents*…not mine, it's their money, Lucius." At this he rolled his eyes at me and said,

"Then you are foolish."

"Excuse me!?" I snapped.

"Do you really think that just because you didn't earn it that it isn't yours?" I folded my arms across my chest, making the leather of the jacket groan.

"That's exactly what I think, and I don't see how that makes me foolish."

"Sweetheart, your trust fund alone would be one greater than that Sultan's fortune," he informed me like this was a certainty.

"I don't have a trust fund," I told him making him laugh and in turn, me frown.

"Yeah, okay, whatever you say, beautiful," he said in that condescending way that people weren't exactly thrilled about.

"What, I don't!"

"And you know that for certain, do you?" he asked with a raise of his brow like he sure as shit didn't believe it.

"Lucius, my dad gave me a credit card with no limit on it when I left, do you know how much I have spent on it?"

"Knowing you, not a penny," he said guessing right and telling me that he knew this about me. I was very similar to my mum in that sense, as she was the same way. She believed in paying her own way and struggled with my dad's extreme wealth for years after they were married. I had always been independent, and yes, naturally when I was a kid, then I was spoiled rotten, mainly by my dad. But despite this, I still knew when I finally left home, that I desperately wanted to make it on my own.

"Exactly," I said, making him quickly reply with,

"Exactly nothing, as you just proved my point."

"How so?"

"You may have not spent any money on that card but just the fact that your father gave it to you proves my point." Okay, so now I was really frowning because despite the answer I gave, I now had that nagging feeling that maybe there was truth to his words.

"No, it doesn't!"

"Oh, so you think it is beyond the realms of reality to believe that he would give you a limitless card and not also think of your future. You think your overprotective and extremely rich father wouldn't have set up a trust fund the day you took your first breath." Okay, well there it was! As with the way he just worded it then yeah, now I did, and my face must have said as much.

"Yeah, that's what I thought. Not that any of this matters," he added in a tone that suggested what he meant was obvious, which yet again in Lucius' world, it so wasn't. Which was why I asked,

"What do you mean?"

"I care not for any money your father wishes to thrust upon you, so it should be of little concern." Oh Gods, but this sounded like another can of worms to me.

"Erm, well I agree it's of little concern, but I have a feeling we don't mean the same thing when we each say that?"

"You won't need his money," he said as more of a statement and yep, totally a can of worms.

"Care to elaborate," I asked, knowing instantly that this was most likely a mistake, one I made despite knowing this.

"I think we established I am rich, comparable to a Sultan wasn't it?" he teased but I ignored this and moved straight along with,

"Yes, but I fail to see what that has to do with me?" At this Lucius rolled his eyes and started muttering to the roof of the Lambo and doing so in a language I didn't know this time.

"I think we established already that you are mine, Amelia, and seeing as you are a smart girl, then it wouldn't be hard for you to figure out the rest." Okay, so at this my mouth dropped at what he was implying.

"Oh no! We are most definitely not opening that financial can of worms, in fact, let's just bury it now and never talk about it!"

"You're right, we don't need to talk about it as there isn't really anything *to* talk about, for it is simply an absolute that is happening." Now I was the one to roll my eyes and start muttering, only unlike him, I did my asking the Gods for help in English.

"I am starting to understand what my mother went through," I said before thinking about it, always feeling weird about mentioning my mum around Lucius for blindingly obvious reasons.

"Yes, and it is also common knowledge what a pain in the royal ass she is, so I am starting to understand what your father went through," he replied back in a curt tone.

"Oh, because wanting to pay your own way in life is such a bad thing, is it!?" I snapped.

"It is when it gets in the way of getting me what I want!" he snapped back.

"And what is that, some gold digging eye candy on your arm with the IQ of a 90's turtleneck?" Well, at least now he was laughing.

"I don't think your IQ will ever be in question, sweetheart, and as for eye candy on my arm, I would rather that eye candy in my bed laid out for me like a feast, after all, I know how fucking addictive you taste," he said making me blush and have to roll my lips to stop my smile.

"I think it's safer we don't talk about this either," I said in a shy voice as it was clear we would never agree on this and I already knew how pushy Lucius was in trying to get his own way.

"Do you mean sex or money?" he asked with a smirk he wasn't trying to hide.

"Until we get to where we are going, then I would say both," I said then nodded down at the obvious erection straining against his jeans in an overly obvious way due to his size. He chuckled and said,

"Yes, well around you, it is a common occurrence, so you'd better get used to seeing it, sweetheart," he said in a totally unashamed way that had me blushing and secretly high fiving my inner sex kitten.

"Mmm, looks like my girl likes this," he said to himself making me unable now not to bite my fingertips giving into my habit. Of course, Lucius noticed this and reached across so he could pull them from my mouth. But then he didn't let go and instead brought them to his own lips to nibble on before sucking them into his mouth. Gods, but it felt so possessive and was undeniably hot!

It was only after he had released them, that he asked,

"Why do you bite your fingers?"

"Well, I started off biting my nails, but then I would make them bleed and they would get sore, so I decided to force myself out of the habit…because, one oww, and two, I like have something to paint. So now, instead of biting my nails, I sometimes find myself biting my fingertips instead, but I am in the process of trying to break that habit as well." This last part granted me a look before he asked,

"Why?"

"Why what?" I asked with a little shake of my head as I was taken back by what it was I had said that he would be questioning.

"Why are you trying to break that habit…does it cause you pain or damage?"

"Well, no but…" I started to say but Lucius getting enough of his answer, interrupted me.

"Then don't stop."

"But it makes me look…"

"It makes you look fucking cute and adorable, that's what," Lucius said, interrupting me yet again and in a way that was sweet because, really, could any girl ever get enough of being called that by someone as hot as Lucius… *err no, I don't think so!*

"Is this you *asking* me not to stop?" I asked in a shy voice.

"Yes Amelia, this is me asking you not to stop doing something that's cute and obviously brings you comfort," he said in a gentle way that melted my already gooey insides.

"Okay," was my breathy reply, because like I said...*gooey.*

"Okay?"

"Yeah, okay I won't stop." He laughed once and muttered,

"And this she doesn't argue with me on."

"Well, you asked nicely," I told him with a wink, and he shook his head at me a little before the sign for a gas station was coming up.

"Are we stopping?" I asked knowing that I could very much do with using the bathroom and also a drink after it.

"I need to fill up, and I take it you need to use the facilities." I frowned in silent question asking how he knew.

"Because you have been sat cross legged and bouncing in your seat for the last ten minutes." I suddenly looked down at myself and noticed that he was right, I had been. I decided not to comment on this but instead remained silent as he pulled into a Shell station. One that was empty other than one car that was already driving away. So, we pulled up to a pump and Lucius turned off the engine before getting out of the car. I did the same, only to find Lucius by my side granting me his hand so I didn't struggle. Because, well I may have been a bad ass, but I was a clumsy one at that!

Once I was out of the car, I mumbled about not being long and turned about to walk inside when his question made me pause.

"Do you want to get anything?" he said nodding to the store,

"Yeah, I was going to get a few...erm, no, actually it's fine, I don't need anything," I said quickly knowing that he had asked me this because he had pulled up to a 'pay at the pump' and knew that if I did want anything that he would need to pay for it. Damn it! Okay, so I know this may have been petty. But considering I had spent what felt half of this drive trying to explain what my independence meant to me and how I liked to pay my own way, then I think only minutes later for him to hand me some cash over was so not proving my point, but the exact opposite in fact.

So naturally, I backtracked.

Problem was, he knew it too. He proved this as when I took my first step away from him and doing so trying to purposely avoid his eyes, he snagged my hand. Then, after a quick tug I was pulled back, practically falling into him. But he wasn't satisfied with this as his leather hand fisted in my hair so he could pull my head back so I had no choice but to look into his eyes. I swear but the look he gave me had me desperate to bite my fingers. His eyes practically danced with mirth and narrowed a little when he growled down at me in a playful tone,

"I call bullshit."

"What? I just changed my mind is all," I said making them deepen and near glow with that knowing look he gave me.

"Uh huh." He made the disbelieving noise as he nodded in that patronizing way that Gods if he didn't look so bloody sexy doing it then it would have been infuriating.

"Lucius, I swear…"

"I'd rather you not, considering it would be a lie, so let's try this another way…" This was when he paused so he could get really close to my ear to whisper the rest in that totally dominating way of his,

"You are going to walk into that store, do what you need

to do and then you are going to pick out whatever it is you want and I will be in shortly after to buy it for you...pride or no fucking pride...am I understood?" I tensed and was about to shake my head, when I was forced to stop, and this was down to two things. One was the way his hand fisted in my hair to the point of pain had I moved an inch and the second was the way he suddenly had a mouthful of my neck held between his teeth. And I knew it was nothing short of a warning, something he confirmed about ten seconds later when he released me, licked at the ghost of where his teeth had been to soothe the sting and said,

"Now go and be a good girl." Then he spun me and smacked my ass to get me moving. And I swear had I not been momentarily blinded by the lust he just forced upon me, then I would have said something witty or snippy in return. As it stood though, for once I simply did as I was told...damn him!

But then I couldn't help but look over my shoulder at him only to find him now leaning back against his gorgeous car, looking every single inch of the sexy bad boy he was! Especially with his arms folded, his upper body resting his weight back against the frame and his eyes solely on me, watching my every move as I walked away from him. Now, if I thought he looked sexy before, well then, this was a whole other level of hot!

And in that moment, it was a hotness I tried to ignore. You know, just so I could focus on my bladder and not on my libido. So, I finally made it into the store and quickly located the restrooms at the back. I tried not to think too much about what I must have looked like, so ignored the obvious stare from the woman behind the counter. I hurried into the bathroom and headed straight to a cubicle, determined not to look in the mirror to see if I looked as bad as I felt.

I swear these tight leather pants actually squeaked as I pulled them down and I sat there the whole time having a pee worried that I wouldn't be able to get them back on again. Visions of me trying to climb through the small window and actually land without breaking something, all so I wouldn't have to run through the shop half naked, was all I could focus on. Oh, I could just picture Lucius' face now after running for the car half naked and my shame when I had to tell him why.

Well, no way! Not going to happen! I would rather catapult myself into the buggers than do that. Or I wondered then about stealing some thread? This was so I could cut up the bloody things, just so I could then sew them back together like some lame version of cat woman. Like when she hit 'bat shit crazy' levels (see what I did there) in Batman Returns and started sewing like…well, like a crazy cat lady!

Okay, well pee done, and it was the moment of truth, oh and time for me to discover that I had been worrying for the last three minutes for no good reason…*the pants did up just fine.*

However, my victory was short lived as with all these thoughts about leather pants and I forgot my rule not to look in the mirror when washing my hands…jeez, I was a mess.

"Oh dear, Fae." Suddenly every hit came back to me and my hands found the edge of the sink. I knew my elbow was bruised along with my stomach, as I felt the tenderness there from being kicked and falling to my side. And looking down at my hands when I felt the sting of soap was from killing that one guy with the lamp cord, one that ended up cutting into my hands. Thankfully though, these weren't deep, but that's where the thanks ended as it was my face that was the worst.

I remembered being punched in the face and then having my head hammered into the floor, which would explain the cut above my nose and the angry purply red mottled skin around my cheek, eye and nose. It all seemed mainly on one side at least and I raised my hand first to pat it before then moving to the back of my head to find the large lump there. I winced one more time before turning away from the pitiful sight, hating that Lucius had seen me like this.

All I could hope for is what little blood of his I had in my system, that it would heal me sooner than a bruise this size would normally take to heal and let's face it, a yellow and green face wasn't ever going to look sexy.

After this and my plummeting self-confidence freak out, I walked back into the store and had no choice but to walk past the cashier again. She was a middle aged lady who looked as though all of her facial features had been pinched. Everything was close together and looked small in such a round face. She narrowed her eyes at me and then, just as I was making my way to the door, said something to me in German.

"Sorry, I…" I muttered this at the same time trying to translate in my mind what she had said.

"You American, huh, it all the same with you girls!" She scoffed and tutted and I knew I should have just left it alone and walked out of the store, but I couldn't.

"What is that supposed to mean?" I snapped back given that her tone with me was less than friendly.

"He is rich so it's worth it...worth the pain," she said shaking her head and I swear my blood started to boil. Because Hell no, I wasn't letting this woman insinuate what I think she was! It didn't matter what Lucius was, or had been reborn into, a woman beater sure as shit wasn't one of them!

"Oh no, you have that completely wrong lady," I said but she just huffed again, making her large chest puff out before she waved a hand at me.

"I know your type."

"Oh really?" I said in a sarcastic tone and folding my arms across my chest, because no, she fucking didn't! I just beat the crap out of four guys, killing three of them for attacking me, so yeah, in reality I was so far from her 'victim type' that I might have lived on a damn space shuttle for the distance apart I was from the picture she tried to paint.

"He rich, good looking, the bad boy..." oh she had no idea!

"And you stay with him, because that matters more than your body. Where is your pride?" Oh no she didn't just say that! This was when I took a few steps closer to her and said,

"Right, now listen up lady, that man out there has saved my life more times than anyone should ever have to. He is kind and thoughtful and has never laid one Gods be damned finger on me in anger! He has never physically hurt me and would kill anyone who tried. You get me?!" I paused to see that, no she totally didn't get me, so I carried on,

"That man out there, the one that you think to judge so easily, well he is the type of man that holds you when you cry, soothes you when you're worried, leaves you little notes telling you to eat because he heard your stomach growling, arranges to get your whole flat refurnished because it got trashed and even remembers to buy your favorite cereal...all because he cares for me!" I shouted this time making her eyes go wide as if she was starting to accept her mistake, but I still wasn't done,

"You see my bruised face and you automatically assume that it must be the man at my side! Well, shame on you lady, because you just accused one of the best Gods be damned people on this planet and the man I love more than anything else in this world, so you should be ashamed of yourself!" After this I turned on my heel and was about to storm out of there in the biggest huff, when a single sight stopped me.

A gorgeous sight and one that looked as though he had just witnessed something mythical. Which was why his name escaped on a breathy question, asking him without any added words if he had seen everything I think he just did.

"Lucius?"

And with one look in return. The one that spoke of so many things. So many emotions. I knew that in that moment he hadn't just witnessed the last few seconds of this fight for his honor.

No instead, he had heard...

Every. Single. Word.

CHAPTER EIGHT

IN A NUT SHELL

"*Lucius,*" I whispered softly as time seemed to standstill for both of us, although Lucius recovered a lot quicker than I did. And the second he broke free, he only had one destination in mind...

Me.

I suddenly found myself with his hands framing my face and lifting it up so he could kiss me, being mindful of my bruised face for his touch was gentle, even if his kiss wasn't. No, this was because the second his lips touched mine it was as if someone had lit a fuse and the burning passion between us simply ignited!

I swear but it felt as if it had the power to consume me whole and, in that moment, I would have let it. Because if I had died right then, I would have done so having known how it felt to be loved by just a single kiss alone. Because Lucius had said once that we didn't need words, and despite the many things that he could have referred to at the time, it still rang true now in this moment.

We didn't need words.

Because we had spoken of so much more in actions alone. It was the desperation I knew he felt. It was the gentle touch in which he cared. It was the taste of his essence bursting across my tongue and drowning my senses in everything that was him. I swear, just the feel of his fingertips on my skin and I was lost to all else in the world. Now this gentle hold was enough for me to lose myself but then for him, he wanted more. More of me, more of us and I swear the thought of it created a heat in my belly that felt as though I had swallowed a small sun. Like he was lighting up my insides.

It was what I imagined kissing an Angel blessed by Heaven was like.

One that loved me.

But then my angel turned dark and that once bright warming sun was replaced by fire. A burning desire that needed more than a kiss, and I wasn't the only one who felt this way. Lucius' hands left my cheeks and instead found my ass, lifting me from the ground and wrapping my legs around his waist as he started walking us both backwards. I didn't know where he was headed, and I didn't care as long as his hands didn't leave my body. His lips however, travelled from my own towards my neck and it was only then that a brief niggle in my mind forced me to look to the woman I had been shouting at only moments ago. But what I found was her frozen in place.

Then I looked to the windows and saw that a darkness was sweeping through the whole gas station, clouding it in a thick black rolling fog, making me suddenly grow scared. It travelled along the floor and started to consume the car, swallowing it whole before coming closer to the glass.

Lucius felt me tense in his hold and left my neck so he could look at me, seeing for himself the worry in my gaze. He glanced back over his shoulder and just when I thought his own concern would now show for what was happening, instead all I received was his knowing grin.

"Lucius?" I said his name in question, as it was clear that he obviously knew what it was but then with a single look, so did I ...*as he was the cause.*

"I'm not sharing you with the world...*you're mine."* Then he crushed his lips to mine and claimed me again, making me release a breathless sigh that was swallowed up by his kiss. And as his tongue duelled with mine, my hands found their way to his hair as I ran my fingers through it, before they fisted at the back. One at the base of his neck and the other at the crown, just so I could anchor him to me. He growled low in his throat and just as I started to move them, thinking I was doing wrong, his demon spoke to me,

"Don't you fucking dare pull away from me." This growled warning only managed to turn me on even more as it had been combined with the feel of his hands fisted in my jacket. In fact, I could hear the leather groaning in protest over the pounding of my own heart and this combined with my heavy breathing made for an exhilarating backing track for what was about to happen. Seconds later and he pushed me up against another space I discovered was somewhat softer than the other shelf, and when I heard the crunch I knew why, seeing with just a glance it was a display stand full of potato chips.

"I have to have you, damnation of Gods, but I am going out of my fucking mind!" he hissed before he pried my legs from his waist and the combination of his words and actions didn't mix as he let my feet touch the ground. But then, the second I felt him yank my button open in haste, I knew why. He then ripped my leather trousers from my legs making me briefly smirk to myself when thinking back to my earlier inner turmoil back in the bathroom. Seeing as they were coming off now no matter what and sort of in front of someone…frozen lady or not.

Then, once the sound of my boots hitting the floor, along with a slap of my trousers, he ripped open the bottom of the bodysuit I still had on underneath my clothes, tearing it at the crotch. After this he unbuckled his belt and yanked at his own. But unlike mine, he just did it enough to allow his straining erection to burst free. And with a startled breath I was back in his arms and a single action later I was being impaled on his cock, making me throw my head back and cry out in screaming pleasure.

Then he hammered into me, the sound of the chips being ground to crumbs in their bags behind me. But then, when the stand started to bend due to the strain, we rolled and found ourselves against another stand, this time one with candy bars. I only knew this as the second I placed my hands back against the shelf to hold on, I felt them fisting chocolate in their wrappers that snapped in my hold.

"More…I need fucking more!" he growled before moving me again, this time it ended against the fridge doors which were substantially more stable…or at least they were until we turned up. Because the second I felt it start to build inside me, I squeezed my thighs around him, and started to rock in a frenzied way on his cock. This drove him even wilder, if such a thing were possible. But it did so until the point that the second I screamed out my orgasm, I heard a mighty crack of glass, and barely looked to the side where in a blur I saw his hand flat to the glass. One now framed by cracked branches cutting through the glass, like tiny lightning bolts from his fingers.

This was when he decided the doors weren't up to the task either, so he moved me, now finding a small chest freezer with a clear lid that kept popsicles and ice creams in. However, the second he placed my ass down on it I screamed,

"Fucking cold!" I shouted thinking he would move me. However, he just gave me an evil badass grin and said,

"Then I'd better be quick, sweet cheeks." Then he thrust into me even harder and I cried out again, feeling myself on the cusp, as he continued the maddening rhythm that I was quickly getting addicted to. Also, from the sound of things I wasn't the only one as the second I lifted my now freezing ass up, both to relieve myself of the cold and push him inside me even deeper, I knew he wouldn't last. And neither did I, for a heartbeat later and I too was screaming my release yet again, one quickly followed by Lucius.

"Fuck...fuck...FUCK AHH!" He roared quickly, his hand finding the base of my spine, so he could force my body to stay locked to his, and as close as I could get the second he erupted into me, spilling his seed as deep as it would go. I felt him shuddering inside the core of me and I never expected to get such a high from the feeling. Then I felt him lean forward, resting his forehead to mine as his breathing evened. But then he said the very last thing in that moment that I thought he would,

"I love you too, sweetheart."

And there it was.

The words we didn't need to say but both found ourselves declaring anyway and in the most unconventional of ways. Mine was about him said to a stranger when arguing in his defence and his was after fucking me on a freezer. Which in a way kind of summed up our relationship, I thought with a hidden grin. Which was why I knew I could raise my hand to his cheek and whisper back,

"That's great, honey, but can you get me off this fucking thing before my ass gets frostbite and falls off." To which he burst out laughing and lifted me off with one arm banded around my back.

"And we can't have that now can we, not when it's one of my favourite bits." At this I rolled my eyes and he shot me a knowing look before saying,

"Did you just…"

"Roll my eyes, yes so you can just go right ahead and knock yourself out Mr Slap Happy McGee, as right now, it's not like I would feel it anyway!" I said making him chuckle before lowering me to the floor and tapping me on the nose saying,

"Poor baby." Oh lordy, but even the way he said this made me want to go for round two, only on something warmer this time…like the sun! Especially the way Lucius then zipped up his jeans and buckled up his belt, which seriously made me wonder if I had a screw loose, seeing I found something so simple so much of a turn on!

But then again, there was just something so raw and

passionate about two people that wanted each other so badly, that they couldn't even wait the seconds longer it would take to strip each other naked. That frenzied need, one so great that nothing else mattered in that moment but the connecting of two lovers.

In fact, I could barely function which was why I think Lucius took my hand and led me over to where the leather pants had been discarded on the floor.

"Oh, I am just going to quickly run and clean up first," I said finally coming to my senses before walking in the direction of the bathrooms. But then, once again my hand was snagged and I was tugged back to Lucius, as was quickly becoming his habit. Then he tipped my face up to his so he could get closer before telling me,

"I need this on you…" He paused and I sucked in a startled breath when I felt his fingers run through the soaked folds of my abused sex so he could gather up some of his release before he brought them back to my lips.

"…The scent of me on you…*inside you*…it helps erase the scent of another male you wear and makes me feel less murderous…now open that pretty mouth for me," he said and to be honest, my mouth dropped in surprise anyway without him needing to ask for it. But then he slipped the tips of two fingers inside and nodded for me to taste him, which I did, doing so with a blush upon my cheeks. It was also one he growled at when he saw it. A response he repeated the second I swallowed his seed down, moaning around his fingers when his unique flavour burst across my tongue. Then suddenly he quickly pulled them from my mouth and replaced them with his mouth, tasting himself on my tongue.

It turned out to be a short kiss and had dazed me enough

that before I knew it, my leather pants were yanked back up my legs. Then they were refastened at my waist before he patted in between my legs, as if sure of himself now that his leaking seed would stay where it was supposed to be.

"Good girl, now pick out what you wanted to get before trying to bullshit me earlier and let's go." Then he turned, walked to the counter, placed a note down and left the store. I then watched as he walked through the thick, dark blanket of fog as it curled around him, as if responding to his presence in a sinister way. Then, with a flick of his hand, it started to roll away and evaporate around the edges of the gas station it had once kept hidden from the world.

"Kaufst du etwas?" the woman's voice asked, which translated into if I was buying anything. I shot her a questioning look, that only prompted a reaction out of me when she nodded down to the large bill Lucius had left. Then she looked even more confused as I quickly stuffed my feet back into the men's boots before saying,

"Erh, yeah." Needless to say, that after this, I got my cold ass in gear. So, I grabbed a packet of chips, ones that weren't from the stand and therefore more than just humped crumbs. Then I grabbed a bottle of water, a box of pain killers and a chocolate bar, one that hadn't been squished and had my nail marks embedded. Then, as she was about to give me money back in return, I took one look around the mess we had made and said,

"Keep the change." Then I left the nosey and judging woman to the rest of her night.

I found Lucius waiting by my side of the car and as I approached, he asked,

"Did you get everything you wanted?"

"Yeah, thanks," I said with my booty nestled in my arms, resting against my lady shelf...*thank you C cup breasts*. But then, as I was about to lower myself into the seat, he stopped me,

"Hold up, beautiful, do you want to tell me what those are?" he said suddenly plucking the pain killers from my arms and now reading for himself the packet, even though he'd just asked me.

"They are just ibuprofen," I said now dropping the rest of my stuff on the seat so I could reach for them, something that wasn't easy to accomplish thanks to him being considerably taller than me. Meaning he didn't have to try very hard to keep them out of my reach.

"Yes, I can see that, now do you want to tell me what you need these for?" he asked, his tone serious and suddenly stern. But despite this demand, I didn't really want to tell him as I knew it would just piss him off more. In the end, however, I knew that I had no choice, especially when he asked in a regretful tone, one that seemed difficult to ask for fear of my answer.

"Did I...*did I hurt you?"*

"No! No of course not, I just have a headache, and well looking in the mirror I don't have to guess why. I know I look a mess." I said, unable in that moment to look at him, so I found my 'too large for me boots' instead. Of course, this was Lucius I was stood in front of, which meant that he wouldn't allow this for long.

"Give me your eyes, Pet." His soft demand was combined with the slight pressure under my chin as he lifted my face up to his. His gaze was so tender, it could have been classed as a weapon against my senses and I swear I felt my whole body relax. Gods, but the power this man held over me and my heart, well, it was near terrifying.

"You are beautiful and although I wished I could have been the one to kill the bastard that did this to you, it doesn't change the fact that seeing this mark upon your face is only a reminder of how strong my girl is, and it makes me proud that she made him suffer," he told me and I swear it was so sweet that I couldn't help but throw my arms around his neck and kiss him, which I could tell took him by surprise. But even then, the second he felt my body plastered against his own, it was like an automatic response for him to wrap his arms around me, lifting me slightly so I didn't have to strain to get to him.

"Thanks my handsome, bloodthirsty warrior man," I said making him smirk down at me before saying,

"You know, I think I will pick that over honey." Of course, I burst out laughing and shook in his hold.

"Come on, my pretty, bloodthirsty warrior woman," he said making me chuckle and tell him,

"You know, I think I will stick with Sweetheart, but thanks for giving it a shot." His lips twitched at this before he nodded to the car and said,

"Right, well in that case, it's time to get your ass in the seat...*sweetheart.*" I huffed and folded my arms after first plucking my tablets out of his hand and said,

"Nice to see you're back to playing my bossy manhandling boyfriend that wishes to be called my eternal life partner," I said making him growl at me playfully.

"Get your ass in the car, Amelia!" he snapped, now only pretending to be grumpy. Then I watched him walk around to his side and I gave him a salute and said,

"Sure thing, Bossman Hippy." At this he growled louder this time and I laughed as he grumbled under his breath,

"Shackles and a gag...I am getting shackles and a gag."
At this I folded into my seat trying in vain to keep the smirk from my face, because well, teasing Lucius was almost as much fun as when he teased me. Which is why I couldn't help but ask,

"That could be fun, did you want my help putting them on you? As I can imagine at least one of them being tricky to do on your own." Again, this granted me a lip twitch before a full-blown bad boy grin emerged as he pressed the start switch, then he revved the engine, telling me what revenge he had planned.

"Lucius, don't you dare...AHHH!" This ended in a shout as he sped out of the gas station like he was coming out of the pits on a racetrack. Smoke billowed around us as the tires burned on the tarmac and he spun the car, now doing doughnuts and making me grab onto the door just for something to hold onto as I screamed. I mean there was no danger, I knew this, as it wasn't like there was anyone else here but still, the action kind of made you want to hold on for dear life!

Then he pulled out of the continuous circle and the car whipped around before straightening up so he could drive up the slip road before rejoining traffic, still doing so with speed. Then, once we had joined the fast lane, he opened her up and drove with ease.

"I think you are safe to let go now, Amelia," Lucius said with humour in his tone.

"I would but I am afraid I would kill you and if I

throttled you to death then we would crash." At this he laughed and said,

"Still think I need those shackles, sweetheart?"

"Most definitely, actually no, make it an iron maiden only without the spikes, because lucky for you, I like your handsome face," was my witty reply.

"Lucky for me then," was his cocky retort, one I couldn't help smile at. Then he asked,

"How's your ass, still cold?" I could tell he was also trying not to laugh but failed when I growled at him.

"Cold enough not to feel you spanking it!"

"Well, we can't have that now, can we." Lucius then flicked a switch and was soon making me moan in pleasure.

"Heated seats, oh my, there is a God, and wouldn't you know it, he works in the car business," I remarked, making Lucius chuckle back,

"Amen to that."

After this, Lucius actually made a conscious effort to slow down, at least somewhat. But then, just as I was about to speak, I noticed flashing headlights behind us, as a car seemed to come out of nowhere.

It was weaving in and out of the lanes at speed and I swallowed hard, knowing that once again, our time was up...

The bad guys had found us.

CHAPTER NINE

A DRIVE TO REMEMBER

The second I saw them my whole body went rigid and I was in half a mind to scream, 'not this shit again!' and the other half of me wanted to curl up and pretend they weren't there. Seriously, could we not catch a break!

"Amelia, what's wrong?" Lucius asked me as it was obvious by his concerned tone that he had felt my unease and no doubt heard my heartrate kick into high gear and speaking of high gear,

"I think you should go faster!" I said in a panic.

"What?"

"Go faster, as in as fast as this thing will go!" I screeched suddenly wishing we were in a James Bond car with every corny gadget known to man!

"Amelia, you're not really making sense here…oh," he said once he finally caught sight of the car behind as it flashed us one more time, only what it hoped to achieve by this I didn't know. Were they trying to intimidate us, or warn us that if we didn't stop, they would ram us off the road?!

"Yes oh! So hit the damn gas would ya!" I shouted making him reach over and place a hand at my shoulder, so he could tap his thumb on my pulse point, before saying my name, this time in a comforting way,

"Amelia, sweetheart...just relax, there is no need to wor..."

"No need to worry! Are you joking, they are..."

"My people," he stated quickly before I could hit XL on the panic mode.

"Oh," was my calmer reply.

"It's Clay driving, I called when you were using the bathroom to let them know what had happened," he told me softly, and thankfully not mocking me for my brief moment of panic. After this I didn't say anything as he explained most of his people had been ordered to leave Transfusion, now that it had been compromised. Instead they were all to meet at Lucius' stronghold. Which was basically, on all accounts heard, a mammoth castle hidden inside an actual mountain!

Clay and Ruto had been the last to leave after tying up loose ends, which I gathered was getting rid of the bodies before the 'human officials' were allowed to enter. What this job actually entailed I really didn't want to know, but for some reason visions of a great big vat of green steaming acid came to mind, with body parts melting on the surface. Of course, the less gruesome part of this vision was that it was painted in my mind in a cartoon style. Admittedly not quite Disney but leaning more towards Looney Toons, as come on, that shit was violent! It also made me wonder out of the two, who would be holding the big stick, getting to stir the dead bodies?

Now to Lucius, my silence during this time obviously meant that I was worried, which was why it was a few minutes later he said,

"They won't get you again, Amelia, I can promise you, for nothing can break inside my winter home." Yes, and nothing can break out of it either, I thought without saying anything. No, instead I nodded, and Lucius then left me to my thoughts, ones from the looks of things, he knew what they focused on.

Ten minutes later and my headache reminded me of what I still held in my lap. So, I opened up my water and took two tablets, after first gulping down half the bottle. Lucius watched me out of the corner of his eye and waited until I was done before telling me,

"I will heal you once I get you home." It was such a caring statement I almost kicked myself for saying,

"Home?" Then he shot me a look and said,

"I'm sorry, did you want me to unearth that can of worms you so intently wanted buried?"

"Good point, moving on," I replied knowing that if he wanted to refer to his home as such, then that was fine…fine, fine, just dandy, in fact and wasn't even freaking me out in any way, shape or form…*yeah right!*

"Are you in a lot of pain?" he asked, and I found it sweet how this big broody Vampire King, who was a total badass and was, let's face it, rude to most people, was now fussing over me because I had been hurt. So, I reached across the centre console and placed my hand on his thigh to squeeze before saying in an equally tender tone,

"I'm fine, really." He didn't comment at this, but simply nodded as if accepting it. Besides, it might not be completely true at the moment, as I was most definitely sore. But it would be fine when the tablets kicked in, so I didn't think there was any harm in answering prematurely.

After this we sat in silence for a bit and I wondered why he kept glancing over my way, or more to the point at my lap.

"Are you waiting for something?" he finally asked and at first, I had no clue what he meant until he then nodded down to the bit of food I still had nestled in my lap.

"Do you mind if I eat in here?" I asked, to which he just gave me a pointed look.

"Are you hungry?" he asked in return.

"Yeah."

"Then do you really think I would care more about this car than about my woman gaining substance and erasing some discomfort, something she would need after jumping into a freezing, fucking river from a Gods forsaken helicopter?" was his pissed off reply, making me want to ask if he was Bipolar at all.

"Erh…no?" was my own unsure reply.

"Fucking eat, Amelia," he said making me now question,

"And if I hadn't jumped into a…and I quote, 'freezing, fucking river from a Gods forsaken helicopter' would I get the same answer?"

"What do you think?" was his curt reply.

"Erm…no again?"

"Nice to know you catch on quick, Princess," was his naturally dry response.

"I thought we agreed you wouldn't call me that anymore." At this he smirked and teased,

"No, we agreed that I would and often, but wait, what did you hear…not something different I hope?" he mocked making me sneer at him.

"Yes, because the way I heard it, every time you slipped up and did say it, then you had to bend over and let me spank *your* ass."

"Yes, and that will be happening *never,*" he replied. I laughed and then folded my arms and asked,

"Now how do you know if you like it or not if you have never tried it?" he raised a brow at my teasing and said,

"I will remind you of that when walking you into my playroom." At this I laughed, and in a way, I hoped wasn't a foolishly naïve way of believing this was a joke, otherwise…*oh Gods!*

"Wait, don't tell me, you're a secret pinball junkie!" At this I received an unimpressed eyebrow raise.

"Board games."

"Oh, there is a board, and once you step inside, most definitely something I will want to play with, now as for being considered a game, well, by the end of it I will most definitely consider myself the winner." I had to say the erotic picture he painted now was one that had me swallowing hard and almost wishing for that room to be real…if it wasn't already. Something that was starting to look more and more that way when he continued,

"Now, as for being addicted, the door does have a lock, so I am well and truly covered when it comes to getting my fix." This statement ended with him winking at me and smirking when he saw me squirming in my seat, something he had also told me he enjoyed watching. Which is why for peace of mind on my part I shouted,

"You're teasing!" A tone that said, I really hoped that he was, considering I was already nervous about walking in the place, let alone the potential surprises he had in store for me.

"Am I? For I wasn't aware," he said mockingly making me now nibble my fingertip again. Naturally he saw it and grinned.

"Now eat," he ordered nodding down at my bag of chips and chocolate bar. So, I did as I was told, opening the bag slowly at least so the thing didn't just explode open, spilling them all over what I already knew was a mega expensive supercar...because really, this was me here.

"What flavour are they?" Lucius asked after smelling the air like some hungry cartoon character. So, I held the packet at arm's length and read the front,

"They are called, Chipsfrisch BBQ, so I am going to take a wild guess and say, smokey meat was involved." This granted me another lip twitch, which I had to say, I was most certainly racking up tonight.

"Mm, I wonder when they will bring out a rare meat flavour," he said and I laughed and said,

"What like the Northern Hairy Nosed Wombat, only I think Chipsfrisch may struggle with that one...what, you said rare?" I joked making him roll his eyes before pointing out the obvious,

"I also meant bloody."

"Ah, but of course, I was forgetting your new pet name, my bloodthirsty warrior man," I said nodding to myself and then picking up a handful of chips and stuffing them in my mouth.

"And may I enquire as to why you suddenly dropped the handsome?"

"You may enquire, yes," I answered with a mouthful.

"And?" he pressed, continuing on the playfulness.

"Oh, you wanted me to tell you...it's so you stay pretty and don't get a big head...I've never seen you in a hat and with Christmas not too far away, well then I have to think ahead...get it, A head!" I said laughing at my own joke and then muttering the punch line to myself again as I took another swig of my water. I noticed him shake his head to himself again in that typical, what am I to do with my goofy girlfriend/ eternal life partner.

"Alright, well I will make it easy on you, I don't wear hats and I don't celebrate Christmas." Okay, so talk about dropping a massive bombshell on a girl! He didn't like Christmas?! Okay, so given what the origins of this particular celebration was, then yeah, I could understand considering I knew he had a real problem with Jesus Christ. But seriously, not even a tree?

"Okay, why do you now look like you're about to cry?" he asked giving me a double look after needing to look at the road as he overtook what he considered to be a slow car. I, however, considered it a normal speeding car but hey ho.

"So, not even a tree, or a single stocking...not even one present?" I asked, with the sound of my voice telling him of my utter heartbreak.

"Trees are for outside, stockings to peel off a woman's legs and I can buy whatever the hell I want, whenever I want, so why would I wait until a single day of the year in hopes of receiving it from someone else," he said making me go completely silent, not even a crunch which promoted him to look my way.

"Gods woman, but you look like I just maimed your childhood teddy bear!"

"You lay a fang on Mr Smooney and we are so over," I warned making him laugh before saying,

"Do I want to know why you slept with a spoon as a child?"

"Oh, he wasn't a spoon, he was a moose," I informed him, and he rubbed his forehead a little before asking in a strained tone,

"I know I am going to regret this, but why was he named this." At this I laughed and said,

"Because he used to smoon me and I will give you all of one guess as to who named him this and I will even give you a clue, the moose was dyed green by the same person." Lucius chuckled and said,

"Ah, it's making sense now," he said whilst checking his mirror to once again overtake.

"I miss my aunty Pip," I said mostly to myself as I continued to munch my chips. Lucius shot me a look but didn't comment, so instead I decided to continue the Christmas talk, testing the waters so to speak,

"So, it looks like I will be going home for the holidays then, oh but don't worry, I will stay clear of the mistletoe," I said before crunching some more and making him growl.

"You will be going nowhere!" he snapped, obviously furious at the idea.

"Well, it's not like I can invite my family to spend Christmas with us, seeing as you are the Grinch's long lost cousin and all."

"Amelia, what in the Gods names are you talking about?" he snapped, again having no clue.

"What I am saying is what if I want a Christmas, are you going to refuse me something I have celebrated since I was born?" Lucius again looked thoughtful a moment and instead of giving me his answer, he decided to remind me yet again,

"I think this also constitutes as that can of worms, sweetheart." I scoffed at this knowing he was so using this as an easy way out. But despite this, I didn't reply. As he was right, it was most likely another argument for another day, one in the long list of arguments that was currently growing longer by day. But then again, I had to ask myself, could I really see Lucius spending any time with me and my family? Not even bringing into it the awkward 'mother thing', but mainly my dad who I was pretty sure wasn't exactly going to warm to the idea of us dating any time soon!

Oh yeah, I could see it now, us all stood around the piano singing, with some very real nuts roasting on an open fire, although I could pretty much guarantee that they weren't the type anyone wished to eat!

Gods, but this thought actually made me shiver, because that was one family announcement I didn't ever want to make! Maybe an email was going to be in order.

A very *short* email. Something like...

> Mum, Dad,
> Guess what, I am dating...
> *Lucius*.
> Bye, love Fae.

This was why the next thought to form and make it out of my mouth was,

"Wow, we are going to have a lot of worms to sort out, aren't we?" I commented making him mutter back in annoyance,

"Or step on."

"I will pretend I didn't hear that," was my reply,

"And I will pretend that you did, *whilst naked...* " I shot him a questioning sideways glance.

"Well, whilst I am pretending, I might as well enjoy it to its fullest." At this I burst out laughing, making him grin at obviously being able to make me laugh. I think this was one of the things that shocked me most about Lucius, he was actually a really funny guy, especially when he was teasing me. But then this was another shocker, how playful he was, and I had to say I was starting to become addicted to that side of him. Oh, but who was I kidding, I was addicted to all sides of Lucius even his growly side, because even when directed at me, it was still panty melting hot!

Which was why I found myself more and more trying to either make him laugh or I was trying to encourage more banter between us. Reason being why I looked down into my nearly empty bag of chips and smirked.

"Oh sorry, did you want any?" I asked now holding out the bag to him and like I said, after I had finished consuming most of the bag first. Lucius glanced over and then gave me a look as if I had just offered him dirt on a plate. Then he said,

"Ah, I see I get the scraps, you must love me indeed." At this I would have laughed but instead I blushed to my roots, remembering how he had first heard those words being said. Or more like shouted at some random person.

"Aww come on, I will tell you what, how about I create a new flavour for you, I can let you bite my finger so I can bleed all over them and then we can call it BBQ Princess, Lucius Limited edition…sound good?" I asked loving the way he threw his head back and laughed, gifting me the sight of that sensational smile of his…*another addiction of mine to confess.*

"Ah, well now it *is* confirmed, you must really love me," was his reply, making me smirk as I granted him a wink. Then I shook the bag at him in a tempting way which in the end despite all his teasing, he declined. So, I rolled up the bag and tucked it out of the way so I could move onto my next target. The best course…dessert.

"Are you aware that you are humming to your food?"

"But of course I am, its chocolate," I said like this should have been obvious. Then I broke a few squares off my Milka Caramel Chocolate, and instead of just biting into it, I broke it open and started scooping out the dripping caramel with the tip of my finger before sucking on it. I did this a few more times before all that was left was a chocolate shell that I popped in my mouth. Then I repeated the process.

"Gods in Hell, grant me strength." The sound of Lucius muttering to himself had me pausing just as the caramel was hanging off my finger. Then, just before I could pop my finger into my mouth, it was snatched from me and in between his lips in less than a second. Once there and held captive, he sucked on it, making sure to tease his tongue round to gather every sticky drop. Only then did he let me go.

"Mmm, delicious," he said as though he really did enjoy it, and this was confirmed when he added,

"Save me some."

"You like chocolate and caramel?" I asked with wide eyes.

"Melted and dripped over your body, then licked from your skin like I intend to do at the first chance I get, *most definitely.*"

"You're teasing me again," I stated, wondering if he was because his knowing grin told me differently. And besides, with Lucius I could never tell.

"We will just have to wait and see now won't we, because look, we are almost there." Lucius nodded to the first sign that said Königssee and I knew then that my time was quickly running out.

Because I hated to admit it, but instead of feeling as though I was coming home, I felt instead as if I was about to step inside a prison.

A prison as Lucius'...

Willing Captive.

CHAPTER TEN

LUCIUS

WRAPPED IN LEATHER

A short time after seeing the first signs for Königssee, I realised Amelia was more than just silently contemplating our arrival, questioning what would soon become her new home. But she was in fact, fast asleep. Not that I was surprised at this, as her mortal body had endured a lot throughout the night and it was bound to take its toll. However, it wasn't her body that concerned me, although somewhat bruised and no doubt sore, it was her mental state of mind that was my biggest worry.

But of course, on the drive she had been her usual playful self, but I was no fool and knew this was a coping mechanism she defaulted back to when hiding the true nature of her feelings. Fears and doubts I had tried to get her to speak of during the journey in hopes of easing her hidden anxiety of the future.

But despite trying, I soon learnt that I wasn't yet able to break through her defences and if I were honest, after what she had been through, then even I knew when not to push too hard. Because even the few fears she had mentioned, had given me more than enough food for thought. This being down to an array of questions I couldn't yet give her the answers to, not in regards to what her future held.

Because I knew the depth of near desperation she clawed at, one that would enable her to try and keep the life she had built for herself around her.

Her safety zone.

But seeing as I knew that the truth would only panic her more, I refrained from answering her questions, as keeping her old life would simply be impossible. Because in reality, she simply couldn't have both. No matter how much she believed she was able to merge the two lives, she just couldn't be my queen and continue her 'normal' and safe little mortal existence in a world that was as far from my own as you could physically get. So, I knew the day would come that she believed she would have to choose. But what she didn't yet know was that it had in fact been chosen for her a long time ago.

For she was mine.

And I sure as shit wasn't letting her go, not even if she begged me to do so. No, instead I would simply spend my time trying to convince her that she wanted this new life more than her old one. But my plan was simple and based on the hope that it wouldn't come to that, not when I was intent on making Königssee a home for her. Which meant surrounding her with the things that made her comfortable and at its most basic nature, manipulating her mind until it forgot all about the world she'd left behind.

For I would become her safety zone.

I had hoped spending more time at Transfusion had been the key into easing her into the new life I had planned for her, but well, that plan had literally crumbled and was no doubt still crumbling as these thoughts assaulted me. My anger at this made my hands tighten dangerously on the steering wheel. Because I didn't like it that my options had practically been taken from me and now I had less time to put my plan into motion. Because I had a list in my mind, a list of her fears that I needed to conquer and now fucking Christmas being one of them!

Gods, but just her look of disappointment when I told her I didn't celebrate the fucking pointless holiday, one that left nothing but disdain in my mind. Oh, but there had been times in the past that I had let Pip decorate the place as she saw fit, knowing that left to her own devices, she would have done far worse. But other than this and giving her the day off to celebrate alone with her husband being the usual practice that time of year, then it was just another fucking day in my eyes.

But speaking of eyes, well, I couldn't then help but remember the way hers had gotten wide and beseeching, after hearing what she no doubt classed as a character flaw of mine. Well, then it almost made me want to swallow my fucking words and choke on them and with it that fucking smelly tinsel shit mortals seemed to love putting on fucking trees!

Oh yeah, the drive had most certainly ended up adding to my already mounting list of shit I had to try and figure out. But I knew the problem was one of my own doing. This was thanks to my actions seven years ago that had given her the last push away from her own people that she had needed. I had been the one who had pushed her into embracing the mortal world and therefore foolishly managing to sever ties between her's and my world too.

Her energy was then spent on building the safe one she believed she had independently built. And now I just had to figure out a way to tear it down without her even knowing. I had to destroy her world and rebuild it around my own, doing so in a way that she wouldn't even notice until it was too late. Until she was so deeply entwined in my net that she couldn't escape it even if she wanted to. I wanted to consume her world and make it all about my own.

This was my plan.

It always had been.

Granted that during this drive I had taken the opportunity to discover the obstacles set against me, something admittedly she had given me very little to go on, other than playing with Lego, having a constant supply of her favourite cereal and spilling shit on a rug, something I hadn't understood in the slightest. Oh, and then there was her all-important pop culture obsession, which was one problem I knew how to solve, with the aid of a little expert help of course.

But then there were harder aspects to face, like her job and apartment, both of which I knew she was attached to in a way that wouldn't be as easy to dislodge as I'd first hoped. And now there was bringing her here, which I knew from only one panicked look she viewed as being more of a prison than a potential new home.

I confess, that knowing she felt this way was a blow, not to my ego but solely in a sentimental way. For it was true, I was greatly attached to my home, knowing that throughout all my years on this Earth, Königssee had been the first and only place I felt connected to. And in such a way that became rooted to my soul.

Naturally, being who I was, I wasn't a sentimental person by any means, but with this place, well there was always the exception. But then I had to force myself to view this from her point of view. And seeing as she had fought herself on whether to try and run from me or not, doing so since being at Transfusion, then by being here now simply took that option away from her. An option I didn't believe she truly wanted in the first place, but that was beside the point for it wasn't the outcome she was looking for, but simply the choice.

Choices in her life she was quickly losing control of making. Because it was true, I was rapidly taking them from her one by one and if I wanted her to eventually admit defeat and submit to me fully, then I needed to slow the fuck down. No matter how much my dominant and selfish ways were screaming at me to simply take, take, and take, until everything that was her was mine.

Which meant I had to give her the illusion that she had a choice when really, *she didn't*. But then I knew it was like breaking something beautiful and then expecting her to trust me to put it back together the way she wanted. When in reality, I would only do so the way I wanted, with the picture of her being the same, but then placing it inside a box for safe keeping.

Because yes, she was perfect for me and I wouldn't have changed one Gods be damned thing about her. But all that surrounded her, yes, I would change it all.

She wanted to be free, whereas I wanted what was mine safe and pretty much locked away in a clear glass cage she couldn't see. But she wasn't stupid, far from it and knew the true nature of Königssee. For it was a fortress I controlled and one she would have no way of escaping. Gods, but I was a sick bastard seeing as that thought alone had me growing hard.

And deep down she knew this.

Now, as for her family, then yeah, I agree that shit was going to be awkward. Me and Dom had history that was like a fucking thorn bush overgrown with far more thorns than flowers. And then there was Keira, who for me, the past had been a mere flicker in time.

Amelia was my eternity.

But Amelia didn't know this, and I knew making her believe it would be my biggest challenge yet. But that wasn't to say that Keira meant nothing to me. As like I said that history may have been a mere flicker but the respect I held for her now was down to what she had gifted me... *My Chosen One.*

And as much as it fucking pained me to admit, then in turn Dom also deserved that same respect, even though I was pretty sure he would want to rip my fucking dick off when he found out about who his daughter was to me. Did I care, Hell no. Would it ever happen, fuck no!

I was Dom's equal in a fight and he fucking knew it! But my winning hand over him and his fucking rash temper was something he could never ignore. I had saved his Chosen One's life more than once and in doing so had made her one of my turned. Meaning that like all my people, she was literally bound to my life, one Dom would not ever dare risk taking. For I was her Sire.

So yeah, to say shit was complicated was an understatement and one I knew Amelia would struggle with far more than I. But then again, I knew my ties to Keira in the past had only been because of what the Fates knew she would one day grant me. So, they had used me to protect her, just like the rest of the Kings who had found their Chosen Ones thanks to their ties to Keira.

And mine had been their fucking daughter! Talk about a fucking cosmic joke, one I would kill over if ever I heard a single being laugh about it. But it was a fated connection even Keira knew about and thankfully encouraged, after of course she first tried to kick my ass when she discovered it. But then Amelia had only been sixteen at the time and still considered a child by both of us. So, I vowed to protect her and keep my distance until after she was of age, as was best for both our sakes. Because even though my connection with her was strong, even at that age, I wanted a woman in my bed, not a naïve, spoiled girl who was still yet to discover the world.

Meaning it was a promise to Keira I made easily but then as the years had gone by, that promise turned into my own vow, for the timing was never right. Something I was now starting to regret, for at the time I had made a deal with Keira to wait until after she was twenty one, before I came to claim her. Also stating explicitly that I would be doing so with or without Dom's fucking approval!

But that time had come and gone, allowing her to not only discover the world, but forge her own into a comfort she was still now clinging on to. And really, after all she had been through since that box turned up in her life, then could I blame her?

Then again, thinking back on all she had endured and overcome in a way that I could have never imagined she would, then she was nothing short of astonishing! I thought I had known her. I thought I had seen it all where she was concerned. I had watched her life from afar and been arrogant enough to believe that I knew her inside and out. Gods, but how wrong I had been.

I remember all the times I had been handed a daily report on her routine, most of it very much the same as the day before. It was mundane and more than anything else, it was safe. Mainly because I made it that way and wouldn't have allowed it to be any other way. But as for everything else, then I would watch as her mortal life blossomed around her into something so far from my own world, I worried when the time came how she would cope.

Well, those fears were well and truly ground to dust, from not only witnessing her bravery firsthand, or the fact that she was clearly able to handle herself in a fight, but mainly from the second I saw her getting off that shitty bike, all dressed in leather and shaking her hair from that helmet as though she was some fucking warrior woman getting from her horse after conquering the battle.

And as much as I had been furious with her for risking her life like that, I was also in fucking awe of her as well! She had indeed saved the fucking day and one glance behind her seat to see the box sitting there and not in the hands of my enemies, then her courageous actions couldn't be ignored.

But like I said, hearing her account of events, I swear to the Gods, it had nearly sent me into a rage. The only things that held me back, was one, I didn't wish to frighten her, and two, she was finally safe, alive and within my reach to touch, something I found increasingly difficult not to do. Because the second I got her in my arms, I felt my world and soul right itself again. However, the moment I got her in the car, I could focus better and what I scented made me want to growl. She smelled of two things, the river Isar and of another male, one of which was driving me to near fucking insanity!

So, instead I focused on her conversation, which was playful and lighthearted, which still surprised me given the circumstances. Reason being why I endured and tried to ignore it the best I could, all the while feeling like some wild beast needing to stake my claim. And well, short of pissing all over her, which I was almost certain was a sure way of getting my balls kicked... or knowing her, my arm broken... then I knew it would have to wait. Because I needed her in my bed, with more of my blood in her system and my seed leaking out of her sweet core. Only then would this calm my primal and demonic instincts.

But then we had stopped for fuel and thank my fucking sanity that we had, for two wonderous things had happened next. One that had quickly led onto the next. I thought back to it now, glancing over at her sleeping form and remembering how she gallantly defended my honour to some clueless, insignificant mortal. Yes, for anyone to insinuate that I had harmed her in such a way had pissed me off, for I would rather cut off my own fucking hand than lay it on her in anger.

However, her words had started to penetrate and when they did, they cut to the core and would stay there forever. And it looked to be that I hadn't been the only one this had happened to. As it started with a list of my past actions and what they had meant to her. This telling me instantly that I had also cut to her own core in the best way possible and remained there ever since...a place I very much intended to fucking stay!

But then I had never been affectionate with a woman before and romance wasn't exactly something I believed myself capable of. In the past, I had picked a female, fucked her and then swiftly moved on after sating the sexual thirst.

Then came Amelia and I found that these things

weren't something I needed to work on but found myself just...*doing.* She simply brought it out in me. Like when seeing her upset or worried, I had instinctively wanted to soothe her or hold her until her tears ran dry. But always done through choice, not as just some unspoken duty. I hadn't once asked myself what to do or how best to act during these times. It had just been like a hidden part inside myself that she had dragged to the surface unknowingly.

Like when hearing her stomach growling, my instincts then had been to feed my woman and take care of her. Just like when she had been hurt, the need to heal her was one I ended up battling myself with, as I knew time was of the essence and I needed to get her safely situated inside my mountain home before anything else could befall her. After all, I had underestimated my enemies once, I most certainly wasn't about to do that again!

But then this mission had gone out of the fucking window the second she had said,

'Well, shame on you lady because you just accused one of the best Gods be damned people on this planet and the man, I love more than anything else in this world, so you should be ashamed of yourself!'

After that, then nothing in this world would have stopped me from claiming her, as a frenzied need had taken over all other senses. I was even surprised that I'd had enough thought of mind left to focus on bringing forth the demonic fog that surrounded my home in Hell. It was one that had the energy to destroy anyone who dare cross it, but topside, it only had the power to disguise and keep people at a distance without understanding why.

That way, I had been free to make her mine after I had also dealt with the mind of a single mortal, knowing that claiming Amelia was for my eyes only. And her passion had been fucking addictive to experience, for she may have been inexperienced in ways of the flesh, but she was by no means lacking in the bedroom.

She was naturally beyond compare and quite frankly, the best I'd ever fucking had.

But the lingering smell of another on her skin had still been fucking with my head. Something which had gotten mildly better once I could scent my seed seeping out of her. But then I was also a sadistic bastard for I enjoyed the way she squirmed in her seat whenever I knew she felt it there captured in between her legs and leather. Needless to say, that I spent the rest of the drive hard as the fucking rock I could see above the tunnel I was now driving into.

From a distance you couldn't see much, and the secret access road was one no mortal would ever find. It was the only way in or out of my castle and again, you had to be welcomed or one of my turned to gain access.

As was the same with leaving and I instantly looked to my sleeping girl to know that there would be no escaping me now. I had to confess the thought put me at ease for the first time since she walked inside my club. One I had believed secure given the amount of security I had inside Transfusion. But if there was one thing I had learned about Amelia and it was that if she wanted something, then she would always find a way.

She was and mostly likely always would be...

My cunning little Princess.

I drove down the tunnel and soon found myself in my underground parking which mainly consisted of my private collection of classic cars. There was another level to this where others parked, but this one was all mine. It was an overly large, well-lit space with the raw mountain stone above us, that was neatly mirrored below on the spotless marble floor. The cars were staggered in their places for ease of access which I knew would have to change when the rest got here from my club's own underground parking. Because this place was about to get packed and pretty quickly.

The only space that would remain was the central driveway, which was the one I made my way up now so I was close to the doorway. There were many different ways to go from here, depending on where you wanted to get to. My castle was a honeycomb of tunnels and passageways leading all over the place and an easy place for someone to get lost in. Another reason why I would be keeping my girl close whilst here. The other reason was as simple as I fucking wanted to!

However, one of the main tunnels led straight to my personal space, which was the largest natural cavern that had been transformed into practical and even comfortable areas that all connected. This made me wonder what Amelia would think of it when I finally led her down there. I knew that I could have done so now, but I didn't think having her waking up in a cave was probably a good idea, not when I was trying to ease her into this new life. And I wanted to let her sleep, for I also knew how much her body needed it.

So instead, I cut the engine, and got out of the car, noticing as Ruto and Clay pulled in close behind the Lambo.

"Fuck me, but I can't fucking wait to hear what your girl pulled this time." This was Clay's response as he got out of the car and when he slammed the door, I tensed and hissed,

"Shut the fuck up will you, she is asleep!" He winced a bit then leaned round me and saw that, thankfully, she was still asleep, meaning he felt free to comment once more,

"Well, if she didn't wake to that, then I would say she is well and truly out for the evening." I looked myself and had to agree, for she hadn't moved.

"Were my orders carried out without issue?" I asked.

"Yes, my Lord, finally something went smoothly," was Ruto's reply.

"Yeah, about fucking time something went our way!" Clay replied and he looked again at Amelia and I swear I was a hairsbreadth away from knocking him out. Instead I sidestepped, putting myself in his line of sight and folded my arms across my chest before snapping,

"Can I fucking help you with something, Clay?!" At least he had the good graces to look contrite.

"Sorry Boss, just curious to know how that's all." I raised a brow but even Ruto then agreed, speaking up,

"We are all curious, Sire." Now this did surprise me, as Ruto didn't usually give a shit about most things, least of all mortals. But then again, she was to be my queen, which meant she would rule by my side one day and one day soon. So, perhaps this was why. Then again, with my council it was a belief that actions spoke louder than words and in Amelia's case, well recently she had been nothing *but action*.

I released a sigh and said,

"She shot the pilot and jumped from the fucking

helicopter." This made Ruto's black ringed eyes grow wide and Clay release a low whistle.

"Fuck me, Boss, your chick is hardcore!"

"That unfortunately isn't where it ended," I informed them sardonically.

"Gods, but what else did she do, blow up their base with stolen C4?"

"No, but had she had the means I wouldn't have put it past her," I admitted, rubbing the back of my neck with my hand, showing just how fucking tired I was at nearly losing my girl!

"She dragged herself out of the river Isar nearly naked, beat up a couple of punks, stole their clothes and a bike and then overtook me so that I could read the words spray painted on the back of her jacket, giving me a clue to follow her," I said. Clay then looked to his side, thankfully at the car this time and then straightened to look back at me,

"She overtook you?"

"In the Lambo?" Ruto added making me growl low,

"I was following Bitch face, so I wasn't exactly going my usual speeds," I said arguing my point.

"Bitch face?" Ruto then enquired.

"Amelia's name for Layla," I informed him making him shrug his shoulders and agree,

"Mmm, that fits."

"What kind of bike?" Clay asked this time and I suddenly wanted this conversation over with.

"A fucking dirt bike, alright!" I snapped making them both grin at each other.

"Right, well if you two have had your fun pointing out the fucking obvious, Clay, get the box and my sword to my private vault. Ruto, call a meeting, I need to get her settled first, but I want you all to be ready to discuss our next move," I ordered, this time making them both really grin, and as I reached inside the car and lifted my beautiful bundle into my arms, Ruto asked,

"And our next move would be?" This was when I granted them both one more look before saying on a growl,

"My fucking revenge."

CHAPTER ELEVEN

AMELIA

BRUISED EGO

"F*inally, you're home, sweetheart.*"

The second I heard Lucius' voice whisper in my head, my eyes snapped open. I found myself in a room I had never been in before and quickly bolted upright, moaning in pain as I did. This was thanks to my bruised stomach. Fortunately, the room wasn't too dark, as someone had left on what looked like a bathroom light. Which meant I could also see enough to tell me that it looked as though I was in a hotel room, making me wonder if Lucius had pulled over somewhere before we had made it to his castle.

Maybe he saw that I had fallen asleep and decided it was best to wait until morning. But then again, he also seemed pretty Hell bent on getting me there and with my safety being his main concern, it now had me questioning if I wasn't already at Königssee.

I glanced around the room again and winced because when I scrunched my face up it hurt. Damn it but I really needed to start remembering about these stupid bruises! I also wondered where Lucius could be and why he had left.

I hated to feel needy here, but I did kind of just wake up in a place I had no clue as to where I was. And other than waking with his voice in my head, then I had been expecting a little more than just dumping me in some room somewhere and walking out the door. But then again, knowing Lucius, he probably had people to kill or at the very least, order to be killed. Well, he was my handsome bloodthirsty warrior man after all, I thought with a smirk.

But still, despite this argument in his defense I was having with myself, I had to say, it was a hit to my ego.

"Well, there is only one thing for it," I said aloud before whipping back the covers and finding that other than my leather jacket, I was still wearing my stolen goods. I found this odd also, as I was sure Lucius would have wanted to get me out of these clothes as soon as he could.

In the end, I shrugged my shoulders and got up, ignoring the aches and pains my body was trying to complain about and padded over (as my boots were also gone) towards one of the windows. However, I soon discovered this was a pointless endeavour, as it offered me nothing. I then gave up squinting at the glass and walked over to the bathroom. I opened the door fully, which then managed to flood the room full of light and now offered me a better view of the space.

It also meant that I could find the light switch, which unsurprisingly was by the door. I raised the lights, as they were on a dimmer switch. This made not only the spotlights on the ceiling illuminate but also a feature wall that had a recess above it that cast a soft white glow downwards. This wall was covered in what looked like reclaimed wooden panels that had been painted with the black and white silhouette of a winter forest. Only with the light now shining down on it, ended up giving it a cool 3D effect.

The rest of the room was neutral colours, with dove grey walls and white and grey bedding, with a dark grey comforter covering the bottom of the bed. The bed was a plain wooden frame, one whitewashed to match the bedside tables. There was a large black rug on the floor underneath the bed so this was the first thing your feet touched when getting up in the morning, not the light grey tiled floor.

The bed also faced a floor to ceiling window that at first glance you would have believed might have been a door onto a balcony. However, it wasn't and the view outside could have been facing a stone wall for how dark it was.

I decided to check out the bathroom and found it mirrored the bedroom décor. Grey tiles, white bowl sink, white roll top bath and slightly darker grey tiles in the shower. The only difference was like the rug in the bedroom, there was a single statement of black.

It was the onyx stone vanity top, one that the sink sat on top of as an overly large bowl. Once again, it looked like something you would have found in a fancy hotel and right now, after what I had been through, it was like finding Heaven. Especially when all I wanted to do was strip naked and wash every inch of my body until I no longer smelled like river water, weed and leather.

So, I did just that.

Of course, getting naked now and I had no choice but to see the damage for myself thanks to the large white framed mirror over the sink. I turned one way and then the other to see it was worse than I first thought. For starters, there was actually a boot shaped bruise forming sideways on my stomach and just under my breasts. But there was also a bruise on my upper thigh which looked to have grown in size and one on my elbow from my fall. There were also a few on my back, both by my shoulders and one just above my backside. I remembered that the one on my shoulders must have been from when he threw me to the wall. And the other must have been from when that bastard had held me down to the floor with his knee to my back.

Gods, but Lucius was going to freak!

This certainly made me get in the shower quicker, trying to get done and maybe wrapped in one of the robes I could see on the shelf before he came back. I mean, this was Lucius we were talking about, so I doubted I could hide it for long. But right now, well I just didn't have the strength left in me to deal with the angry Vamp.

But oh, Gods in Heaven, just feeling the heat of the water on my aches had me moaning aloud and staying under the water longer than what was needed. I did find myself having to be gentle when washing my hair, so as not to forget about the lump I had there, doing the same when washing my body in gentle circles around my bruises. I also washed my face with my fingertips, even though I would have loved to have given it a good scrub. But hey, it was most definitely better than smelling as I did, even if I was now washing away the evidence of Lucius which he had demanded I leave behind.

I had to say but even the idea of washing him from my

skin felt as if I was committing a sin, no matter how uncomfortable it had been in the car. But this was overridden by how much of a turn on it had been. It was so possessive and primal, it made me wish I had the time to pleasure myself whilst in the shower just thinking about it. Admittedly, I even checked to see if the shower head came off the wall but unfortunately not. Damn it, but what was with me since being with Lucius? Could I not even go a few hours without an orgasm!

Gods, but the man was addictive.

But then should I really be surprised? I mean this was Lucius I was talking about. The man I had been obsessing over like some religious cult I had unknowingly signed up to years ago. I laughed at the thought and turned off the water, purposely ignoring my sexual frustration. Then, after stepping from the shower and as I was reaching for my towel was when I heard it.

An angry growl.

It was one I knew well, so when my head eventually braved looking up, I knew what I would find before I found it.

"Lucius?" I whispered his name in question the moment I saw him stood in the doorway panting like some wild beast. He had both hands on the door frame and it was as if this was helping in holding him back. The rest of his body was leant forward beyond the frame in an intimidating way and one that made the large muscles at his shoulders and arms stretch the fabric to near splitting.

Gods, but what was it about this man that made his casual clothes look beyond amazing on him. The dark denim that moulded to his perfectly muscular thighs, the belt buckle that was just slightly bigger than regular but not overly stated like some wannabe cowboy. Then there was the way his black T-shirt was moulded to his muscular frame, like a second skin. One that was now raised slightly from the position of his arms that allowed me a tantalizing strip of skin to be seen at his waist. A strip of skin that was teasing me with the abundance of muscle and solid abs I knew were there barely hiding underneath.

Then there was the powerhouse of a man above all this in the sheer mass of upper body strength I could now see was barely holding himself in check. Even the doorframe started to give way in his hold, and I knew in that dangerous look of his, that he barely even registered the fact. Because that deadly gaze was rooted elsewhere and it wasn't at my face, but at my body.

"Lose the towel," he ordered, his voice strained and tight. I looked down at myself to see in fact he was right, I was now holding it to my front as if at some point my body reacted on its own accord in self-preservation. I looked back up at him in surprise, before my eyes changed and spoke of something more. A pleading, beseeching way that asked him silently not to do this. Because as much as I would have liked to have thought his reaction was one done out of arousal, I knew it wasn't.

It was one bred from rage.

Because I knew what he had seen beneath this towel and that was the full extent of my injuries. A sight that had him seething mad and had quickly warped his once silver grey eyes into crimson pools of fire. Which was why I decided to add words to my gaze,

"Please Lucius, don't do this"

"I said, lose the fucking towel!" he snapped back making me sigh and look down at myself knowing that there was no use in denying him. Not when he was like this and as much as I hated what I was about to show him, he would see it eventually. So, I did as I was told and let the fabric fall from my grasp, leaving my wet, bare bruised body for him to see.

I also heard the curse word being hissed from his lips, but I still couldn't look at him. I wasn't brave enough, not after tonight. But then I felt his presence get close and before I even had a chance to move, his finger and thumb were gripping my chin and he was forcing my head back.

"Look at me," he demanded, at least somewhat softer this time. Which was why I did as he asked and looked. His eyes, even though still blood red and burning, at least managed to soften slightly or enough to know that he was capable even in his rage of being gentle with me.

"Amelia, my sweet, adorable girl…I…*fuck…I am so sorry.*" He whispered this last part after first hissing the curse, and I swear I did a double-take. Because I swear I just heard him apologize? But why? Why would he…oh, and finally this was when it hit me. I knew why he was furious. As yes, he no doubt wanted to kill the bastards that did this to me all over again, but right now, he was more angry with himself. Which was why I raised a hand to his cheek and stroked the pad of my thumb under his eye before doing the same across his lips. Then I told him in a soft voice,

"You have nothing to be sorry for, honey." At this he closed his eyes and lowered his head to mine, holding himself utterly still and immobile. Doing so without touching me as if now he was afraid to. As if he would only end up hurting me more than what he irrationally believed he had.

Then he confessed his thoughts and Gods, my heart broke for him,

"I took you hard...took you rough." Of course, he was referring to the gas station.

"It's okay, honestly you didn't..."

"No! You don't get to do that, Amelia," he snapped making me flinch before I asked,

"Don't get to do what?"

"You don't get to ease my suffering when it is only yours that matters here." I frowned at this before pulling back slightly, something he allowed because he still wouldn't hold me.

"Why is it mine that only matters and excuse me, but I think you will find I was screaming my release right alongside you in that store, or did you forget...or better still, did you momentarily go deaf because of them?" I snapped making him growl,

"I could never forget."

"Good, that means you will also remember, did I once ask you to stop?"

"Amelia." My name was said in reprimand, but I was having none of it.

"Other than when you decided to try and freeze my ass off?" I added making his lips twitch, but I didn't get the full smile that I had aimed for, as they soon turned back into a hard line.

So I pushed,

"Answer me. Did I ask you to stop, Lucius?" I asked, this time more forcefully.

"No," he growled.

"And when I cried out, did I do so in pleasure or pain?" I asked, making him turn his face from mine.

"I don't…"

"You remember, Lucius, so answer me," I interrupted and when he wouldn't answer me, I once more placed my hand on his cheek and forced him to look at me this time.

"You know the answer," I told him again making him drag in a deep breath instead of answering me, so I told him,

"It looks bad, I know it does, but I am not made of glass, Lucius, despite being human, I am not as breakable as you or your kind would believe." At this he finally looked up at me and said,

"It is my job to protect you, not hurt you." Gods, but my heart ached for this man.

"You do protect me but more than anything else, you give me what I want and what I need, and right in that moment after I said I loved you… well, Lucius…*I needed what you gave me,*" I told him fervently before then crushing my lips to his and thankfully not having to wait too long before he took the hint and kissed me back, doing what he did best and dominating it. Then when I realised he still wouldn't touch my body with nothing more than a gentle hand on my neck, one to hold me to him, I pulled back a little. Something he allowed, now being overly cautious with me. So, I told him on a whisper,

"So, give me what I need, Lucius." At this he growled low and instead of doing as I asked, he unfortunately let me go. He quickly turned his back on me and raked an angry hand through his hair, one done out of frustration.

I would be lying if I said it didn't hurt, especially after the tender moment we just shared.

"Fuck, Amelia! Why didn't you stop me! Why didn't you fucking say anything?!" he shouted in annoyance and I quickly snatched up my towel, ignoring the bite of pain as I did. Then I wrapped it around me, tucked it in at my breasts and without answering him, stomped my way out of the bathroom. Or at least I would have had the door not slammed shut before I had chance to. So, I just folded my arms over my towel covered chest and turned to face him.

"Open the door," I demanded but he just mirrored my stance and folded his own arms, making me try really, really hard, to ignore the delicious way his biceps bunched...*damn him!*

"No," he stated firmly.

"Fine, then do what the fuck you want!" I shouted back before walking over to grab another towel so I could start drying off my dripping hair, ignoring his irritated growls and standing purposely in front of the mirror. This continued for a few minutes before I heard him release a heavy sigh. Then I felt him step up behind me and I finally allowed my eyes to find his as his hands came to rest on the vanity top either side of me. Then he lowered his head to my shoulder so he could confess gently,

"I'm struggling here." On hearing this I stopped breathing, holding my breath as I waited for more.

"I...*fuck*... all this...us...I am not used to these emotions, Amelia." Once again it came out as a confession and one that eradicated all my anger before even his last word was uttered.

"It is beyond my control and..." the moment his sentence trailed off I couldn't stand it, I had to ask,

"And...?"

"I think you get that I like control here, sweetheart," he said, telling me something, *like he said*, I already knew.

"And me?" I braved the question.

"You are not something I can control, no matter how much I try."

"Then stop trying," I offered, making him laugh once without humour before he kissed my bare shoulder and lifted his head up to pin me with a knowing gaze.

"That, I am afraid, is not in my nature."

"Then where does that leave us?" Again, it was a question that took all my bravery to ask, as I feared the answer.

"When one of us learns when to submit and the other learns patience for when it doesn't happen," he replied and I actually closed my eyes as his words hit me. That's what he needed, *my submission*. I decided now was not the time to discuss this and because I didn't have the answer he wanted, instead I reverted back to my greatest defence…

Humour.

"Fine, then I will learn patience as I wait for you to get down to your knees and worship me." At this I saw the flash of his teeth as he grinned, before swiping away my wet hair and whispering in my ear,

"I have to say, Pet of mine, I like your idea of submission and look forward to seeing it…soon."

"Good, I'll get you a cushion." To which he chuckled and kissed his way up my throat making me relax back and let out an involuntary moan. But then this ended in a shriek as I was suddenly swept up in his arms and carried from the room, after he made the door open on its own of course.

"Where are we going?"

"I am going to give you what you need," was his husky toned answer and I sucked in a deep breath having to stop myself from muttering up a thank you to the Gods. But then something in my face must have given away my thoughts as he lay me down gently on the bed before placing a fist either side of me. Then, whilst looking down at me, he said in that annoyingly knowing tone of his,

"To heal you, Pet, not fuck you." At this I rolled my eyes at him and tried to squirm out of his space, which he wouldn't allow. I knew this when one hand came to my neck to still me and his head lowered, all the while holding his body weight up with one arm. It was as if he was doing a one armed press up with his body at an angle seeing as his feet were still on the floor.

Gods, but just the sight had me near panting and flooded my mind with delicious images of him in his training room. Of course, in this flicker book of sexiness he was always shirtless and holding something heavy enough that it tensed his muscles. Or maybe he was just beating the shit out of a punching bag before coming to me to throw me over his shoulder, his sweaty shoulder. Oh, but there was always the option of him tripping me up and lowering me to the floor and making love to me on the mats like he promised.

Okay, so I was most definitely starting to see the benefits of letting him train me in his style of fighting, especially if it ended in one of my sexual fantasies.

Now making me wonder when he was just going to crawl up over me already! But instead of doing as I was screaming at him in my mind to do, he gently ran his nose up along my cheek, the one not bruised, and asked me in that dangerously seductive tone of his,

"Did you just roll your eyes at me...*again?*" At this I smirked and lifted my head as much as his hold on my neck would let me. Then I said in a challenging voice,

"Yeah, I did, so what you gonna do about it...*stud?*" At this his lips twitched as he fought a grin and told me...

"Oh sweetheart, you have no fucking idea!"

CHAPTER TWELVE

TREE OF DEATH

Cold…I was so cold.

I don't know what had happened but when I opened my eyes, I found myself outside surrounded by snow and a near crumbling arched wall. I gasped at the sight before me, asking myself had I been sleepwalking? By the Gods, but it was one of the most spectacular sights I had ever seen, like stumbling into some winter wonderland that was equal parts exciting as it was disturbing.

It was that eerie silence that was as if the entire world around you had been put on pause, for not a single thing moved. Nothing that was, but me. It made you feel like an intruder. As if nothing living was welcome here and as stunning as it was, you had to decide if seeing it was worth what it could potentially do to you. The secrets it held. The memories written into the very stone that surrounded it. It was as if the entire garden was an entity of its own and its spirit started to warn you against entering its domain without its master's permission.

It was a feeling so strong that it made me wonder if a witch was involved or was it some kind of casting that Lucius himself had someone put in place. Either way, I decided to brave it as the sight of the place was just too alluring to ignore.

I started to scan the vast space, starting along the wall that framed this secret winter world. It was one that seemed to be held together by the roots of some fallen tree. Either that, or it was the thickest vine I had ever seen that ran along the top of the wall. A wall that framed a truly incredible space and one you would never expect to find here.

The garden didn't hold much in way of design. Nothing more than snow covered hedges that seemed to line the wide walkway in the centre. Something that led to a single dead tree in the middle that was all twisted roots and beaten bark that was nearly as white as the snow that surrounded it. But the difference was the shape, as its base was big enough to actually fit people inside, as it was hollowed out. It also had a sizeable opening facing me and one that looked as if an age ago some beast had ripped it open at the belly and peeled back the edges to create a door.

Despite its harrowing appearance I found myself drawn to it. And even though it was dead there was a startling beauty about it and I couldn't help but find myself taking my first steps in its direction.

So, I walked closer, feeling the cold penetrate my bare feet as though I was stepping on icy shards, something in itself that should have stopped me. But despite this, I still continued on, feeling compelled to do so as if something inside its bare core was calling me to it.

I walked down the centre walkway, briefly looking to the side and expecting the view of the mountains from the strength of the moon's light. It was the brightest I think I had ever seen and it lit the whole garden in a midnight bluish glow that made the floor sparkle and glisten. The only sound to be heard was the crunch of snow beneath my own feet, and one I made with each footstep I took.

It was surprising then that by the time I made it to the tree, the faint sound of laughter could be heard. It was almost as if a ghost had made the sound and I frowned before whispering the only name I could think it belonged to,

"Mum?" I asked, knowing that I would have recognized her laughter anywhere. It was just so familiar to me that I even found myself running my hand along the bark, as if this action too was also familiar. As if I was actually stepping into history and being led to do this by someone in the past that was trying to pull my presence back there. Could these have been the actions of my own mother, some 30 years ago?

This thought made me shiver as it was far from a pleasant thought for obvious reasons. The story went that Lucius had kidnapped my mother and held her ransom for something he wanted in return from my father. By this point they had been enemies for a while, since the second world war, so it stood to reason that my father wasn't Lucius' biggest fan.

But once again I knew little of the details as it wasn't like anyone was telling me anything of the past. I knew this was to shield me in some way but to shield me against what, was another question. But then, looking around my surroundings now, and I felt anything but shielded. For starters, I didn't even know how I'd gotten here and I looked down at myself to find I was wearing Lucius' black T shirt and for once my usually tanned skin was deathly white.

But then my heart froze, and my fingers curled, with my nails scraping against the bare tree. Because this time when I heard the ghost of laughter, it most certainly didn't belong to my mother. My head whipped one way and then the other as I tried to search out the cause, my loose hair fanning to the sides and looking even darker than usual.

Then I heard it,

"You don't have his love." I frowned and narrowed my eyes as I tried to find the person that would dare question how Lucius felt about me. The whole garden was vast in its size and went far beyond the tree, with what looked like a thickly dense woodland at its end. I knew then that the voice had come from that direction and I looked back over my shoulder at where I knew was the safety of the castle.

"You don't believe me…come…see…for…yourself." The voice spoke again, in a taunting way that had my teeth on edge. I wanted to discover who it was, I really did, but then something inside me was screaming in my mind that it would have been a mistake. That it was what they wanted, and they were using my fears against me. So, I pushed away from the tree and instead of being fooled into going nearer to the forest, I stepped away from it. I turned back towards where I knew I could gain access back inside but after one footstep the next voice I heard was directly behind me, making me silently scream,

"The silent garden wants your blood…*and it will take it!"* This last part was hissed at the same time I felt a painful hand take hold of my shoulder and turn me suddenly. I was whipped around with force giving me no other choice but to face my stalker in the night. A blood red cloaked figure stood looking down at me with a hood framing nothing but ominous darkness. Then two white eyes started to glow, and I opened my mouth to scream but yet again, the sound was stolen from me.

"This place will feed from your screams young one, and the tree of death will feed from the blood of Kings...*once it has been found.*" A voice spoke from within the darkness of the hood and I shivered in the spirit's grasp. Then it raised a rotted hand, one made of nothing but chipped and hacked bloody bone, barely buried beneath burnt flesh. Blunt, bloody fingertips void of nails, gruesomely looking as if the tips had been chopped off. I thought the sight a sickening one but as it pointed towards the tree I screamed again with no luck of a soul hearing it, for the spirit had been right.

The garden had stolen my scream.

A scream that should have disturbed all life around me had there been any, as the horror that faced me was worthy of the reaction. For the tree had been transformed and mutated into the stuff of nightmares! Gone was the alluring tree of stark beauty, now being replaced by one of death as it was covered in so many dead bodies it was hard to make out where one began and another ended. Pieces of people all wrapped around it and held in place by thorns of the likes I had never known. Its spikes were impossibly big, like daggers that had managed to pierce right through even the thickness of thighs, pinning them to the wood in a bloody mess. The whole tree was covered in blood as it seemed to pour down from the branches, overflowing over the bodies and pieces of people, I thankfully couldn't make out.

It was the most grotesque sight I had ever seen in all my life and I fell backwards, ripping myself from the hold of its bearer, the one who wanted me to witness this nightmare. Then, just as I started to fall in a slow motion, doing so now as if time had slowed right down, the person spoke one last time,

"The blood of Kings must be spilled…

"Soul bearer."

CHAPTER THIRTEEN

FINGER OF PUNISHMENT

I woke with a start, but I wasn't screaming like I thought I should be. No, instead I just had my mouth open as if I had wanted to do it, but my voice had been robbed from me. A sight that I could imagine was nothing short of creepy. Especially when finding me suddenly awake with my eyes opened wide with fright and my mouth open agape, screaming with not a sound penetrating the air. Well, it was no wonder I was just glad a certain someone hadn't woken up and seen it.

And speaking of that certain someone…

Lucius was still asleep next to me with an arm still curled around my waist and a hand curled possessively at my hip. I had to say that the sight and feel of it there certainly helped to make me feel safe, which was why I sucked in a deep breath before releasing it again.

It had been nothing but a dream. Just a stupid dream that's all and one most likely as a result from the night I'd been through. But I knew instantly it was one that would rid me of sleep for the rest of the night and I looked to the window to see that it wasn't yet near to morning. So, instead of disturbing Lucius with my fidgeting, I decided to get up and use the bathroom. Besides, I could imagine that after the night Lucius had also had, then he could most definitely do with the sleep.

So, ever so gently I lifted his arm, knowing I had a chance to escape when it felt like a dead weight in my hands. Then I shifted from under it before placing it back down on the bed as gently as I could. After this I grabbed the first thing I could feel and put it on, before quietly tiptoeing to the bathroom, only putting on the light after I was inside, and the door was closed.

Once inside I used the toilet at the far end as it was tucked away behind a wall. Then I started thinking back on what had happened before Lucius had exhausted me enough for me to basically pass out on him. As it turned out, Lucius' punishment wasn't a spanking to my ass, as was per his usual threat. No, this naturally was because I wasn't yet healed. Something that was established earlier as being a definite sore spot for him. So instead, he decided a more fitting punishment for me was more of the prolonged suffering kind...*sexually speaking.*

Now it has to be said this wasn't fun for me, that was until he finally allowed it to be very fun for me. Something that started with him sitting upright in the bed and the second I also sat up to give him space, he snagged me under the arms before dragging me up to him. This ended with my back being held to his chest and sat in between his legs with us both now facing the window. This was also when I started to squirm.

His answer to this was by way of banding an arm across my chest as his other hand collared my throat. I sucked in a quick breath and this time, it wasn't in fear or trepidation, it was pure lust. It was such a dominant hold that it had me swallowing hard, something he could feel sliding down his palm.

"Ssshh, my captured little bird, it's time for me to play with you," he whispered seductively, making me actually feel like some erotic pet of his. Then, in one swift action, my towel was gone and a girly shriek followed. And well, if I thought I was squirming before, then now I was really moving, something that seemed to amuse him greatly. But I also noticed with the way he held me, that he was avoiding hurting me further by staying clear of my bruises, which was why when I didn't still, he whispered,

"Be still, or you will hurt yourself." I did as I was told, because he was right, I needed to stop twisting and force myself to relax. After he was assured that I wasn't going to move again, his arm over my chest relaxed too before his gloved hand went exploring. The feel of leather clad fingers caressing gently over my skin felt amazing and soon had my head falling back against his shoulder. I knew he was looking down the length of me and with his head angled to one side, that obviously gave him the best view, he muttered,

"Fucking exquisite." Naturally, I blushed at the compliment, before releasing a series of soft moans when his hand cupped my breast, testing the weight in his palm before digging his fingers in for a firmer hold. Then he started plucking at my nipple, one already hard from being exposed

to the cool air and I swear my moans increased in speed and volume. I even found myself arching my body and therefore pressing the round soft flesh firmer into his hold. But then with his other hand still shackled around my neck, he held me to his shoulder so I couldn't move too far.

"Now for your punishment, my pet," he hummed against my cheek before swiping at me with his tongue and kissing the wet mark he made. At the same time his hand left my heaving chest and my now beautifully abused nipple so it could travel further south. But his journey took him along my ribcage and then to my belly, where his feather light touch caressed the worst of my bruises, making me feel so protected that I released a breathy sigh.

"I wish I could have been the one to make him suffer, for no one marks my beauty and no one touches what is mine and lives to recall the memory...*now spread those pretty thighs for me,*" he said making me try and take in all the things he'd just said but other than asking me to open my thighs, I couldn't think. Which meant like the good girl he owned, I did as I was told, letting them fall open. I thought that this would be enough and waited for the moment that his leather hand would snake further down to where my sex was exposed. Something that was both exhilarating and shameful at the same time, messing with my emotions.

"Good girl, now spread yourself for me," he whispered in my ear and I tensed in his hold.

"Wwhhat?" I asked again on a stutter, one he chuckled at.

"I said spread yourself for me."

"But I...No, I can't do..." Again, I tried for words.

"Yes, you can, and you will...now start by touching

yourself," he demanded more forcefully this time and when I still didn't move, he reached across me and took hold of my wrist. Then he brought my own hand to the juncture of my open thighs and even extended a finger before placing it at my core. Then he applied enough pressure that he swiped my finger through my folds, gathering up my obvious arousal before raising it up for him to see it now glistening on my soaking wet finger.

"Mmm, too tempting not to taste," he said before forcing me to bend my arm and bring my hand to his lips, so he could suck in my slick finger. His tongue swirled around the digit and it soon became his turn to release a moan. Then he let my finger go with a pop and said on a growl,

"Fucking delicious!"

After one last wet lick with his tongue, he forced my hand down and said,

"Now again, only this time, fuck yourself and feed me from your dripping core." I shuddered at his crude demand finding that 'my core' just gushed with even more arousal thanks to his rough and sexual demand of me. So, with his forceful guidance, yet again I was made to touch myself, only this time he angled my finger in the right spot and using his own fingers against mine, forced two digits inside, making me finger myself. Then once he pumped them a few times, causing me to cry out at the building sensation, he pulled them free and fed from them again.

And this was to become the start of my torture.

Over and over again I was made to repeat this action, and each time he would force me to pleasure myself for longer and faster, letting it cruelly build until again pulling my hand away from completion. Then his mouth would suck and lick every bit away before guiding it down once more.

"Please." I ended up begging and I could feel his pleased grin against my cheek. Only instead of granting me my request for him to let me make myself come, his hand left the column of my throat. He did this so he could play with my breast, making me cry out even more, as the pleasure became almost too much to bear. But yet, it still wasn't quite enough to push me over the edge and he knew it, the bastard!

"Say it again," he said as his hand worked me with my own, this time paying more attention to my clit.

"Please," I uttered as I felt it building but then the second the word was out, he forced me to stop.

"No! Please, please Lucius, don't stop, don't be so cruel," I pleaded making his chest rumble with a different type of growl this time.

"But I am cruel, Amelia, it's who I am...*it's what the Devil made me,"* his Demon whispered and this time when I shook against him, it was his Demon that cooed me,

"Ssshh, my delicious one, a feast for the eyes and for my tongue must be rewarded...now, say it again like I asked." This time he went back to working me but stopped directing me with his fingers as they were no longer over my own. No, instead he started running his leather fingers up through my dripping wet folds and I swear I was close to meowing and crawling up him like a damn cat!

"Please...oh no, please don't stop, I am doing as you asked!" I cried out in dismay when his hand shackled my wrist and started to pull it away and damn him, I had been so fucking close!

"That is not what I want to hear you say, sweetheart," Lucius whispered down in my ear before biting it a little and adding a clue,

"Now, tell me what I really want to hear…*said only to me this time."* This was when it finally hit me, and he let go of my wrist and urged me to continue as he started to do the same, so we were both now working the tight bundle of nerves. So, I turned my head, to reach his ear and told him,

"I love you, Lucius."

This was when his reply was to finally grant me what I was desperate for. Only added to it was when he suddenly inserted a finger inside my channel, fucking it and fingering me with incredible speed. I rubbed my clit only a few more times before I was coming, doing so now by screaming out my release for the power of it felt as if it could tear me apart!

But this wasn't enough for Lucius as he was far from done. Something I discovered when he pulled back a little from behind me, so he had room to bring his own wrist to his mouth. I only caught a glimpse of this before he was placing his bleeding wrist to my mouth and telling me in a forceful, demanding tone,

"Now drink me down, my love, and come again!" Then I had no choice but to do both, as he added an extra finger at the same time thrusting his wrist to my lips and snarling,

"Open your fuckable mouth and drink!" I did as I was told and the second I did, he groaned in pleasure behind me, making me feel the abundance of muscles at my back all tense from his own pleasure gained at having me feed from him. But soon this became a shadow of my own, for once again, I was screaming out yet another release, one not as strong as the first but one that lasted a lot longer. I ended up convulsing as I rode each wave of pleasure that assaulted me, at the same time drinking down as much of his blood as he wanted me to have.

Then, before I knew what was happening, he tore his wrist free and grabbed a fistful of my hair before yanking my head to one side.

"Again! Give me another one!" he shouted and just before I could utter in protest that it would be impossible, he swooped down and sank his fangs into my neck and feasted on my blood, and at the same time added yet another finger.

I cried out at the double assault, as he fucked me harder with the extra intrusion, one that made my insides clamp down on him, and I screamed in pleasure with the sensation he created when touching what felt like every erotic nerve. Then with his thumb he worked my clit himself, as I had nothing left in me to do anything but sit in his hold and let him take complete control.

Unsurprisingly, a few seconds later I was screaming my release up at the ceiling in such a powerful orgasm that my vision blurred, and my body started to sag. This was obviously Lucius' cue to stop and he retracted his fangs, making them slide out of my pierced skin. I vaguely felt him licking up the mess he had made and when he softly whispered down at me one last order, I could do nothing in my power but to obey,

"Sleep now, my sweet, tasty love."

CHAPTER FOURTEEN

THE BEAST AWAKENS

I finished on the toilet and walked over to the sink to wash my hands, still deep in thought and only just noticed that my bruised face was no more.

"Ha!" I said making a happy noise as I lent closer to the mirror and at the same time prodding at my cheek and nose, where the worst of it had been. Then I straightened up and looked down at myself, lifting up Lucius' T shirt to check out the rest of my body. I was rewarded by the sight of unmarred skin, and even poked at my stomach just to check, smiling when I felt no pain.

In fact, I was still smiling when I looked back up at myself and the sight that welcomed me, quickly snatched it away and replaced it with a scream.

"Lucius!" I shouted his name in fright as there he was, a looming figure behind me, completely naked and looking less than happy. Actually, he looked positively pissed off! Then he took the last steps into me, doing so from behind and crowded my space. This in turn meant that I had no choice but to step right up to the slab of marble, putting my hands out on the cool stone so as to steady myself.

"Have to say, Princess, not a fan of waking up and finding you gone," he said in a dangerous tone and I knew I was in trouble seeing as I was back to being 'Princess'. Something I had quickly learned was a sure sign.

"I just...well, I just needed to use the bathroom," I said in a shocked voice.

"Then you wake me." I frowned at this, totally blindsided,

"Erh...come again?" I asked, now making my dumbfounded state fully known. This was when he leaned in close and said,

"You heard me. If you wake up, then you fucking wake me!" he snapped making me now narrow my gaze at him,

"Are you serious?"

"Deadly," was his single word hissed back at me and my next question was a toss-up between 'why' and 'are you fucking insane'! Thankfully, the first one won, seeing as he was seething mad.

"Why?"

"Why? Because I fucking said so that's why, because when your body is in my bed, then your ass is abiding by my rules," was his infuriated reply.

"Your rules?" I questioned with a little shake of my head, thinking that this was totally barbaric behaviour.

"Yes."

"Your rules?" I asked again, needing this repeated in case I did, in fact, believe I was the one that had gone insane and was now hearing shit. But it was at this point that his hand curled around my waist, fisted his fingers in his own T shirt I wore and yanked me back hard against him.

"My. Fucking. Rules!" he said this time growled against my cheek.

"That's wacked!" I said making him snarl.

"No seriously, I don't know what is worse, the fact that I am getting reprimanded for not waking you up because I needed a piss, and may I add was considerate enough not to wake you, or the fact that you have a set of rules I must abide by if I am to be in your bed!" I shouted, losing my own damn temper now!

"Okay, sweetheart, then let me fucking elaborate this for you. I am not a fan of waking up in a fucking panic to find you not there and fearing the worst only a few hours after…*the worst fucking thing happened and you were taken from me!* that is one!" Okay, so he was making somewhat of a point here, even if he was using his super scary voice to say it.

"Secondly, seeing as it is you and you are my Chosen One, a person who I think you will get by now, means the most to me in this fucking world, then yes, in my bed, you come with fucking rules!" he snapped only I managed to focus on only one part of that as I asked,

"I mean the most to you in the whole world?" At this he closed his eyes and groaned down at the floor, as if speaking directly to Hell this time,

"But of course, that is the part she focuses on."

"Oh, I am sorry, would you like me to go back to focusing on the part where my boyfriend is being totally irrational and barbaric?!" I snapped back, now trying to

185

dislodge his hold on me, something that wasn't exactly working out the way I'd hoped.

"You really think that after tonight my request is irrational?" Again, this question was snapped at me in annoyance.

"Request?" I said knowing that this was bloody far from it!

"Demand," he reiterated, now using one more fitting with both his mood and his irrational needs.

"So, let me get this straight, you seriously want me to wake you every time that I want to get out of the bed, even if it's just to take a piss?"

"Even if it's to take a piss," he repeated making me shake my head before telling him,

"That's crazy." To which he shrugged his shoulders and said,

"My bed, my rules." I frowned back at him through the mirror where this strange and totally 'beyond my normal world' argument was taking place and said,

"Okay, so I guess I am not sleeping in your bed anymore." Then I shrugged my shoulders and tried to move from his hold, one that told me not a chance when his arms tensed around me.

"Newsflash for you, sweetheart, any bed you find yourself sleeping in will be my bed and *I. Will. Be. Fucking. In. It!"* he seethed, grinding out each word.

"Oh yeah, and how do you figure that, uh?"

"Because I will have chained you to me until you can *learn my fucking rules!"* he said, taking my challenge and crushing it, especially when he looked down at me side on and started to trail his fingertips up the back of my naked thigh.

"These fucking legs of yours, this perfect peach ass..." he said on a growl and forced my 'peach ass' into his crotch, letting me feel the length of his hard cock now pressing along the line of my ass cheeks. Then his hands came to the front of me, with one snaking under his over-sized tee, so he could palm a breast, taking a firm hold at the same time cupping my now dripping wet sex with the other.

"These perfect tits, and this fucking addictive pussy...all fucking mine...whenever I want it and it is always, and I mean always...*In. My. Fucking. Bed!*" he said and suddenly his hands left their bounties and came to frame my hips. Then with his fingers biting into my flesh in a painful but erotic way, one that made me want cry out in pleasure, he yanked my ass back. Then he angled me down so my chest was being pressed firmly against the marble slab.

"Mine!" he roared as he entered me quickly, making me cry out and instantly claw at the vanity in a hopeless attempt at holding on. Then he pulled almost fully out of me and then, like the first time, thrust in deep and hard, bringing me to the tips of my toes from the force of it. Gods, but I was sure it should have been painful, but it wasn't. No, instead it was pure and raw and intense and to the point that it only took him six more times for this action to have me coming quickly around his cock, screaming out his name,

"LUCIUS!"

The very second I erupted, Lucius fisted my hair and pulled me back, so I was forced upwards where he growled down at me,

"I want to see the woman I love come again!" And he did, oh boy did he! I threw my head back, despite his hold and screamed at the mirror, trying my best to keep sight of him as he powered into me. Gods almighty, it was incredible, coming to the sound of him calling me the woman he loves as it echoed through my mind to the feel of him taking my body in a hard, rough and unyielding way! As if it was his to use how he wanted it and there was nothing I could do to stop him. And by the flaming rivers in Hell, that thought was fucking hot and turned me on more than I ever had been in my whole life!

"Just look at you, look at yourself! Fucking spectacular, the way you take me so perfectly into this hot little body, one made solely for me and me alone! *Fucking. Perfection!"* Lucius growled and the sight of him behind me, still forcing me to take even more pleasure, had me unsurprised to find it building again.

Suddenly, thoughts of him tying me to the bed and spanking my ass, or playing with me as he had earlier, all the pleasurable ways he could punish me…Gods, it was all assaulting my mind and twisting all thoughts of what I thought I wanted sexually, until these dirty scenes were all I could see.

It was unsurprisingly then that my body was so close to coming again and the second he felt it, he held my body to his in a near crushing hold as he growled in my ear,

"You come when I say you can, for we find our release together…now hold the fuck on," he said fucking me now with greater speed and I had nothing to do but as he demanded of me. So, I held on to his arm, one banded across me under my T shirt, with my breasts slapping against his forearm with the force. Now this truly was fucking…wild and untamed fucking that felt deliciously like being owned…

Like being claimed.

"I can't…please…please Gods hurry, Lucius," I said begging him to find it and soon because I could barely hold it off much longer. As every quick and powerful caress his cock made inside me was driving me near crazy with the need to erupt.

"Fuck! Come, Amelia! Come now! Fucking my Heaven made, fucking what's mine! Now milk my cock and come!" he shouted at me and I erupted full around him, my core quaking against his length and dragging him inside me as far as his impressive size would go. Lucius in turn threw his head back and roared at the ceiling, swearing,

"Fuck, FUCK!" The sound was unbelievable and true untamed beauty to my ears, for I knew that I had done that…

Me.

A moment later and Lucius curled his body over mine and held me to him as we both came down from the immense high together. Naturally, Lucius recovered first and lifted me into his arms. Then, as he was walking us both back towards the bed, I nestled my head against his chest and said in a mumbled, out of breath way,

"Maybe you're right…maybe waking you up in the middle of the night is a good idea." On Lucius hearing this, I soon felt my body begin to shake with his quiet laughter. Then he placed me down, whipped his tee off my body and then used that to soak up my dripping core below, cleaning me where I clearly didn't have the strength to. And I had to say, it felt so intimate to be cared for in this way, I couldn't help but smile. Then I felt him get into bed behind me, and

position my back to his front, wrapping me in his arms and resting my head on his bicep.

"It's not just a good idea...*it's the best idea, love.* Now go back to sleep," Lucius said, giving me a squeeze. This was one order I had no problem accepting as the second my eyes closed, I felt myself drifting.

And that morning...

I woke with Lucius cupping my sex possessively.

CHAPTER FIFTEEN

TORN HELL

The next day Lucius woke in a far better mood and I suppose it was easy to put this down to a number of reasons, the main one being he was essentially home. This became obvious when the first thing he declared that morning was the day's plans, this being a tour of his mountain castle.

However, before this better mood began, two things happened. The first being that after I had woken to finding Lucius' hand resting in between my legs, I had strangely fallen back to sleep, and doing so with a knowing grin on my face. Then the next time I had woken, it was to find Lucius gone. Which lead on to the second thing to happen and that was realising how sore my eyes were.

I sat up and tried to focus, blinking away the sleep that seemed to cling to my vision thanks to sleeping with my contact lenses in...*again*. Unfortunately, this also meant that by the time Lucius was walking out of the bathroom already dressed for the day, he caught me like this. And well, naturally one look at me when I started blinking rapidly and I soon found my head framed in his big hands, as he started tipping my face up to look at him.

His growl of disapproval wasn't a surprise.

"Amelia." Again, my name being said in the same disapproving way also, *wasn't a surprise.*

"It's okay, I just need…"

"What you need to do is remember to fucking take them out!" he snapped making me narrow my blurred and sore eyes back at him.

"Well, I would have done but then I didn't exactly fancy a day of feeling for the walls and walking around like Mr Magoo!" I argued back, knowing that just from his face alone, he had no clue as to who Mr Magoo was and really, was I surprised? If anything, I think I might have fainted had he said, 'oh yeah, that's true, honey, you do resemble that cartoon of a near sighted retiree that finds himself in comical situations'. But of course, instead of this I got a clipped,

"Who the fuck is Mr Magoo?!"

"Never mind, the point being I don't have my glasses as I packed them in my bag and left them at…"

"You mean that bag over there," he said interrupting me and motioning to the sofa in the room where I could kind of see a dark spot.

"Oh," was my award winning, witty reply. After this he cut me some slack and walked over to where my bag was to retrieve my glasses for me. Then, as I got up from the bed, ready to grab his Tee, yet again to wear, he snatched me up in his arms making me squeal.

"Hey, what are you…?!"

"Well, I wouldn't want you to hurt yourself…*Miss Magoo,*" he said making me chuckle as he walked me into the bathroom. Once there he placed me on my feet in front of the vanity.

"Now time to get ready, sweetheart, and I will be back in a little while, as I have a bit of business to attend to," he told me, whilst running his fingertips down the valley of my breasts to my stomach and making me shudder against him. Then when he paused, his hand splayed out against where the worst of my bruise had been and said,

"It eases my soul once more to see you as you were." I inhaled a quick breath and held it there, letting his words roll over me like a warm blanket.

"I…"

"Twenty minutes, Amelia, no more," he said interrupting whatever it was I was about to say in response to his tender words.

Then he placed my glasses down and put one of my hands on top of them, letting me know where they were. I pursed my lips and frowned.

"I'm not that blind!" I shouted back as he walked from the bathroom and but of course, doing so now,

Chuckling.

A little time later and after what felt like trying to win a losing battle to gouge my own eyes out, I was just putting on a pair of sneakers when Lucius walked back in. He also found me wearing a pair of stonewash skinny jeans with zips up the ankles and a navy blue T shirt that was dotted with little white stars clustered at the hem. To this I'd added a navy and white striped long knitted cardigan that was soft and baggy in its design, even to the point of being called slouchy. It also had large pockets to keep my hands warm just in case as I had no idea how cold it would be when walking around inside a mountain. As let's face it, it wasn't exactly the type of advice TripAdvisor would be able to offer.

I had also tied my hair up into a messy bun, and was wearing my trusty thick black rimmed glasses, that yes, I knew made me look like a geek. However, it was clear that after last night, my eyes needed the rest.

Lucius found me kicking my feet into my shoes and I looked up, speaking as I did,

"It's a great view out…whoa!" This ended because I found myself in his arms and plastered to his front before he grabbed my soon to be even messier bun and kissed me as if he hadn't seen me in days, not the twenty or so minutes ago.

The kiss didn't last long, but it was one that would have curled my toes had I been an evil Disney villain. On the other end of the Disney spectrum, it was also one that would have had birds singing and mice blushing, before a pixelated screen flashed up with a warning saying, 'no longer suitable for younger audiences'.

Needless to say, my glasses were slightly steamed, and I was panting by the time his lips left mine. Then he tipped my head back and said,

"There's my beautiful girl."

After this he took my hand and started to walk me to the door, but I pulled back slightly and asked,

"Where are we going?" as I didn't know why, but I found myself nervous.

"We are going to have breakfast in my private living space."

"Erm, but I thought this was your room?" I asked, looking back behind me now and if I was honest, even thinking to myself that it seemed a little tame for Lucius' taste. That and smaller than I would have imagined. He laughed once and said,

"No, Amelia, this is just one of the guest rooms, my space is…well, let's say it's a lot more…*spacious.*" He said this as if it was an inside joke, one I would no doubt get once I had actually seen it for myself.

I had to say I was surprised by Lucius' behaviour as he seemed almost excited for me to see it, grinning a lot more than usual. But then, this could have been down to seeing the trepidation in my eyes and he was enjoying making me squirm. Something that was fast becoming his new favorite hobby, I was sure. Well, other than making me come a lot, I thought with a hidden smirk and a silent Hail Mary for that one!

I had to say that his home was a strange mix of castle meets manor home, meets a large network of tunnels inside a cave. Some parts were long large hallways, with smooth walls and hanging tapestries made to depict what I imagined was Hell in its different beliefs. For example, there was one that was clearly Ancient Mesopotamia, as the Sumerian afterlife was a dark, dreary cavern located deep below the ground, one which was shown on the tapestry.

It also showed where Hell's inhabitants were believed to continue a shadowy version of life on Earth, a bleak domain known as Kur. It was also believed to be ruled by the goddess Ereshkigal, if memory served me right. Which was why I asked to be sure,

"Is Kur ruled by the goddess, Ereshkigal?" Lucius paused, with my hand still in his and looked up to see what had triggered that question. Then his eyes came back to me and they crinkled at the sides with the smile he gave me.

"You know of Sumerian history?" He looked impressed, which in turn made me blush.

"Yeah, a little," I said lying. He raised a brow in a way that told me he didn't believe me.

"Sumerians believed that all souls ended up in the same afterlife, and that a person's actions during their life had no effect on how that person would be treated in the next world to come," Lucius said in a way that made this belief sound utterly foolish to him.

"A bit contradictory then when it was also believed that the souls in Kur were thought to eat nothing but dry dust and was the reason why family members of the deceased would ritually pour drinks into the dead person's grave through a clay pipe, thereby allowing the dead to drink," I said thinking out loud and Lucius gave me a look before commenting dryly,

"Oh yes, *a little,* indeed. "

This was in reference to my earlier comment about knowing only a bit about the history we spoke of. But then I was often used to downplaying my knowledge, as I always feared that I came over as a know it all and also, well...*boring.* In fact, Wendy flatly refused to watch any more quiz shows on TV with me, as I would just spend the entire time blurting out the answers and moaning when they got them wrong.

So, naturally I ignored his comment and went back to focusing on the dark and gloomy scene in front of me.

"Mmm, I wonder which other cultures you will recognise?" Lucius wondered aloud, now setting a challenge for me.

"Well, back there was somewhere in Asia, as I noticed a red dragon, but I confess I don't know too much about that one." He smirked at this but didn't comment, instead nodding for me to continue.

"And you also had, Africa, with the Hell of Swahili mythology that I believe is called Kuzimu, and it is thought that this developed under the influence of Muslim merchants at the east African coast," I told him no longer holding back. He folded his arms and leant his body against the wall next to the Sumerian Hell and said,

"And I am curious, what in the art gave that one away?"

"Well, it's believed to be a very cold place, unlike most depictions of Hell and well, the scene of people all looking like they are freezing their asses off, kinda gave it away." At this he threw his head back and laughed before pulling me to him, holding me close and rubbing his chin on the top of my head.

"Mmm, rightly so, my smart little scholar."

After this sweet endearment we carried on, with me pointing out those I knew, which was almost all of them. Of course, I got so excited when I saw my favorite subject,

"Ancient Egypt!" I shouted, quickly pulling him back. I then stared at the tapestry and it was so beautiful I actually reached out to touch it, stopping myself just in time. I then looked to Lucius and blushed, mumbling a quick,

"Sorry, I couldn't help…"

"Amelia." He said my name again in that soft reprimanding way of his before explaining why,

"You're my Chosen One." Erm…or should I say, more like just adding to the confusion with that statement.

"I don't understand, what has that got to do with…"

"It means if you want to touch it, then touch it… fuck, make a dress out of it if you want to, I don't care so long as you treat this place like your own," he said in his usual forceful manner.

"Erm…" This was when he got closer and said,

"Which means you are free to touch whatever the Hell you want, for if it belongs to me, then it belongs to you… now do you understand?"

"I, erm…well, I'm not sure…" I started to say when he decided for himself,

"She understands," he muttered to no one, as if this was final. So, I went back to the art on the wall and to prove a point and (to basically make Lucius happy) I reached out and started to trace one of the forty two divine judges it was believed a dead person faced at a tribunal. This was to determine if they had led a life in conformance with the principles of the goddess Maat. A deity who represented truth and right living, who would welcome the person into the Heavenly reed fields.

However, on the opposing end of this, if a person was found guilty, they were thrown to Ammit, the "devourer of the dead", and would be condemned to the lake of fire, which showed on the image below the divine court. It was also believed that the person taken by the devourer was subjected first to terrifying punishments and then annihilated. So not really a very happy ending I thought wryly.

I felt Lucius watching me with great interest, which meant I felt the need to fill the silence.

"It does make me wonder…"

"Um, about what, Pet?" he asked in a knowing tone as if what I was going to say next was a sure way of amusing him. This being one of the reasons I chose not to look at him, as I could see even from the corner of my eye the way he was tapping two fingers over his mouth as if to hide his grin.

"I wonder if these depictions of punishment may have influenced the medieval perceptions of the inferno in Hell found in early Christian and Coptic texts?" He made a 'humming' sound and said,

"That's a coincidence, as I was wondering the exact same thing." At Lucius' comment I totally fell for it when asking in an excitable tone,

"You were?!" At this his gaze softened and he ran the back of his finger down my cheek before saying,

"No sweetheart, I was wondering how soon I can make it so as I am fucking you again, only this time on my bed." At this my eyes widened before I smacked his arm and said,

"No, you weren't!"

"Oh, I can assure you, I fucking was, and despite how adorably cute I find your intelligence and passion for giving me a history lesson, I also find it a fucking turn on of the likes you wouldn't believe." Okay, so now my eyes really widened, and I uttered a breathy,

"Seriously?"

"I swear to all these Hells and back," he said getting closer and whispering it only an few inches from my face. Then he straightened and said,

"So, if you are finished with your studies, or should I say, *finished with mine,* I have something far more interesting for you to focus on." This sentence ended with a wink and I groaned before commenting,

"You mean your cock, don't you?" He turned with a smirk, took my hand and said in a confident tone,

"Yes, yes I do." I laughed at this and let him pull me along, but then at the very last tapestry I couldn't help but notice the major difference in this one.

First, it was from classic Greek mythology. The image of what I could make out, was a deep, gloomy place, like a pit or abyss used as a dungeon of torment and suffering of those that resided within Hades' domain. But then below this, was something far worse and the moment I saw the fiery mountain in the middle of a vast wasteland, I knew exactly what it was.

Tartarus.

Of course, nothing about this version of Hell depicted on this tapestry would have screamed out of place, for it was just another belief. Another civilization's version of Hell and where the sinful ended up. And this should have been it. This should have been like all the rest.

But it wasn't.

Because this one wasn't like the rest.

No, this one had met a destructive end. This one had met the force of someone's temper.

Someone's claws.

Had met…

Lucius' rage.

CHAPTER SIXTEEN

SIGIL OF LUCIUS

Tartarus

This was what my thoughts were stuck on and it didn't take long before Lucius started to notice my mind was elsewhere. However, on this occasion he must have chosen to give me this time, no doubt putting it down to how strange my surroundings were. I mean, just trying to get your head around the fact that you were inside a castle, cocooned inside a hollowed out mountain, was enough for more than just a few deeper thoughts.

But then this was me we were referring to, so naturally my thoughts were still rooted in Hell. I just wished that I knew all the details surrounding the past. Or should I say, *his past*, as I just knew it was something big. It had to be if it was purposely being kept from me. In that moment I couldn't help but look to his gloved hand and ask myself if that had something to do with it?

Of course, I knew that Tartarus was real, as Hell and

Heaven were not as a single person would have believed them to be. No, it in fact consisted of everyone's beliefs. Just like the Gods, whose greater power came from the strength of that mortal's belief in them. And this was no different in Hell. Each of the tapestries do, in some way, actually exist in Hell and the ferrymen simply get you to your final destination depending on factors that surround how you live your life.

This was similar to Heaven in a sense, but then again, each of the two were worlds just as complex as the Earth was in between. Factors, consequences and rules were everywhere to be found, just as there were species, deities, fates and angels, who all ruled their own pieces and ran these sectors with their own set of rules. It was literally a minefield and Hell was no different, if somewhat more brutal in its punishments.

But Hell wasn't exactly all fire and brimstone like most depictions would have you believe. There was order, there were rules and with these the rulers that enforced them. There were palaces, realms and kingdoms that were fought for and conquered by the strongest. There were rivers and mountains, deserts and fortresses, strongholds and castles and more. Jeez, but even my father had his own palace in Hell!

Of course, I was solely mortal, so I had naturally never been there as unless you croaked it, then it was impossible. I had heard it slip out once that my mother had been there a few times, even encountering my grandfather on one occasion. A high ranking Demon who was actually the Prince of Lust and part of the guild of the nine circles. But then, the nine circles of Hell did make up for seventy percent of Hell, so it meant he was kind of a big deal down there.

My mother, of course, hadn't actually been completely human, hence being granted access without needing to die first. Which made me now wonder, did Lucius have a place there?

"Now that look intrigues me," Lucius said not exactly bringing me out of my thoughts, but instead choosing to voice them when I blurted out,

"Do you have a home in Hell?" At this he burst out laughing and the sound echoed down the tunnel we were currently walking down.

"Why do you wish to know?" he enquired without answering me.

"I was just curious, you know after…" I let my sentence trail off and instead looked behind me to indicate where we had come from.

"Yes, Amelia, I have a home in Hell, an entire kingdom actually and one I have no inclination to rule as of yet," he said surprising me.

"But then if you're not there who rules it?" At this Lucius' features hardened and his curt reply only ended up adding more questions I felt I couldn't yet ask,

"Someone in my place."

Naturally after this serious tone, I decided not to push.

After this we continued walking and I wondered at this rate if we would ever get there. The place was as incredible as it was intimidating, seeing as I knew it would take years for me to get used to a place like this without getting lost. It was tunnel after tunnel, many of which all looked the same and I couldn't help but say,

"You know I am thinking you should invest in some signs. That or an app on your phone, that acts like a sat nav." To this he chuckled and then suddenly I was tugged into his hold, the flaming torch he had been holding to lead the way, now held back. Just the sight of the flames flickering against his skin was pulling me in. This, combined with the alluring shadows of the dark space which were creating equal strips of darkness against his handsome face, made it nothing short of striking.

"But I like the idea of you needing me to guide you…that way I know you won't be able to get yourself into trouble." I grinned up at him and said,

"Well, that's going to be annoying for you every time I need to take a piss." At this he threw his head back and laughed again, the sound this time echoing through the tunnels with greater strength, making me wonder how far it travelled.

"I think I would cope," he commented before placing a sweet kiss on my lips, one that didn't deepen but was still a tender gesture all the same.

"You know how to get to this point?" he asked after retaking my hand in his and leading the way, with the torch in front.

"I think so, why?"

"Because beyond this tunnel you will find your first sign," he said, something that only made sense when we finally reached the door at the end. This opened up into a large room which the only purpose of was like a lobby in its barest form. Carved rock walls that only showed themselves when Lucius raised an arm and lit some sort of shelf that surrounded the whole room. I then watched as it caught alight and flames travelled along the narrow reservoir that framed the room about a foot from the ceiling. This created enough light that it enabled me to see the room in detail, not that there was much to see at that.

It was pretty much a space you stepped into before picking your chosen destination, as what faced us now were four large doors. Each were the same size, being about eight foot high, arched and heavily studded. The only difference was the demonic looking symbols that had been carved into the dark red wood.

"I will take what's behind door number three please, Monty," I said making Lucius laugh and say,

"Lucky for you that's the door you will want."

"Your sigil I take it?" I asked referring to the marking on the door that was different from the rest. This was something that influential demons were usually issued with. But then, the most powerful of these were granted a different sigil, and these were usually two circles, one fitting inside the other. Then within that ring were symbols that basically indicated rank, power, strengths, loyalties and the strength of your army, that type of thing.

It was a little like trading cards and the thought always tickled me. Of course, I didn't understand the ancient language as unfortunately it wasn't as if there were books to teach you. No, it was a case of, if you were in the demonic club, then you were just reborn with the knowledge. Which I think sucked to be honest. Especially for knowledge thirsty bookworm mortals like me.

"It is," Lucius replied with a grin playing at his lips as he looked down at me.

"So, what does it mean?" I asked making him now raise a brow.

"Oh come on, I am the daughter of a Demonic Angelic King. Are you really surprised that I would know this shit?" Lucius' lips twitched and he said,

"No, I am not. I am however surprised that you would have to ask."

"Oh… right… well, I uh…may know what it is, but I can't decipher it," I admitted taking the hit to my intelligent ego, which was basically the only ego I had.

"This surprises me, you were never taught?"

"Erm, that would be a no. Basically if it wasn't in a book that I could get my hands on, then I didn't learn it," I confessed making him give me a gentle look.

"They protected you too much," he stated, one that could have been a question also. I scoffed a laugh and said,

"Erm, yeah, that's the understatement of the year." Lucius made a 'umm' sound as if deep in thought before he announced,

"Then I will teach you." At this my eyes grew wide and I couldn't help my reaction as I blurted out loudly,

"You will?!" He laughed softly and nodded,

"If you wish."

"Aaahh! Oh my Gods, yes! That would be, Oh my Gods so awesome!" I said before throwing my arms around his neck so I could kiss him. He wasn't expecting this clearly as he actually went back a step when I launched myself at him. But his arm automatically banded my waist so as to pick me up to his height. Then he started chuckling and told me,

"Gods, but finding you gifts for occasions will be

fucking easy." I laughed at this and pulled back a little from his face, and said,

"What, you mean like a Christmas present?" I then winked at him making him groan before muttering a noncommittal,

"We shall see." And I swear my love for this man just soared to even greater heights. Oh, and I think he could tell when he saw my face light up at just the hope of that statement. He then kissed my forehead before placing me back on my feet so he could walk over to his door.

"Many Sigils have names around the outside with a single symbol at its core. These are known even in the mortal world. In mortal demonology, sigils are pictorial signatures attributed to demons, angels, or other beings. They were used for ceremonial magic, mainly in the Middle Ages, where they were used in the summoning of these beings and were the symbolic equivalent to their true name," Lucius said giving me a little lesson and insight, which I confess, I found fascinating. In fact, I didn't know whether I wanted to pull up a chair and pop some corn or jump on him and thank him in other, more delicious ways.

Of course, I knew which I would prefer and would win given the choice.

"However, in our own world these Sigils show something more than just our names… come and I will show you," he said nodding to me seeing as, strangely, I must have looked rooted to the spot and on the other side of the room. So, I walked over to him and he quickly positioned me in front of him so that his arms came around me. Then he took my hand in his and told me gently,

"Extend your finger." I did as I was told and his own

hand covered mine just as he had done last night, assaulting me with the memory enough to shudder in his hold.

"Behave Pet, for I know where your thoughts venture to," he told me in an amused and knowing tone. Then he ran my finger along the grooves of the symbols, starting with those at the top of the ring.

"This one symbolizes my origins," he hummed close to my ear and I swear but could his voice be any more seductive? But then with his free hand, he started to walk his fingers along my side, gathering back the sides of my cardigan so he could get to my waist, making it increasingly more difficult to concentrate. Even as he shifted my hand to the next symbol down, my mind was screaming sex.

"This here speaks of the many legions at my command," he said again, using that voice of his as if luring me into something only he knew what. Of course, his hand continued exploring until it crept under my t-shirt finally making contact with my skin and enticing another shudder from me. His knowing smirk could then be felt at my neck before he started kissing up its length.

"Concentrate, Pet," he hummed against my skin and I released a sigh before saying,

"I am trying but that's hard...oh..." I ended this sentence quickly, as thanks to when I said the word hard, he suddenly pulled me back against him even harder, so I could feel what else was 'hard' now digging into my back.

"Hard indeed," he said before moving my hand on to the next.

"This is a mark of power," he said and I found myself asking,

"And if it increases, what then?" Again, I felt his smile against my flesh before he whispered,

"Ah, my clever little scholar, that is a good question."

"Well?" I pushed.

"The Sigil will change and re forge itself in accordance with its bearer," he answered more seriously this time, making me twist back and look at him over my shoulder to say,

"Well, that's convenient." He grinned down at me and said on a tease,

"Yes, indeed and saves me a fucking fortune on doors." I burst out laughing and this in turn caused him to grant me another gentle look.

"So, what about the next?" I asked turning back to the door.

"This one speaks of what type of demon I am." I ran my finger along its grooves and confirmed,

"So, this means Vampire?"

"It does," he answered in a firm tone that went alongside the possessive squeeze at my side. But then his hand started to move on and continue exploring.

"And the next?" I asked now somewhat breathy as his fingers reached just under my bra line.

"Who I am loyal to." I narrowed my eyes at the scorched edges and just before I had chance to ask, he said

"It has changed throughout the years." Then he moved my hand to the last on the outer circle and said,

"This stands for Kingdom."

"Your own?" I asked and this time I felt him humming just below my ear before kissing me there.

"And this one?" I finally managed on a breathy whisper

as it was the last one in its centre and suddenly I was flipped around to face him, and he pushed me up against the door.

"It means I am a King!" he growled and then lifted me under my breasts so I was at the right height for his lips. He then pinned me to the door and kissed me fervently. In response, my arms rested on his shoulders so my forearms trapped the back of his head and locked his lips to mine. He growled low again and nipped at my bottom lip before kissing me once more in a rough and demanding way.

"I see I am going to enjoy teaching you the ways of my people," he said over my lips and this time I was the one grinning as I asked,

"I agree, only at this point I am a little unsure as to what I will be learning exactly, as the subject lines just got a bit blurry, professor." At this he laughed long and hard, a sight that I had to admit, I fucking adored!

He lowered me back down and then retook my hand and said,

"Then I'd better get you there quickly, before your next lesson ends up being taught against my Sigil."

"Mmm, that doesn't sound so bad...hey, maybe we could make a few of the symbols change, you know...as you 'powered' into me," I said wagging my eyes at him and making him chuckle, only this time it was with a shake of his head, as if he didn't know what to do with me. But then, he decided exactly what he was going to do to me as he growled,

"Fuck it!" Then, I was over his shoulder with a shriek and he was kicking open his door and striding down the tunnel now with greater purpose.

"Erm, I can walk and fast when given the right

motivation, which I think this would easily constitute as being one of those times," I remarked.

"Good to know, but still not fast enough," he said before snagging an unlit torch from the sconce, and with snap of his fingers by my legs, it ignited. Then I muttered from dangling behind his back,

"You know, I think living here I am going to have to invest in a bulk pack of matches." This granted me a little shake from his silent laughter, before he said,

"Or you simply agree to become my shadow, little pet." I growled at this making him chuckle out loud this time.

"Well, like this and I don't really have a choice," I grumbled and the second I felt his hand running up the back of my thigh he said,

"I could make the journey more pleasing for you, just give the word, sweetheart." Then he skimmed his fingers down the centre of my ass making me squirm against his shoulder.

After this he continued on, not really giving me much of a view to speak of. He did, however, give me lots to think about as he continued to tease the backs of my legs, ass and even skimming my sex when I wiggled enough on his shoulder to allow him access. This was naturally done on purpose but not so as it was obvious.

I swear that I was so turned on, that by the time we got there I was worried the only appreciation for my surroundings I would show would be for his bed! I swear, the man was turning me into some sex crazed lunatic who was in constant need for it. Of course, this was prompted not only by Lucius' sexual teases, or his constant touches, but also by the mere sight of him!

To say that he was the sexiest man I had ever encountered felt like too weak a statement. He was beautifully raw with a presence that was born to dominate those around him, including me and most definitely in the bedroom.

Oh yes, I was becoming well aware of how much Lucius craved control.

These sexual thoughts were jarred from me when he pulled me forward and I soon found myself opposite yet another set of doors.

Only this time, these looked more like a fitting entrance into,

Well, into...

Hell!

CHAPTER SEVENTEEN

DAVE IS THE KEY

The crimson doors that faced me right now didn't exactly scream welcome, come on in and put your feet up. No, all it screamed was run for your life, DANGER, DANGER, DANGER. Needless to say, I wasn't getting fuzzy warm snuggly vibes coming from whatever was behind that door.

The set of double doors in question stood at least ten feet high of solid wood and each was coated in a deep blood red colour painted in a high gloss that made them look as though they were bleeding. Both sides were also adorned with lots of thick heavy ironwork, like the hinges that were curled three times over before a point in the middle pointed towards heavy iron rings. It reminded me a bit like a wilting flower on its side, one minus the head with a spike taking its place. And as if the doors weren't intimidating enough, they were also framed by two solid pillars, reminding me of guardians standing to attention in the sizeable stone corridor. I looked back over my shoulder to see Lucius watching me with interest and after ignoring the multiple entrances at his back that led into this space, I spoke.

"Erm, who did you say lives here again, Dracula?" I teased making him snarl playfully at me before he grabbed me to him as quick as a heartbeat and flashed his fangs down at me. Then he snapped them twice as if he was going to bite me, making me flinch back to avoid them further.

"You were saying, Pet?" he asked when I swallowed heavily.

"Erm…That those doors are awesome and very fitting for a badass Vampire King who doesn't resemble a corny Dracula in any way shape or form?" I answered making him grin before his fangs sank back to their normal size and he kissed my forehead, telling me,

"And there's my good girl."

After this playful reprimand he released the one hand he had fisted in my cardigan so he was free to place the flaming torch into a holder on the wall. The pointed metal spike that Lucius had been holding then scratched its way down into the natural grooves marked in the stone. This from the Gods only knew how many years of use.

Then, once he had both his hands free, he used them to push both doors open, bending his torso slightly as he put his weight into it. This offered me a delicious sight of his T shirt tightening as his back muscles tensed.

"Ah!" I shouted suddenly when the sound of them booming echoed in the space beyond as they hit back against the walls inside. Another click of his fingers was all it took for the space ahead to erupt into light making me turn to him and say,

"You know, it's like dating a magician." His lips twitched and his eyes spoke of his amusement.

"Mm, well that would make you my lovely assistant…in that case I should invest in a skimpy gold outfit for you and a box and handsaw for me," he commented with a wink before walking past making me giggle. But then I started to take in the room we had just stepped into and my mouth dropped open.

Holy shit, now we were in a castle!

This was because what faced me now was a room totally worthy of the title. Three large open arches stood opposite me and had been cut from the mountain stone, being as smooth as the walls that surrounded us. I watched as Lucius stepped down into the square room that acted as a lobby of some type, making me wonder if his private space would finally be beyond the arches? Something I would only discover once I had descended the steps after Lucius as from up here, I couldn't see beyond them, making me question, was his space below? Well, there was only one way to find out as I followed him down the steps towards the grand arched entrance.

The white marble floor looked like liquid for how shiny it was and as my eyes followed the diamond pattern along, I found the expensive looking stone now carved into something much more than just the floor.

"Wow!" I uttered to myself as I took in the two massive statues of pure white that stood like sentinels either side of the three arches in between them. Okay, so the red Hell door had nothing on these guys in the intimidation department!

They each carried a sword that was held upright almost touching the high ceilings they were aimed at. They reminded me of Egyptian warriors, with the lower part of their bodies covered in carved skirts hanging low on their hips and touching the floor hiding their feet. Each was also adorned with a long belt hanging down the centre.

But then stone flames were carved into the design, as if these warriors had to endure the tortures of Hell by being burnt alive whilst still remaining steady enough to serve their king. It was most certainly symbolic.

Just like on their bare chiseled, muscular chests that, at further glance, had pieces of their smooth flesh cut away to reveal the hidden reality of their true nature. These mortal bodies were nothing but a façade, with hints telling you a story in the way of spiked flesh. Small palm sized window frames of flesh displayed an armored demon beneath the marble skin.

However, moving on from their impressive torsos, ones that mirrored both sides of their beings, I found the top half was all demon. Two massive horns grew outwards from their shoulders and curled around, coming to a point at the tops of their gold masked heads, ones that gleamed bright in the firelight.

Their demonic features hidden to the world with nothing but painted thin black lips and holes where the eyes should have shown through. Like I said, the whole scene was nearly as grand as the first entrance way, but far more intimidating. However, this was also me we were talking about and nothing kept me from exploring. So, I stepped right up to one and ran my hand down the lower half, making Lucius growl low. My hand dropped away and I glanced at him over my shoulder to find him looking annoyed.

"What?"

"I would rather you didn't," he snapped.

"Why, are they expensive or something?" I asked totally missing his point.

"No, it is, however, a male form and you feeling it up isn't an image I want branded to memory." At this my mouth literally dropped before words took over the dumb looking action.

"Lucius, it's a bloody statue!" I argued but my only reply was in the form of one pissed off male now folding his arms and giving me a pointed look. I shook my head, reserving the roll of my eyes for when I faced it again before muttering,

"Sorry dude but looks like my old man's being a drag."

"I heard that!" Lucius declared and was something I also chose to ignore. Meaning I moved on and was just about to walk through the centre arch when Lucius' arm banded around my waist stopping me.

"Not so fast there, sweetheart, it's not safe yet." I frowned at this now wondering exactly what was beyond this archway and how he intended to 'make it safe'. I didn't have long to wait. Lucius walked us both back in front of the statue and I couldn't help but comment dryly,

"Oh look, it's my other boyfriend. Hi, Dave." Lucius tugged me closer, growled low and nipped at my neck before holding the tender flesh captive between his teeth.

"Aa aah." I moaned as he did this until it was just on the cusp of being too painful. But before that happened, he let go and soothed the bitten skin with a kiss.

"Behave, little pet," he warned with one last squeeze before letting me go.

Lucius then walked up to the statue I had just dubbed as Dave and grabbed its sword, before twisting it around so it's tip now pointed down to the ground. After this he reached up and pulled down on the golden mask making it open thanks to a hinge at the chin. Naturally after this, I moved closer and side stepped to get a better look as I was curious to see what was beneath it and the second I did, I sucked in a breath.

"Okay, so Dave isn't looking so hot right now," I commented making Lucius chuckle as I now referred to the demonic face hidden beneath the face of wealth. Its face now looked to be made more out of baked cracked sand, with high cheekbones and elongated features. Its mouth was open in a creepy, overly wide way and was framed by rows and rows of deadly looking teeth. Ones that didn't seem to be anything but real this time.

But it was hard to pinpoint just one animal involved as there looked to be everything from tiger's fangs to shark's teeth. Even more startling was seeing Lucius now actually putting his hand in there and I couldn't help but hiss,

"What are you doing!?" But then he made a motion like he had released something inside the mouth before he was pulling his hand back and walking over to me. And what he had released was a hidden doorway off to one side that had appeared from behind the smooth rock wall.

"What did it look like?" Lucius replied stepping up to me.

"Like you could have hurt yourself!" I exclaimed making him smirk down at me before patting me on the cheek and saying in a condescending tone,

"Aww, were you worried about me, Princess?" To which I huffed, folded my arms and said,

"You know what, I missed it the first time, could you just do it again please, only this time, give your hand a good wiggle and have a nice long feel around in there!" Again, Lucius walked away chuckling.

I followed him, because, well I didn't have much choice in a place like this and when I did, I did so walking through the secret door muttering,

"What is your aversion to keys anyway, because I will tell you right now, there is no way in Hell damnation I am sticking my hand in Dave's mouth...*oh... my... good... Gods!*" I ended this on an astonished whisper the second I noticed the sight now in front of me, as it looked as though we had just found the belly of the mountain!

It was an utterly enormous sized cavern that could easily have been the size of a cathedral. Its ceilings went up forever and its floor was a made up of a series of deadly drops. Falls that if by some miracle you managed to survive then the colossal spikes from a playground of lethal stalagmites would most definitely turn you into a human Shish Kebab! And well, there was just no dancing away from that.

The door he had created, or should I say Dave had created, led to a small platform roughly the size of a car, which then led onto steps down to a larger platform. This one was directly in front of the three open arches on the opposite side. But then it was no wonder I wouldn't have gotten far, seeing as two steps in and I would have seen the sheer drop down. Especially seeing as the platform I was now stood on was a good four metres away. Meaning that the arches hadn't been doors at all, they had been large glassless windows.

"Okay, so now this is so cool!" I said seeing a bridge across the deepest part of the cavern, about a metre wide. Lucius gave me a curious look as if something about this moment struck him as strange.

"What? It is cool and in fact reminds me of one of my favorite movies growing up, Indiana Jones and the Last Crusade, which got me into wanting to be an archaeologist," I told him, as I crossed the bridge with no problems. However, I couldn't miss the way Lucius kept close behind me as if he feared I would trip and fall. Which, seeing as this was me, he was right to be cautious.

"You're not scared of heights." He stated as it clearly wasn't a question but more like a surprised observation. I chuckled and said,

"Uh, I think it would be a bit silly to be, considering my dad has wings and all, plus I always sat up in the cockpit when my dad flew his private jet." I made it to the other side without incident and was standing on the large platform when I threw my hands up and said,

"Tadaa, see I made it…Whoa!" This ended up with me tripping on some uneven floor and nearly falling to my side when Lucius caught me on a growl.

"Okay, so almost," I muttered embarrassingly. Lucius scowled down at me and then hissed,

"I am starting to rethink things." I didn't know what to make of that and would have asked, only to be honest, I chickened out. All I could hope for was that it didn't include bringing me down here or even worse, being with me down here. Or even worse, worse…*being with me altogether.*

An irrational thought that disappeared back into stupid land the moment he decided that instead of letting me walk, he thought it safer to simply scoop me up in his arms. Meaning I had no choice but to let Lucius carry me the rest of the way. It then clicked that this had been what he had meant when saying he needed to rethink things.

Damn that stupid land!

To one side of the raised platform we were now on after crossing the bridge there was yet another passageway, but at least this one looked as if it may lead further into the cavern, as it cut through the rock. Like I said, I knew the place was huge from when we had been stood near the arches. But with the way the rocks were formed, it had been hard to see much beyond it other than the sheer size of the place from the vast stretch of its rock faced ceilings. Meaning it was mainly below that had been hidden.

I had to say that by the end I was glad Lucius had picked me up as it was so dark inside the tunnel that I fear tripping this time would have been inevitable.

Thankfully though, it led out to the other side pretty quickly and after blinking a few times, I was awarded with an amazing sight.

An incredible sight and one startlingly beautiful just like its owner.

It was…

Lucius' home.

CHAPTER EIGHTEEN

VAMP CAVE

"*Gods, Lucius.*"

I muttered this in total awe, as I scanned the large open living space and the first thing I noticed, one that surprised me, was how warm and inviting it looked. The walls were bare and untamed natural rock, but it seemed softer with the warm glow reflected against it. This was from the many lit lanterns that were fitted to the walls and I was amazed to see that, unlike on our journey getting here, they were actually electric.

"This place has power?" I asked too astonished to comprehend what a feat that must have been.

"It took a bit of engineering, but it was accomplished only a few years ago," he told me and I couldn't help but look up at the incredible chandeliers that hung down on lengths and lengths of cable. They were a work of art in their own right, with layers and layers of twisted black ink coloured branches in what could have been dipped metal. Attached then to this giant knot of branches was an abundance of blown glass shards in the same glossy black. It was overflowing with them and each hung down like deadly, stretched tear drops. The light part was a huge cluster of bulbs inside the black rooted sphere that cast shadows against all the rocks in a gothic display of beauty and elegance.

Even the jagged rock of the mountain that surrounded us didn't take away from the fact that it was clearly a home. Just the staircase alone was more than just rough carved stone. It was one that led down to the first level and had been decorated with charming intricate patterns carved into each step. Swirls of interlaced symbols even kind of told a story as each step was different, giving it an almost whimsical feel and, combined with a black iron banister, it felt like being in a fairy tale.

It was only when he descended the steps into what was obviously the main living space that Lucius put me down, lowering me to my feet. This was also inviting and instead of the usual shades in Lucius' contemporary living space back at Transfusion, this was totally different. The room, if it could be called that seeing as it was without walls and was basically a large island, was as big as an apartment itself!

Other areas could be seen as everything was all open plan, except a few doorways that were this time cut into the rock face, situated against a cavern slightly above where we stood. There was even a kitchenette on one of the connecting, smaller platforms, as well as a grand dining set on the one closest to it. Then I took a wild, stalagmite stab in the dark and guessed the other enclosed caves were no doubt a bathroom or a bedroom.

Each of these different living spaces were connected by a series of connected walkways or decorated steps that had been carved right out of the rock, creating a unique living space. It certainly gave a whole new meaning to the 'baddie's lair' persona. Which was when I couldn't help but say,

"Wow, I take it back."

"What?" he asked clearly intrigued to know my thoughts. So I turned back to face him and said,

"Dracula has nothing on you, babe." At this he rolled his eyes but again, he was getting really bad at hiding the smile that wanted to come out and play.

"Come on, my little comedian, let's get you fed before I decide to make a meal out of you just to shut up that pretty little mouth of yours," he said dragging a thumb down the center of my lips and walking away, catching my hand as he went so as to drag me with him.

Although, one look at the extra deep, rich navy blue sofa and all I wanted to do now was sink into it. The cream cushions and soft knit throws also gave it a homely touch, along with the scattered array of rugs in greys, creams and blues that all crossed over at some point on the stone floor.

Gods, but was that...

"Is that a TV?!" I shouted in excitement, as there was a cabinet at the far end of the space that the sofa faced. It was one that looked as if it could be hidden inside the dark wooden frame it was situated above, at just the click of a button.

"Later, food first," he said walking up the curve of steps onto what I discovered was the dining area I had seen from below. The table was again in keeping with the décor of the place, being made from thick heavy wood. It was one that was smooth all the way around three sides, with one edge that still had the rough bark along it. It was a long straight rectangle in shape but that natural side remained in the curve from the tree it had been cut from. It was highly polished and had a beautiful grain.

I then glanced at all the food spread out on the table and then back at the kitchen level that was only three steps up and looked as though it could be fully equipped and much more than the kitchenette I had first thought it to be.

"Has it always looked like this?" I asked curious to know.

"The TV is new," he replied with a knowing look, making me blush because he was saying without words, it had been installed for me. Then he came to the back of me and pulled out a chair, combining the gentlemanly gesture with an order, as was very Lucius,

"Sit."

I did as I was told, mainly because there were donuts involved and delicious looking pastries. Lucius took his seat next to me, which of course was at the head of the table, one big enough to sit twelve people at least.

"It has changed over the years and added to when electricity was available."

"Hence the kitchen I gather," I commented making him nod and I removed my napkin from my plate and started to reach for an array of stuff, *all of it sweet.*

"I am starting to think that you are addicted to sugar," Lucius said nodding down at my selection.

"So?"

"You are sweet enough, Pet." I smiled at this and then took a big bite, then to make a point, I spoke with my mouthful. Only admittedly, doing it in a way that wouldn't end up showing him my food or spitting it out. More done so for comedy value.

"I could always be sweeter." Then I winked at him making him grin one of those bad boy 'I am going to eat you like a hungry wolf' type way.

"That sounds like an offer," he returned and I laughed before saying,

"Or a challenge." He hummed once and said,

"Indeed."

After this we ate breakfast, or more like I devoured it, before Lucius continued to give me the tour, which consisted of very few places left. One of which was a hot springs pool hidden behind a massive boulder in a bathroom carved right from the stone. It was also one made private thanks to the connecting wall. The same wall that contained the countertop and sink, both of which were a smooth wave of curves, the same as the toilet. There was even a small waterfall over what was essentially a giant bathtub, that acted as a shower and seemed to be continuously running, feeding the pool below. In fact, the sight made me want to strip off and dive on in there, as it looked so inviting.

But then came the last room in the cave and that was Lucius' bedroom. He led me up there as it was at the highest point and I didn't know why but I suddenly became nervous as to what I might find. For some reason a BDSM club sprang to mind!

I walked inside and I had to say, I hadn't been too far off the mark with his bed alone. The room, like the rest of his home, seemed to be on different levels, with the bed being at the highest point and situated in the centre like a statement, *which it was*. For it was unlike any other bed I had ever seen before, and consisted of four massive beams, that were square cut carved wood. On top of the wooden beams were large heavy iron brackets that held four thick chains fixed there, chains that were easily the width of my arm.

These chains were then fixed to the four angles of the bed's frame by even thicker brackets, each bolted to the corners so as the bed didn't touch the ground. On top of this was a thick mattress covered in a rich deep red material that matched all the dark wood in the room and light soft neutral colour of the natural stone walls. All other furniture in here matched the chunky wood of the bed, and even framed a doorway into another room off this one. The only things decorating the walls were old fashioned wrought iron lanterns with big glass tops that held modern day lighting.

"That's...erm...quite a bed you have there," I said making Lucius chuckle.

"I had something similar once before, but had it redesigned, replacing it with wood," he said letting me know without being obvious about it that he had a new bed. Even so I found myself asking,

"How new?" He tugged me to him, after hooking a finger in the belt loop of my jeans and said in a husky voice,

"Very new."

"And the chains?" I asked, my voice thick and also now husky.

"They make great support," he said rubbing his chin down my neck and shoulder.

"For the bed," I surmised.

"Yes, *amongst other things."* This time his reply was whispered by my ear and his knowing grin followed my sexually induced shiver. I decided it was best to focus on something other than being chained to his bed and nodded towards the doorway.

"And in there?"

"Nothing but a closet and another bathroom," he said in a nonchalant tone and as I walked away towards it, he grabbed my arm and pulled me back to him.

"I don't think I am finished showing you my bed yet." Then he leaned down to kiss me, doing so in a way that I knew would soon land me in this bed. But then he started to move from my lips, and I couldn't help but ask,

"Does it rock?"

"Only when it needs to," was his reply whispered against my jawline, his flaxen stubble brushing roughly against my skin. The bed was at his waist height which meant that instead of me trying to figure out a way to get into it, he was one step ahead of me. As he just framed my waist and lifted me onto the thick mattress, so I was now sitting on it, with my legs dangling over the edge.

I was surprised that the bed barely moved, well that was until Lucius placed his hands either side of my hips and leant all his body weight towards me, making the bed shift from the strength of him. This was when I giggled nervously, which was ridiculous considering how many times we'd had sex now.

But then I felt my bladder scream at me and thought it best to use the facilities before we started getting into it. So, just as he was moving back up my jaw to claim my lips again, I quickly said,

"I need to use the little scholars room." He groaned in annoyance making me chuckle and said,

"Very well, but may I suggest using the one down on the main level." I jumped off the bed with a swing of my legs once he gave me room and told him,

"Nah, it's okay I will just..." I was saying this but stopped when Lucius grabbed my hand, stopping me from going further and said more seriously this time,

"Use the other one, Amelia." I frowned up at him, knowing that he was hiding something from me, which I didn't like...as in, *at all.* Which was why I nodded and pretended to walk back through the door we had just entered, only at the last second, I bolted for the closet door, running through it before he could stop me.

"Amelia!"

The room was bigger than what a normal person would have considered 'just a closet' as it was bigger than my whole flat back home. And well, speaking of flat, I took one look at the now empty side of the closet space and then again to the floor. A floor that was half consumed by boxes labeled with only one name...

Amelia.

I then looked back to Lucius with accusing eyes as there was only one question left to ask him,

"Why is all my personal stuff here?" He released a heavy sigh as if he knew what was coming next and replied sternly,

"Because I ordered it to be here." An answer that was swiftly followed by an astonished,

"But why"

His reply this time was most definitely one for concern…

"Because I moved you in."

CHAPTER NINETEEN

MOVING IN

"You did what?!" I shouted this time, making him fold his arms and grant me a look.

"Oh no, you don't get to act like the injured party here and be all, I am macho man, you little woman will do as I command, shit!" I snapped, whilst mimicking his bad ass stance and making his lips twitch.

"Amelia."

"You don't get to do that either!" I added when he said my name in that soft, reprimanding tone. He released a sigh and took me in his arms, now going for a totally different tactic. I decided not to make this easy for him and started squirming in his hold.

"Come now, be still for me," he cooed making me scowl back up at him as with my arms trapped by my sides, pulling his ears just wasn't an option!

"How about you hear me out and then decide...yes?" I rolled my eyes and said,

"Fine!" He didn't comment on my behaviour, but his look said it all... annoyingly, he was finding it adorable. So, I let him pull me back into the bedroom and even pick me up to put me back on the bed, so I was once again opposite him. However, this time swapping the end of the bed for the side of it. And I knew when he didn't join me that he was going to use his size to intimidate me in some way. I just needed to wait for it, knowing it wasn't long in coming.

"It was no longer safe, and as your flat had been compromised once before I thought it best to get your personal stuff packed before it could once again get damaged," he said making me resist the urge to roll my eyes and instead made my feelings known in another way,

"And naturally you had it sent here," I said dryly, now crossing my arms over my chest after first pushing up my glasses.

"I think you can guess that Transfusion was no longer an option," he stated and I snorted in an unladylike fashion and muttered,

"Conveniently."

"Hardly," he responded and yeah, so I knew he was right but still, I felt like he was just using this as an excuse to get what he wanted.

"You could have arranged for it to be put in storage...*in England!*" I said, adding this last part in a tone that was trying to make my point.

"And why the fuck would I do that?!" he snapped, dismissing said point.

"Okay, so I guess it's time to let the worms out then, yeah?" I said making him now cross his own arms across his chest and Gods, when he did it, I had to force myself not to look at his gorgeous body. Bloody Hell, but those arms… was it hot in here or just me?

"Open that can all you want, Amelia, but I am telling you now, if you think this conversation will end with me agreeing to send your shit back to a fucking storage unit in England then I would save your breath for something more productive."

"Ha, like what?!" I yelled, making him uncross his arms and get in real close like he usually did when he had a point to make.

"Like for when I ravish that talented mouth of yours."

Well, okay then.

Seriously, can a person's libido actually fan itself?

"I see my girl likes that idea," he said leaning in further and like he did before, placing his fists either side of me, caging me to the bed.

"Wait, we aren't…"

"Oh yes we fucking are," he growled before kissing me and when he did, he did it hot and heavy.

I was then being dragged up the bed with his arm curled around my back, and once he had me there, he lowered down over me, holding himself just slightly above so as not to crush me. Then I felt his hand trail down my thigh before lifting it so my leg was being hooked over his very, very, fine ass. After this he started kissing his way down my neck, yanking my T shirt to one side to give him better access to my bare skin.

"Lucius, we need…"

"I know what you need, sweetheart," Lucius replied and when pressing his hips into me I could feel the hard length that was obvious as to what he needed also.

Needless to say, two things happened after this.

The first being Lucius gave us what we both needed and the second was a discovery. As he was right,

The bed only moved when it needed to.

About an hour or so later after Lucius had exhausted me to the point I could barely lift my head up from his chest, one I was now making circles around with my fingertips, currently focusing on around his nipple.

"And if I tell you we still need to talk about me moving in, will that translate to you as round two?" I asked only half joking.

"Technically, I think you find it will be round three, as I took you twice," was Lucius' cocky reply, making me smile. We were both naked, and in his bed, which wasn't exactly a surprise. We were also entwined together with me held to him with his right arm curled around my back resting at my shoulder. This ended up with my body plastered to his side and my leg bent, resting against his thigh. His left hand was at my hip, making the leather groan slightly every time he squeezed.

"Lucius." This time I said his name in that telling way and he released a sigh and said,

"Alright, here it is Amelia. I want you to move in with me, it is where you belong…"

"But…" his hand left my shoulder and covered my mouth quickly before he said,

"Please, let me finish." I nodded letting him know that I would, making his hand go back to holding me to him.

"I also know that you have your concerns, and I understand that this may be going too fast for you, which is why I am willing to compromise here."

"That's good of you." I replied with dry humour making him this time pinch my nipple and as I shrieked, he said,

"Are you going to behave, Pet?"

"Okay, okay!" I shouted and once satisfied he let go and went back to explaining making me now rub the sore spot.

"Now, if you decide things need to change after a time, then we will discuss our options, as having your stuff here doesn't mean they can't move again if we decide they need to. But whilst the threat is still out there, then it makes sense for their relocation and really, what is the harm with you feeling more comfortable here?" he asked, sounding remarkably sensible about the whole thing.

"Okay, so put like that, then yeah, maybe it kind of makes sense," I admitted as really, he annoyingly made a compelling case. But then he smirked as if he had just won a victory making me quickly add,

"But it's not permanent! It's only for now…okay?" At this he nodded in that condescending way that made me smack his stomach and say,

"Stop it!"

"Stop what?" he enquired with fake innocence.

"Stop looking so damn cocky like you just won something or are thinking, 'yeah right, my girlfriend's words mean shit' that type of stop it!" I snapped making him laugh so I smacked his stomach again.

"Oww," he moaned, feigning pain and rubbing his hard abs. But soon was laughing again in the hilarity of his pretense.

"Baby," I muttered and rolled my eyes, pausing the second I realised my mistake and I knew it when his eyes narrowed at me in a stalker playful way.

"Did you just...?"

"NO! No, I didn't and besides, even if I did, if you want me to unpack, then you are definitely letting this one go," I said making him laugh and he pulled me to him for a kiss, before agreeing,

"I'll let this one go."

And my cheeky reply...

"Good call, Captain."

Shortly after this, we both showered and dressed, after first fooling around in the shower. A time which ended with me on my knees recreating a not so distant memory. Needless to say, Lucius ended up having to once again fix the tiles in that bathroom too.

We were now walking down into the living space after I had asked if there was anything planned for the evening that I needed to know about. Lucius had told me sweetly that he wanted to give me time to settle.

Which meant that I was just in the middle of convincing him that the whole settling in process would go a lot smoother with a movie night and eating junk food in front of the TV. To which he would have replied with something equally as compelling, had his phone not decided to ring in that exact moment. Or should I say, had a certain person not decided to ring him in that exact moment.

"Speak," Lucius demanded in his 'I am King, bow down

to me now' kind of way. Now, I should point out that I was fortunate enough to be curled to his side with his arm around me and resting at the curve of my waist. This then meant that I could hear the whole conversation.

"We have a situation, boss." I was sure this was Clay on the other end who said this.

"Elaborate," Lucius said and I cleared my throat and made a motion with my head that I would leave him to it. However, he shook his head and held me tighter to make his point.

He wanted me to stay.

"Sometime today, Clay, for I think I made it clear I was not to be disturbed, which leaves me one of two options, either I am pissed at you or pissed at the other person who caused this…so which is it?"

"It ain't at me," Clay answered quickly.

"Clay." Lucius said his name in warning.

"Let's just say you're not the only pissed off party here and unfortunately I am the fucking go between." His head of security replied making me frown at the way it was worded. It was as if there was something he was holding back because he knew I was there. I knew I had guessed right when Lucius looked down at me and said,

"Right… well, it looks like he found his limit on waiting. I will be there shortly."

"Sire." This was Clay's way of saying goodbye before hanging up the phone. Lucius stood before slipping his phone into his jeans' back pocket, and it had become obvious quite quickly that, unlike my first thoughts of Lucius, he was more a fan of casual attire than the suits I first believed him to prefer. But then again, before stepping foot inside

Transfusion the second time, I had mainly only ever seen him wearing a suit.

"I guess being King never stops," I said in a lighthearted way making him give me a warm look.

"Having you here in my home, then it makes me wish that it did," he said before pulling me up and raising my face by the chin to kiss me and this time it was as sweet and tender as the look he gave me.

"It's alright, I will just see you tonight and hey, if you play your cards right, I may even let you pick the movie," I said waggling my eyebrows at him, making him grin.

"I thought I'd already played my cards right...*twice.*" This comment naturally ended up with us kissing again and when I heard Lucius' phone beep, he growled low and said,

"Next place I buy will be on a fucking island with no fucking reception!"

"Well, who knows, I may just have the gold bikini and chain by then," I said winking and making him groan before grabbing me to him so he could mutter against my forehead,

"That doesn't motivate me to leave, Pet." I chuckled and said,

"You can always stick around and watch me shave my legs if you want?" I asked making him laugh.

"Oh, but I think you have a lot more to do than that," he replied making me still in his hold. Because now my internal panic consisted of images that included me sat up in bed with my legs spread and knocking down a safety visor, saying, 'Ladies, I am going in' before going at my private parts with a weed wacker / hedge trimmer! I mean jeez, just how much hair can a girl grow down there in the space of a few days... So, knowing my luck, consuming his blood acts like some sort of miracle grow, making me wish I had read the small print!

Of course, I didn't express these thoughts in quite that way. Instead going with the tamer version of that question.

"Erm…you mean like my pits?" Again, this made him throw his head back and laugh harder this time, before telling me why,

"I was referring to unpacking, sweetheart." Okay so big phew on that one!

"Oh that, oh well that won't take me long, I mean it's only a bag of clothes and…wait, why are you scowling now?" I asked because, well, he was.

"Because I told you to unpack, Amelia, not just hang up a few fucking clothes."

"That is unpacking, Lucius," I said with a shake of my confused head.

"No, it's not, that is staying for a few days, a week at best. That is *not unpacking,*" he said emphasising his words with an impatient growl.

"You can't be serious?"

"Do I look like I am fucking joking?" he asked crossing his arms yet again, making me refrain from muttering, 'oh, here we go again'.

"So, you're saying you want me to actually unpack all my stuff, as in …here?" I said looking around the super stylish place and trying to imagine how I was possibly going to mix the two. Lucius however took this statement completely the wrong way and looked as though I'd just slapped him. He even jerked back before growling,

"And what the fuck does that mean?!" Yep, totally the wrong way, so I told him,

"Lucius, you live in a cave."

"And?" he snapped getting more pissed off by the second, so I thought it wise to make my point and make it quickly before he got even more of the wrong idea than he already was doing.

"And it is a very cool cave. An awesome, stylish cave," I said making him now frown at me, not in a scowly way, but more in a questioning way. I was calling this progress.

"I am not following."

"Lucius, come on, you have seen where I lived, you have seen my stuff…and well, as much as *I may* think my stuff is cool, in a place like this…*so not cool.*" Lucius looked as though he was giving this some thought and then said,

"So, what you're saying is that you won't unpack because my cave is too cool for you, am I correct?"

"It's not exactly Twickenham, Lucius," I said thinking this would make my point. Which it didn't, as in so not. No, instead it simply became a challenge he set me. I knew this when he said,

"Then make it so."

"What do you mean?" I asked confused and thankfully resisted the urge to call him Picard.

"You want it like home, then make it like home," he stated.

"Lucius, you don't mean…" This is when he stopped me, and he did this by walking me backwards until the back of my legs hit the couch and I had nowhere to go but backwards. I fell back on my ass into the seat with little choice but to stay there. Especially when he placed a hand either side of my head on the back rest before lowering his face to mine.

Then he said in a serious tone,

"Make it home."

"Eh…?" He narrowed his eyes and said, more forcefully this time,

"Make. It. Home." This time I visibly gulped at this and nodded quickly. This I could tell made him happy as he grinned and kissed me lightly on the forehead before telling me,

"Good girl." Then his presence was done dominating my personal space, giving me room to take a breath.

"Now, I would ask you to remain only in this personal space and not to leave it, for without me you may get lost, for you don't yet know…"

"Yeah, yeah, don't worry handsome, I have no urge to go getting my ass lost in the middle of Mount Doom." Oops, probably shouldn't have called it that, not seeing as he was obviously touchy about his home and well, trying to force me into making it *my home* too.

"Mount Doom?" He nearly snarled the words. I laughed nervously and said on a giggle,

"Did I say Mount Doom, what I really meant to say was Mount Pleasant, Mount 'come on in and take a load off… that type of Mount…but hey if Doom means something different in your world, then hey, that's your bad."

"Um mm," was Lucius' disbelieving reply with a raise of his brow.

"Just so you know, had I been awake when we arrived then I would have been able to see for myself the very inviting entrance complete with welcome mat by the front door." At this Lucius leaned into me one more time and said,

"Alright, you've made you point, love." Then he kissed me quick and said,

"Now, I really must leave, but do me a favour, Amelia…"

"Hum?"

"No getting into trouble this time." I winked at him and said,

"I make no promises, handsome, after all I am sure there are knives kept in the kitchen." At this he groaned and walked away shaking his head, muttering under his breath the same threat as before,

"Shackles… I need fucking shackles and a gag."

After this he left and like the good girl I was…

I unpacked.

But like the naughty girl I aspired to be, I did so to make a point, saying out loud,

"Oh yeah, this is going to be fun."

I didn't know how long it took me exactly as there wasn't a clock in sight and without windows, well then, it was pretty much a crapshoot in the dark. But it didn't matter as I certainly kept myself busy. This started by going back into the massive walk-in closet and finding one whole side of it had been cleared out ready for me to 'hang my shit' as Lucius had said when we had been talking it out in bed. This had been straight after sex…twice, when his first question had been,

"Does this mean you're going to hang your shit in my closet?" Now if this had been said by any other male in existence then I was pretty sure any woman would have been peeved to hear her stuff being referred to as shit. But this was Lucius and that meant, this was actually him telling me that he wanted 'my shit' there and for me to basically, go and 'fucking unpack it'.

But I had convinced myself that he would totally regret trying to convince me to do this and in fact the safer option would have been to simply unpack my clothes, a few girly things and that was about it. Because one look around this kickass cool cave of his, and well, I couldn't exactly see all my geekiness fitting in.

He disagreed.

He was also about to learn.

So that was precisely what I did. Doing so in the most over the top way possible, because really, I had a point to prove. Of course, I also could have done with spending my time a little wiser, like working further on the damn cursed box for example. But seeing as I had no clue where it was and had already embarrassingly felt all the walls for a hidden safe, then I had no choice but to swiftly move on to plan, 'Prove my point to a stubborn ass Vamp'.

This plan started with the kitchen as the first box I found was all of the gorgeous new stuff that had been bought to replace all my smashed stuff after the break in. It was a good job too as Lucius may have had a kitchen built, but filling it with stuff needed to cook with, wasn't exactly a priority for him. However, one thing this kitchen wasn't lacking was food and mountains of it...ha, see what I did there!

The cupboards were full of, well, strangely all the stuff that had once filled my own cupboards. Okay, so that had been weird number one. Weird number two had been the lack of a fridge. This had taken me a while to locate as it was actually hidden behind the wall of cabinets. I imagined this was so it wasn't as much of an eyesore seeing as this kitchen had been made on a platform without any rock face to call a wall. Which meant every bit of it was free standing.

The whole kitchen space was solid dark wooden cabinets with what I first thought was minus all your usual appliances. But like the fridge, that was because these too were hidden. It was only when I started to lift open cupboards and pulling on handles that I started to discover what lay beneath. Like one cupboard arched upwards and had been hiding a counter space behind it that held a state of the art coffee machine, blender and other gadgets.

Another of these handles when lifted actually disappeared into a slot above and showed the standing twin oven and grill. Another handle pulled turned out to be a microwave and yet another hidden cupboard was a dishwasher. I also tried the fancy tap and found it was one that had instant boiling water.

But back to the fridge and the stainless steel door I found behind the 'fake wall' of cupboards. I pulled it open and found it was a walk in design that had on one side a cooler section, with shelves stocked full of everything you could ever imagine for either putting on a sandwich or if you were the healthy type (which I clearly wasn't) making a salad. The opposite side was a wall of freezer drawers, again all packed with my favorite foods.

However, the best drawer I opened was by far the one that made me laugh the hardest, as it was the one filled with my heavenly Cereal. This took me back to when I first moved back into my apartment, after Lucius had arranged to refurnish it when it was trashed. The next day he had left me a housewarming gift outside my door that had been the same box of cereal tied in a red bow and with a card that said a simple,

You're welcome
Lucius

It was no wonder then that I sat eating my first bowl at the table, smiling the whole time I ate thinking back to how confused I was at the time as to why he would have done this for me. Now though, it seemed blindly obvious, but at the time I was still stuck somewhere between, 'I thought he hated me' and 'Gods, I hope he doesn't hate me'.

All I can say is I am glad I am past all that heartache bullshit!

Shortly after placing all my new dinner set and kitchenware in the cupboards that were free, I then moved onto other stuff. Or should I say...*The fun stuff*. Of course, this started with first needing a shelving unit and seeing as there was one in the closet, one I was pretty sure I was supposed to use for shoes, I started trying to carry it all the way into the living room.

This was how Caspian, of all people, found me.

"Just what do you think you are doing, human?!" he bellowed as I was struggling down the steps. I paused and stuck my head around the side to see him stood there, almighty puffed out chest looking impressive and intimidating. However, I just scoffed and said,

"I think that's obvious," but his stern face and folded arms said otherwise. An intimidating stance, that had to be said, looked like a feat in itself due to his mountain man sized arms. When he didn't respond but instead continued to silently expect an answer, I said,

"Well, I did come all this way just to steal a shelf, so be a doll and just pretend you didn't see me...yeah?" This he didn't find amusing and once again his silence told me so.

"Jeez, what does it look like I am doing?!"

"You look like you are trying to cause trouble." I rolled my eyes, knowing I could totally get away with it now and said,

"Yes, that's exactly what I am doing, so are you going to help me or what, before I break my damn neck!?" I snapped as I was currently trying to make the bloody thing walk down the steps like a flat robot out of battery. Needless to say, the, 'side, tilt, tip and repeat' technique wasn't working all that great. At this Caspian sighed and then walked up the steps, taking three at a time and then grasped the large unit like it was nothing but a flagpole he was about to stake in the ground to claim land.

"Where?" he all but snarled.

"Erm, over there I think," I said pointing to the only side that wouldn't hide anything behind it. I mean it wasn't exactly easy deciding on where, seeing as 'the room' didn't even have any walls to put it against. Caspian put it down and I made an 'umm' sound before showing him which way to turn it more. He rolled his eyes and twisted it an inch, then looked behind his mammoth shoulder to see if this was acceptable. I nodded my head to the side twice more and he took the hint.

"There! So, what do you think?" I asked wondering why on earth I bothered.

"I don't give a fuck." Yep and there it was.

"Oookay then. So, in that case, what can I help you with?" I asked now turning my back and rearranging all the pretty scatter cushions I had added from my place, along with my pride and joy, my pink Star Fleet cushion. One, I might add, with its bright pink piping my aunty Pip had given me, totally did not go with the rest of the décor or the kick ass navy blue U shaped couch. But seeing as that was the whole point here, I was pretty happy.

"Luc wanted a report on your activities." I laughed at this. But of course, he did, wanting to know if I was being a 'good girl' no doubt.

"And let me guess, you were the poor bastard that drew the short straw," I commented with a chuckle.

However, when silence was all I got, I turned around and saw him frowning. Then he totally surprised me by saying,

"No, I requested to." I didn't know why this gave me chills, maybe it was the serious way in which he had said it. Something that was ridiculous, as what else did I expect, him to sing it at me in Soprano! I mean the dude always sounded serious and pissed off and with an 'I am looking forward to the day that I can hunt you down at the first chance I get' attitude. But then, despite this, something about it sounded totally off, as if he was even struggling with the idea of what he was about to do next.

I swear if a regular person could have had Spiderman's spidey sense, then watching Caspian approach me now was definitely making it tingle. Fuck that, it wasn't tingling…it was like the Gods be damned Hunchback of Notre Dame was ringing his damn bells at me!

And I was soon to discover why.

Because he wasn't just walking towards me with purpose, he was now doing it whilst pulling something from behind his back. And my only two thoughts now were, there was no way I would win against him in a fight.

And two,

I was a dead woman.

A dead woman, now staring at...

His knife.

CHAPTER TWENTY

MY HANDS ARE TIED

I started to move and wasn't sure that I was even backing up at all, seeing as he was at me quicker than my eyes could take in. Making me now question if I was even moving at all?

"But why, I just…" I just uttered these words, expecting this mountain of a demon to crush me any second, because let's face it, I could be kickass, but with this guy, then I wouldn't stand a chance!

I was a dead woman.

"It is my duty," he confessed as though the words had been torn out of him and whatever he was about to do now, two things were clear, he was struggling with it and he fucking hated that he couldn't fight it!

This was when I finally realised I was in fact moving and unfortunately this registered when I saw myself getting closer to the edge as I was backing away from one danger only to find myself heading towards another.

So, I tried one last time.

"You don't have to do this," I told him in a pleading tone.

"But I must," he said before shocking me enough that it nearly knocked me down. But then out of us both, there was only one of us going to our knees and insanely, *it wasn't me.* Caspian started to lower himself down to one knee before holding out the blade as if making some kind of pledge.

"Err...what's happening?" I asked in that dumbfounded kind of way. Then he turned the blade back on himself and sliced it across his hand deep and long. After this he fisted the meaty paw now letting it drip onto the floor. Then he bowed his head to me, lifted his now blood soaked fist and held it to his forehead. This ended up leaving an imprint there thick enough that blood dripped down his nose over the many metal bars there from all his piercings. Eyes now burning with not just an intensity but glowing white as if he was speaking to me from behind his demon.

"With my blood I pledge my eternal loyalty to you, for my life is in your service should you need the sacrifice to ever save your own." Then he took his bloody fist down to his heart and pounded it twice. This left crimson stains all over his Iron Maiden T shirt, making the bands mascot, Eddie even more demonic looking. Especially as he was already holding a busty redhead in the skimpiest red hooker dress in existence to his demonic body.

"Err...what now?" I said again, in that same dumbstruck voice I couldn't seem to get past.

"I pledge my life to you," he repeated hitting his own chest again like this act was both final and understood.

"Oookay...can I ask why?" I said now backing away

from the edge I had been getting closer to and putting a safer distance between me and it.

"You tried to save my wife, you protected her, worried for her safety, for this I am in your debt," he said as if the idea wasn't exactly a happy one but more one forced upon him. I released a sigh thinking that he believed he had to do it but just needed letting off the burden, so I said,

"Ah, don't mention it," I said waving it off moving now to walk around him but as I did, this was when he decided to finish what he started. Suddenly he was on his feet, with surprising stealth for a man his size. Then he quickly flattened his hand against my chest and suddenly, I found that I couldn't breathe. I took a few staggering steps back, now holding a shaky hand to my chest.

"Push past it, human," was Caspian's stern advice and if I'd had enough breath at the time to yell profanities at him, I would have...especially now knowing he owed me a life debt and I was pretty sure that meant he couldn't rattle me to death!

I don't know how much time passed as he just stood there watching me with his arms folded and looking as if he would rather be doing his wife's laundry than stood here watching as I tried to 'push past it', whatever the fuck that meant!

In the end, I finally had enough breath to speak and could finally feel the pressure on my chest ease until the point it was no more.

"What the fuck was that?!" I shouted making him scoff, a sound that lifted up half his body an inch.

"Your soul accepting my vow, you now have my life.

Now I can go." Erh…what now? He had turned his back to me not even bothering to wipe the blood from his forehead.

"Whoa there, hold on big guy, let's just back this way up and start again," I said after reaching for him and grabbing his arm to pull him back…Gods, but it was like grabbing a tree trunk!

"Start again?" he asked looking down at me as if I were a bug on his arm, one he was no longer allowed to squash.

"Or at least to the part where you said I now have your life…yeah, explain that bit exactly," I said really hoping this was just one of those, 'I will bend the knee' type of things here.

"It means just that. You own my life as debt," he stated so matter of fact, it was as if he were just saying, 'here's my car to pay off that loan'. I mean jeez, it didn't even sound like that 'car' even meant much to him either! I mean seriously, who just threw away ownership of a soul?

"Okay well you helped me with the shelf, and then we can call it even." He frowned down at me before looking to the shelf before raising a wiry brow at me.

"Because I helped you with a shelf?" he repeated as if he was trying to figure if he had heard me correctly, telling me this wasn't going my way. So, I thought to embellish my reasoning with,

"Yeah, we can just say you may have saved my life with that one, as let's face facts, it's a high possibility with how clumsy I am."

"No. You own it and what's done can't be undone," he stated in clear annoyance.

"But I didn't ask for that!" I said throwing my hands up dramatically.

"You don't ask for one, you're granted it. So, I granted it. Why is this hard for you to comprehend, human?" he asked as if questioning my intelligence when really, it was totally the other way around because this guy was clearly riding the loopy train to crazyville!

"Oh, I get it alright! I just don't think you are getting that I don't want it." Oh no, back up Fae, back up right now! And I did, take a step back that was as saying this clearly didn't go down well as he folded his arms again and scowled down at me. And let's just say, that it was a long way down and pee my pants worthy, which thankfully my bladder stayed strong throughout.

"What is wrong with my offering?!" he snapped.

"Okay, so granted that came out wrong as I am not saying there is anything wrong with your soul per se…"

"Per se?" he repeated impatiently.

"Nothing at all other than offering it to me was totally unnecessary. Now let's say, you had come in here with a bottle of wine or box of chocolates to say thanks then yeah, I would have totally snatched those out your hand but your freakin' life…dude, seriously?" I said and on reflection I wasn't really sure why I threw the word 'dude' in there, especially as it wasn't even a word I kept in reserves. But I guess it just felt like a dude type moment and besides, someone giving you their soul kind of did that to you.

"I don't do gifts," he stated firmly.

"No, no, but souls, yeah sure thing, got loads of them lying around," I muttered again without thinking.

"You are insulting me," he stated and this was when I released a big sigh and said,

"Yes, well I don't mean to, it's just a bit of a shock when

one minute you're wondering where to put your frilliest scatter cushion so your Vampire boyfriend will see it and it will piss him off, and the next you find out you own a person's soul!"

"I don't understand you," he said this time and in pretty much the same tone as he used for everything. *The permanently pissed off kind.*

"Yes, well I don't exactly understand myself right now either," I said slumping down on the sofa and looking down at my hands. Of course, I was also hoping they held the secret of how to return a soul, free of charge, as I doubted even Google could help with that shit!

"Alright, human, you want simple, here it is. You are trouble, this is fact. You are with my Master, which means you are sticking around, also fact. So, you get into trouble next time, I will know. Then I can repay my life debt and you can return my soul's oath. That is it... it is done...now can I fucking leave or what?!" he snapped making me think that for a guy who just came all the way down here to tell me he would basically die to protect me, then he sure was pissy about it!

"Err, yeah," I said forgoing the part where I added, 'please do' at the end. He nodded and then stomped off in his usual, I hate all humans and basically everything but rock bands, beer and my wife, manner. I even had the urge to ask him before he went, if owning this soul meant that I had to do anything. You know like water it or make sure it didn't eat after dark, that type of thing. But then I thought that would have really pushed him to the edge and I didn't know enough of this owning his soul shit to do that just yet. However, if it meant he couldn't hurt me in any way then I suppose this could be fun. Like my new hobby whilst here…how many different ways I could piss him off. Oooh, maybe that way he would just give up and take it back. Okay, so that sounded like one of my usual insane plans.

Naturally after that last boat load of insanity, I didn't really have much choice but to carry on with my 'Prove a point to my Vampy boyfriend' plan and this included the next job on my list…*Lego.*

Which was why a little time later Lucius came back to find me sat on the floor, in front of a coffee table I had moved from the side of the sofa to the front. Oh, and I was currently making a show of cleaning my movie figurines whist watching Buffy the Vampire slayer (on purpose as I wanted to get a rise out of him) on TV.

The living space had also been transformed as now either side of the TV held my biggest pieces of Star Wars Lego, along with a shelf full of my geek stuff. My girly cushions were scattered around the U shaped sectional, and my funny T shirt patch blanket had been folded over one arm. I even had some candles and girly magazines dotted about the place, along with my nail kit that looked a mess on one table after doing my nails and leaving my shit there. Because let's face it, he needed to know the full experience of living with a chick and bonus, my nails looked great!

He took one look at me from across the way and his lips twitched in that telling way of his. Then, without saying anything, he descended the steps and made it to the living space, stopping when he was only a few feet away. I tried to keep my face straight and not smile as I knew he was staring down at me expectantly.

"I think this is the part you welcome me back with a kiss, sweetheart," he stated and I said,

"I think this is the part when you say, 'honey, I'm home', Sugar plum" To this I ended up jumping when his lips were by my ear and he whispered,

"Honey, I'm home." Then I suddenly found myself with my back to the sofa and him lowering his weight over me, my shiny Terminator head rolling from my hand along with the cloth.

"I guess it's my turn," I said referring to his welcome kiss, trying not to sound as breathless as I did and act cool instead. In the end, it didn't matter as Lucius totally took over and kissed me first anyway, something that ended up with us fooling around on the sofa. But then, this was when things obviously started to catch his eye, as his distracted glances said as much. But shockingly, he didn't say anything.

"Anything the matter?" I asked faking innocence and just waiting for the 'what the fuck?' I knew was coming. But then something happened that I wasn't expecting, as Lucius' eyes lit with amusement, he simply buried his face in my neck, silently chuckled and muttered,

"Not one fucking thing." This I took was in reply to my question. To say that I was utterly astonished was an understatement and I came close to saying, 'Why the Hell not?'

But then he went back to kissing me and his amusement turned into arousal. Which meant after about ten minutes of getting hot and heavy on the sofa, that nearly ended with me begging him to make me come already, my stomach chose that moment to growl. This then became priority number one on Lucius' list of importance and I knew that when two things happened so fast I ended up doing a double take at the blur of motion above me. The first was followed by the absence of the body above me and the second was suddenly finding myself being tugged upright.

"Okay so...whoa, Lucius, I can walk!" I ended this in a shout as I quickly found myself over his shoulder and now being carried up the steps to the next few levels. But seeing as this was in the direction of the bedroom, I was more than pleased...well, that was until he veered off towards the kitchen.

"Where's the fun in that and besides, it's time to feed me, wench!" Lucius declared suddenly smacking me on the ass and then setting me down before I even had chance to fully register the sting. Therefore, I pushed the now loose parts of my hair back, pushed my glasses back up my nose and said an unamused,

"Ouch."

On hearing this he took my face in his hands and kissed my nose before saying,

"Aww, poor baby...that's what happens when I come home from a hard day at work and dinner isn't on the table waiting." Now at this I had to laugh, as the thought was indeed a funny one. However, instead of asking him if he'd left his briefcase at the office or to be honest, one of my many other witty replies I could have gone with, I decided on,

"Well, sweetheart, if its feeding you want, then I think you will find we are in the wrong room, if memory serves me right, or should I say, *serves you right*, then a bed is more suitable for the act." Now at this he smirked, and I prematurely waited for him to agree and in some caveman style of his whisk me up to his room to do just that. But like I said, *prematurely.*

He tugged me to him and growled down at me and said,

"Behave, little troublemaker." Then he let me go and walked straight to the fridge, amazing me to see him looking so at ease in the kitchen, even if it was his own. I didn't know why but just the thought of him even in here seemed strange and bizarrely...*human.*

"Erm...so you actually want food?"

"That is what tends to happen when people eat dinner together or am I really that out of touch in the human world these days?" he remarked, this last part an obvious tease.

"Well, it usually starts with a sacrifice these days, so I don't suppose you have any virginal beauties lying around ready for the altar, do you?" I joked and once again found myself in his arms because of the comment, his beer bottle now discarded unopened on the counter. This happened just as quickly as most of Lucius' actions when he was being demanding as one second I was facing the countertop and the next I was spun around to face him and my back was now pressed up against it.

"Not anymore," he growled before grabbing my messy bun in his hand, yanking my head back and claiming my lips in a rough and demanding way. Gods, but it was glorious and I couldn't help but fist my hands in his hair, holding him to me, just as he did the same.

But once again my stomach decided to ruin my fun and growled again making him pull back and in turn making me moan at the loss.

"Oh, come on!" I suddenly shouted without thought and he raised a questioning eyebrow at me making me instantly feel the heat in my cheeks. But then I thought, you know what, to hell with this shit, as he wasn't the only one who got to call the shots here. And besides, I was pretty sure my plan was going to work big time once I got him inside the bedroom, although now I was hoping it was after and not before.

"Something to say, sweetheart?" Lucius said now leaning back against the counter opposite with his hands to the edge either side of him and space between us.

"Oh, fuck saying it, I am just going to do it!" I decided and I started this by suddenly whipping my T shirt over my head and throwing it at him before I took off running and I did so in the direction of the bedroom.

"Mmm, run, run now little rabbit, for I do enjoy the chase," I heard Lucius warn from behind me, but then when I turned around to glance over myself at how far away he was, I noticed that he wasn't there at all. I came to a stop just in the doorway to his bedroom, panting because well, I was crap at physical activity. *Well, with Lucius being the exception.*

I looked around nervously, expecting any second for him to just jump out and scare me.

"What's the matter, Pet...?" The second I heard his whisper so close to me I quickly spun on a heel but again, was met by nothing there. And here I was, now panting in just my jeans and sea green lace bra that managed to make me look a size bigger than I usually was.

"...Scared you will get caught?" This time he finished off his sentence with the feel of his hand caressing across my collarbone before he was gone again. Seriously, but where was he? I had no clue but thought to myself that there was

only one way to try and take control back and that was to tease him as he did far too often to me.

So, I started this by backing up into the room, looking over my shoulder one last time to check that it was empty. Then I started to unbutton my jeans and it was only when I could feel the tall thick bedpost at my back that I braved slipping my hand inside the waist band on my panties, saying first,

"Two can play at that game." Then I swiped my finger up through the seam, gave the wood at my back my weight and moaned whilst arching my body.

"Yes, but only one of us will win it," Lucius said, and suddenly I was grabbed from behind, with the post in between us. I cried out in surprise, pulling my hand from inside my jeans only to find both my arms captured and pulled back behind me so they were awkwardly hugging the post from behind my back.

"Lucius what are you…!?"

"Quiet, girl!" he snapped in a dominating voice that snapped my mouth closed instantly. Then I felt something soft and silky tie around each wrist before being pulled tight, and only when I felt his hands leave me, did I trying tugging them free, to find them well and truly caught.

Lucius had tied me to the large bedpost with thankfully enough length between my hands so the corners of the wood weren't cutting into me. Only when assured I wouldn't break free did Lucius then stroll out from behind me, looking as masterful as ever coming to stand in front of me.

"Now it's time I get to play, Pet." he whispered after stepping into me and dragging the pad of his thumb down the

centre of my lips, as he had once before. But unlike then he started to press in and said,

"Open you fuckable mouth, beautiful." I swallowed hard as the pure lust for this man was making it hard to think of anything other than obeying him. To the point where I felt I should have questioned if there was anything wrong with me, that I found this demanding, rough treatment of his such a turn on?!

But like I said, I just couldn't find it in me to deny him, as I seemed to get just as much pleasure being his good girl and pleasing him as I did when I was sucking his cock and being the one to make him come at my demand.

He inserted his thumb inside my mouth and then leant his face closer into mine and snarled,

"Now suck it."

Again, I did as I was told, sucking it inside and swirling my tongue around his thumb as if it was something else. Something considerably larger. Then he pulled his thumb from me abruptly and suddenly my cheeks were being squeezed together in one hand, as he brought my face closer to his.

"Gods, but how I love this fucking mouth!" he declared on a growl before crushing his lips to mine for a bruising kiss that set me on fire. Swiftly after this I felt my breast being freed as my lace cup was torn down now hanging from its wire, and my nipple was being twisted and pulled in a painful but sexual way. One that yet again, had me moaning in pleasure not wanting him to stop his delicious torment. I was so turned on that I could feel my arousal dripping down my inner thighs, soaking my panties and even through my jeans.

Lucius tore his mouth from mine and said,

"Fuck, Amelia! The scent of you, the scent of your wet pussy is fucking with my senses, making me blind to all else…" Then both his hands went to my jeans and, like in the gas station, I felt them being tugged roughly down my legs, before they were gone completely. My panties, however, were torn and instead of being thrown to join the trousers, Lucius had other ideas for them as he put them in his back pocket.

Then, once risen back to his full height and looking down at my body, now mostly naked save for one breast still in its cup and the other hanging free, his smirk deepened as he took a leisurely scan back up until at my mouth, where he said,

"Blind to all else but this sweet mouth of yours, *one I am going to enjoy fucking.*" I sucked in a shuddered breath and his eyes seeped into a warm glowing amber at the sight. Then with a hand on my elbow he stepped close enough to whisper down in my ear,

"Now get on your knees for your King, my pretty little Princess." Then with a little force more so to start guiding me, I was lowered to my knees like he commanded. But even through his dark and dominating control, I still noticed the way he took such good care of me. Like how he helped me to my knees, making sure my tied hands slid down the length of the wood at the same time my weight landed on the floor. Then he ran a gentle, soothing hand back over my hair before cupping my jaw in an almost tender way.

I looked up at him, over the rim of my glasses, keeping eye contact until I heard the sound of his zipper being lowered. Naturally, my gaze shot to the sight of his hard length as it burst free from behind the denim. But his growled demand stopped me,

"Give me back your eyes! I want them on me the whole time, do you understand?" He barked out his order and I nodded looking up at him once again. He caressed my cheek and praised,

"My good girl, now take me in your mouth and relax your throat before sucking me down... As much as you can take, Amelia." he told me and I swallowed hard before doing as he wished and opening my mouth wide so I could take him, getting a high from the control he exerted over me.

Now I had done this before and seeing as I had made him come and he clearly enjoyed it, I knew I was capable of this. However, as soon as it started, I realized the major difference was control. Or should I say the lack of, as without my hands, I was completely at his mercy to take me to my limit and trust him to do this and not take it beyond. And oh boy did he take me to my limit!

"That's it, that's it, take me down into that sweet fucking mouth of yours...Gods, how I love this mouth!" Lucius growled out the praise and when I saw his head fall back, I felt myself trying to take him even further as the pleasure witnessed by what my mouth could do was fucking addictive! I wanted to make him come so badly but not just that, but to make it the best he'd ever had. I wanted his orgasm to be so powerful that it would be burned to his memory for the rest of eternity!

So I did as he said, I kept my eyes locked to his, even if he wasn't looking and relaxed my throat as much as I could, working through gagging around him and holding him there for as long as I could.

"Fuck, FUCK!" Lucius shouted whenever I did and I combined this with the quick bobbing motion down his length, alternating between going fast, and sucking hard, to then holding him down for as long as I could keep him there.

"Gods in fucking Heaven!" he hissed through his teeth as if he could barely even cope with the level of pleasure I was forcing upon him, as I may have been the one tied up, but right now, I knew that I was in control.

"Yes! Fuck yes, my girl, I am going to feed you my cum and you are going to swallow it down like such the good girl you are," he told me and I nodded slightly with his cock still deep in my mouth to tell him that I would. He liked this, I could tell as his eyes burned brighter before he said,

"Do you know how fucking spectacular you look right now, on your knees before me, my cock deep in that talented hot little mouth of yours, ready and eager to swallow me down, swallow every drop I fucking give you! Do you have any idea how fucking beautiful you are!" he said now with his hand at the back of my head, ready to hold me prisoner around him should I suddenly wish to escape. His hips then started pumping to the speed he wanted and all I could do was relax, open wide and let him have his way with my mouth.

"You're a fucking Goddess is what you are! Now fucking swallow me down, Amelia! Swallow it all, my girl, *my fucking heart!"* he snarled and just as his fist embedded with a painful bite in my hair, he pushed himself in the furthest yet and roared up at the ceiling like a fucking demon loose from Hell. All the while as he pumped his cum down my throat, making me gag and swallow around the intrusion.

I continued to swallow and swallow until it finally

stopped, and his hand relaxed in my hair pulling me slowly from his still hard, wet length. He was breathing heavily, obviously needing to come down from the extreme high and as he did, his hand smoothed back my hair and ran a gentle thumb along my now aching jaw.

God, even after his rough treatment of me, he managed to make me feel so cherished, like the way when I gave him one last lick and he uttered a tender,

"My sweet girl." Then he took hold of both my elbows this time and raised me to my feet, making sure I was steady. As soon as I was to my full height, he started to kiss me, but starting with across my chest, then up my neck and finally along my jaw to my mouth. This was when he ravished my mouth, gripping my waist and holding it to his hard frame like he wanted to try and merge our bodies as one. To the point that I was so in deep in his kiss that when he pulled back, I even found my face falling forward a little. This he found endearing as he pushed my glasses back up my nose and ran the pad of two fingers across my tender lips.

"Now it's time for me to play with my girl," he said and the second his hand snaked down in between my legs, I gasped at the connection, for I had been desperate for it. Desperate for the contact, being as turned on as I was, it literally stole my breath. Oh, and judging by his grin, he knew it, as the second he inserted the first finger inside me I cried out at the pleasure, one I had been near frantic to find.

Then with his free hand he collared my throat and held my head back to the post to keep me still, even though there was nowhere for me to go being tied the way I was.

But he did this all the same, along with pull his finger

free, despite my moan of protest. Then he brought the coated finger not to his own lips this time, but to mine.

"Here, now you get to taste both of us," he said forcing his finger in my mouth and letting the flavour of my sex burst across my tongue before he then pulled it free and kissed me again, keeping his finger close enough to slip in there as well. This was so we were both experiencing the taste together. Gods, but it was so erotic, so raw I wondered if I wouldn't come from that alone. But then the answer to that came when his hand went back to my entrance and just as he forced two fingers forcefully inside, he said this time,

"Now it's time to abuse that pretty pussy of yours."

CHAPTER TWENTY-ONE

LUCIUS

COMING HOME

Watching Amelia as she came all over my fingers, soaking them from forcing her to squirt a release on them was like staring into the face of perfection! The way her head fell back, and mouth permanently open, panting and moaning as she was forced the pleasure upon her. The way she begged for me to stop so sweetly, Gods, it was fucking music to my ears! But yet, I would not stop, for I knew there was more in her yet. And each time, she would wheeze out a plea for me to stop, but seconds later begging me to continue. I was such a fucking sadist when it came to my addiction and she was every fucking inch of the only drug I craved!

The way her body arched into the force of my thrusts as I fucked her with my fingers, adding to the size after each orgasm I demanded from her. Her hot little curvy body, bouncing, shaking, shuddering and quaking to my every touch, it was like the most beautiful plaything. A fine-tuned instrument and one I swear I could have continued performing with for hours. But the purpose of my hand at her neck was not just to hold her steady so she wouldn't hurt herself with her thrashing, but it was also to monitor her pulse, knowing through that when she had finally had enough. Because my owned and used little doll needed to be taken care of and as much as I was having fun, I knew it would only take its toll on her fragile and mortal body.

And with her being my first mortal taken since my change, then I knew I had to give way to caution, no matter how hard or rough I wanted to take her. I had to be conscious of what she could handle, for my size alone could hurt her if ever she was not completely ready to take me. And there was the sexual pain to get off from and then there was just pain.

But with this being said, she continued to take me to the edge of losing all control, pushing and pushing at the beast in me every time I took her. I just wanted her in chains! I wanted her spread out on a crux decussata, better known as the St Andrews cross, restrained in a spread-eagle position. Shackled to the X frame so I could do as I did now all over again. I would then release her legs from the crux decussata and fuck her senseless!

But that was what she did to me. She flooded my mind with everything that was her, consuming my thoughts. That infallible icy demeanor I was famous for, all of it gone the second she merely uttered my name. Gods, but just getting her down here in the first place had been a challenge, as leaving her in bed in the morning when waking had been a fucking chore in itself. I had awoken, possessively cupping her sex and it was no fucking wonder considering earlier in the night I had woken to find her missing.

Gods, but the sheer fucking panic had me ready to tear down my own fucking walls to find her! I had been in such a rage, that the second I heard her in the bathroom I couldn't help but react like a wild irrational beast, actually letting my Demon take more of a lead this time.

And in truth, I had felt like an utter bastard for it! Especially seeing as my main objective was to try and make her feel at home and at ease here. But instead, on the very first night, she finds me furious simply because she got up to use the fucking bathroom! Of course, the encounter had thankfully ended well, as in that moment entering her body and fucking her was the only thing that I had needed in order to calm the fuck down. As I needed to take what I owned and her fuckable, hot little body was all fucking mine to take advantage of.

So, I had.

And just like all other times before and since, Gods it was incredible. It was like nothing I had experienced before, as she was that something sweet in my life that I wanted to gorge myself on. I wasn't joking when telling her that I was addicted. And since healing her, then I knew I was finally safe to take her the way I wanted to, without feeling like the utter bastard I had felt when seeing the true extent of her injuries beforehand.

Gods, but I had been so furious with her for letting me take her that way. The thought of causing her that type of pain, was enough to cause a physical reaction within me. For it wasn't often a Vampire would feel nauseated.

But like I had said, I knew the difference between sexual pain and just regular pain, as one she got off on, the other only a true masochist would feed from. And my sweet Amelia was simply an innocent little submissive in need of a firm hand and patient training. Especially when she started questioning why she got off on the things I had made her get off on. Because my girl was a fighter, through and through and I fucking loved that about her.

But the misconception that every submissive was like that in every aspect of their life and not just the bedroom was usually false, for each being was different. Simply put, it depended on the person, along with the hand that led the submissive, as some exercised the need for control continuously. And there were those who liked asserting dominance in the bedroom after spending the day being challenged.

I had always believed I had been of the first type, given my position as ruler. It was well known my need to exert my control over my Kingdom and with a firm fucking hand at that! But since Amelia, then fuck me, the way she turned me on with her playful banter and witty remarks, that personal preference I had been holding on to went and took a flying fucking leap out the window!

The way she most certainly challenged me and at every turn at that. Gods, but it was like a breath of fresh air after being forced to live underground for a millennia. In fact, I never seemed to know what she would fucking do next and the excitement in me at finding out was only making it harder to be without her. For when I was, I constantly questioned what it was she was doing. I worried over the simplest of things. Like had she eaten enough? Had she had a moment of clumsiness and fallen or hurt herself? It was near fucking exhausting if truth be told.

As for her stubbornness, like the battle of having her move in. I knew that I couldn't have hidden the fact her stuff had been delivered sooner than I thought it would have. Which meant I therefore had to tackle the subject matter with her yet again and sooner than I would have liked, as I had believed it wouldn't have been quite so fast but, in a way, I was now glad it was done, for it was one more thing I could cross off the list, one nearly as long as my fucking arm where she was concerned.

It was why the second I took in the changes she had made in my personal space I knew instantly what her game of play was. And well, speaking of play...

"Please...oh Gods, please Lucius no more, I can't...I can't..." she said weakening now to the point she could no longer remain on her feet. Nor the shuddering muscles in her legs, as I had to leave her throat during that last screaming orgasm to keep her upright until finished.

"Alright, ssshh now, I will give you the rest you need," I told her in hushed tones as she was very nearly asleep already. So, I snapped the length of silk I had tied her with. One I'd had at the ready knowing I would spend the night with her tied to me this time, so she couldn't leave again without first waking me.

But then this had more than served a purpose as well, I thought with a hidden grin. However, when she started to slump forward, I feared I had taken her too far. I lifted her fully into my arms and carried her around to the side of the bed, before laying her down to sleep. After this I tore my T shirt over my head and used it to clean her up. She moaned in her sleep and squirmed in the way I fucking adored, trying in vain to get away from my hand. One that touched what I knew was now a well and truly abused pussy, and one I also intended to take again later.

Oh, but she would soon discover my increased appetite for sex now that she had finally been situated firmly in my life. And well, I had a lot of making up for lost time to do. As well as teaching my sweet little scholar a thing or two about her role in my bed and out of it. Starting with getting my way and making her unpack. Something I had most definitely achieved much to her vexation and the reason I grinned now.

But like I said, her game had been clear from the start. For she had thought to purposely irk me by displaying everything she owned, including an array of very feminine pillows now on my couch. This along with a new display unit for all her 'toys'.

When Caspian had told me what he caught her doing then I had been furious. For she could have fallen and hurt herself, or worse, making me decide instantly after that, to change aspects of my home to make it safer for her. To be honest, this had been something I had decided when watching her navigate the bridge. It was one that led into the tunnel entrance to my private quarters and a place that she had nearly fallen over on from her premature victory dance. Something I would have found charming had it not been followed by the possibility of hurting herself.

So, by the time I had arrived back I had been fully ready to reprimand her about moving furniture around without aid, being thankful for Caspian's arrival when he did. This despite his actions that I discovered after the fact!

But then I had walked into my home and the sight that greeted me, had me too moved mentally to do much else other than stare. I knew she hadn't yet spotted me for I watched her for a good ten minutes before letting my presence be known.

I was utterly fascinated. Not just by the sight of her, one that was far beyond fucking adorable but with the way she cleaned her toy figures and added her commentary to whatever nonsense she had been watching at the time. Things like, you go girl, bazooka that demon's ass!

It had actually made me wonder what she was watching at that point, especially when she was so engrossed, she wasn't looking at what she was doing. Something that caused her to catch the pad of her thumb on a pointed piece of her figurine. Then I watched as she sucked it into her mouth and Gods but the sight of her sat there had me hard in seconds. She looked the very epitome of innocent virginity, even one after I had staked my claim and taken it for myself. The way she had started sucking the pain from her thumb, wearing those fuck me glasses and that tight T-shirt that clung to the delicious curve of her breasts. Gods, but my cock could have carved out the fucking rock surrounding us!

I knew then how I would have her sucking on my own thumb, watching those wide blue eyes of her staring up at me in question over the rim of the thick frames. Oh, the corruption, and what fucking sweet delights it had brought me! But then once again as was the way with my girl, the second her delectable mouth had swallowed down my cock she had quickly stolen my control and claimed it as her own.

I had to say, I was looking forward to a future where this little power battle between us would continue and not just in the bedroom. Hellfire, but I just couldn't seem to get enough of her! Even now, looking down at her as she slept, and I wanted to wake her with the slide of my cock penetrating her from behind, doing so as gently as possible and seeing how long it would take for her to wake and realise.

Mmm, perhaps tonight I would sleep with my length still nestled inside her, for staying hard around her wasn't a problem. For that was the damn understatement of the year, for my problem was trying to walk around here without a constant hard on!

Even earlier when dealing with the business of her family, I had entered my office to find my council waiting but with only a glance at my desk and I was assaulted with thoughts of taking her hard against it. This then meant walking the length of the room with the very obvious imprint of my cock down my leg pressing heavily against my jeans. I even snarled and threatened violence at Clay who openly laughed at seeing it. Of course, it was a threat he didn't take seriously as thankfully I had taken her only hours before. However, I found that trying to keep a level head when I hadn't, was becoming a difficult endurance. Like an irritable alcoholic that needed a drink.

Something I thankfully didn't have added to the annoyance of Clay's emergency phone call...*fucking Dominic Draven.* To be honest, I had been surprised it had taken him this long and no doubt this was down to his wife's influence in trying to keep her husband under control. Obviously even she had exhausted her talents.

Earlier...

"Is there anything to report?" I had asked when taking my seat behind my overly large carved partner desk, one topped in red leather. As far as offices go, it was old school, with lots of dark mahogany that both panelled the walls as it did with the coffered ceilings. A grand fireplace made from Egyptian rose marble dominated one side of the room, whilst my desk dominated the other. The stone floor was the same marble as the heavily carved fire surround, done so in the design of two Roman warriors standing guard. A sight that always took me back to a different time. One filled with politics, corruption and the backstabbing pastime of murdering Emperors. And I would know seeing as I was one of them when I seized power shortly after the death of Emperor Pertinax back in 193, this during the Year of the Five Emperors.

But this was my office, a reminder of the many lives lived throughout my two thousand years plus on this Earth. Like the picture above the fireplace that was my first home and place of birth. Queriot, a town located south of Jerusalem in Judea. But no one knew of this or could guess that the mountain in the painting was Mount Hebron. This was the highest point and comprising the bulk of the central Judean Mountains.

However, no one knew much of my past, other than the stories my people fed on like the fucking mortal world of the rich and famous. As even Angels and Demons loved fucking gossip and well, when you were King, it unfortunately came with the territory. But it also made me wonder how much of my history Amelia knew.

She had never asked, and it made me wonder what would come of that conversation. I knew that for her, she had been extremely sheltered so it stood to reason she knew very little of my past, as I couldn't exactly see daddy dearest divulging in our sordid history. Like the fact for more years than not, I had been his personal assassin. Admittedly a role I had much preferred at the time to that of king, a rule I didn't relish in for many years after I had been turned.

In fact, it was only a title to me and not one I had taken seriously until after I had severed all ties between myself and my old friend. Oh, but then it had been a kingdom I would not strengthen and grow in size but use to my advantage when seeking out my revenge.

But that past was long gone and buried beneath my very flesh with the blood of Christ forging my soul into what had been owed to me long ago.

Fuck, but just thinking back over my long life and it made me wonder how such a conversation between myself and my Chosen One would even start. This, of course, included my gloved hand that until yesterday when my rage had consumed me, no-one had ever seen. But seeing as she had never asked me about it, I was at a loss as to her feelings on the matter. Which in the end, had been one of the most surprising things about her, for I knew she wanted to ask, as I had seen her glance at it enough times to know this for certain. My only conclusion was it was the fear of my reaction to such a question that prevented her from doing so and like the bastard I was, I was thankful for it, as it wasn't a story I was yet ready to tell her.

Like many others.

Hell, but I could just imagine the questions now. In that

way she was very much like her mother, always asking fucking questions! However, as much as it had been an annoyance with Keira, I was curious as to why I never found it so with Amelia. No, instead, I found her curious nature an endearing quality and her eagerness to learn of my people's history and culture was nothing but encouraging. Despite how much her father had wished to keep it from her, the fact was that now she was mine and that meant she was my responsibility. She was in my care, so his wishes were a fucking moot point as far as I was concerned. She was my girl to protect and that included what I felt prudent for her to know and not know. And besides, I was the one being gifted the sight of her pleasure when providing her with the source of her addiction for knowledge. The way her eyes had lit up with excitement had been fucking adorable! And well, having her throw herself at me in gratitude was only another bonus for granting her what she desired.

If anything, I guess I should be thankful for the sheltered life they had deemed necessary, as I was the one benefitting from it now. And speaking of overbearing fathers, it was my time to have to deal with hers.

"Nothing to report as such, just a pissed off King threatening to storm the castle should we not have his daughter returned and have her ass on his private jet within the hour," Clay replied and Ruto rolled his eyes at this, muttering,

"It's thirty fucking years ago, all over again minus an Imp."

I scoffed at this and rolled my own eyes, thinking again back to my Amelia and when I caught her doing the same.

"But of course, he did." I answered dryly.

"When was this?" I asked making Clay smirk when answering,

"Sixty nine minutes ago." Now this made me smile.

"Well, I'd bet not keep the royal dick waiting then," I said then nodded to the door for my people to leave, picking up my phone and tapping on the one number named asshole. It was also a number that had changed many times throughout the years, as his anger usually got the better of him and ended up destroying the phone. I wondered then with a smirk if the current one would last the call.

Part of me hoped not. Oh, who was I kidding, all of me hoped not.

A hope that seemed almost absolute when the first sound I heard on the other end was a vicious growl, making me both grin and respond with a dry...

"Draven"

Friend, Old Foes

CHAPTER TWENTY-TWO

FRIENDS, OLD FOES

"About fucking time!" Dom snapped on a growl, telling me he was already at seething levels. Of course, hearing me call him by his last name wouldn't have helped, I thought with a grin. This was something only his wife called him, and he knew instantly the point I had made, for he was no longer my fucking King to kneel to, and I could therefore call him whatever the fuck I wanted to!

But just as I was known for my unsettling and deadly calm, he was known for his temper. So, his reaction was nothing new to me and highly predictable.

"It's good to hear from you too," I said dryly.

"Cut the bullshit, Luc, and just tell me what time my daughter arrives!" Oh, now this made me really grin and gave me a depth of satisfaction like you wouldn't believe.

"I fear you're mistaken, old friend, for if someone gave you the impression she would be on a flight heading your way, then I will find the guilty party responsible and demand an apology on your behalf." I said and then pulled back the phone in preparation for the roar of his demon that was to ignite. Naturally, he didn't disappoint and my smirk turned into a full on grin.

"Don't fucking test me, Vampire, I want my fucking daughter!" Dom roared again and in that moment I would have liked nothing more than to have informed him that she was my claimed Electus and for him to fuck off and take it up with the Fates!

But then I knew that to do such at this juncture would do more harm than good, as I may not only be declaring war but doing so by putting Amelia in the middle of it. Besides, I refused to go behind her back in that way unless it was beyond all reasonable doubt that it had to be done. And unfortunately for me, right in this moment that was not a claim I could make.

"Calm the fuck down, Dom, and uncurl your wings. Amelia is fine and unharmed."

"She is…" he started to say and again I snapped, interrupting him with a growl of my own words,

"She is safe and that should be your only concern right now considering the shit storm you brought down on her thanks to that fucking box!" I threw at him, knowing that I was using what would essentially be his guilt as my weapon here. Oh, and did it ever fucking work!

"Like I fucking knew that would happen!" was his frustrated argument.

"Yes, and lucky for you, my friend, I took it upon myself to continue protecting her, even when I found her sneaking into my fucking club and trying to steal the fucking box back." I informed him knowing Amelia would be pissed but it was this or the truth.

"She did what?!" he shouted in disbelief.

"Oh yes, my friend, that daughter of yours can be quite cunning."

"Gods, but what the fuck was she thinking?!" he snapped and I frowned, disliking this comment and before I gave it thought, I snapped back,

"Perhaps she was fucking thinking of others before herself and ignoring the dangers her actions possessed in order to try and aid us in deciphering the fucking thing!" A moment of silence was all it took to realise my fuck up. This was confirmed with her father's voiced opinion.

"Now that is a curious thing," Dom said making me bark, "What!?"

"Why you would feel the need to defend her, someone who tried to steal from you no less?"

Fuck!

Damn it, for I let my emotions get the better of me

without thinking. I could only hope that my recovery was a believable one, for Amelia's sake if nothing else.

"What can I say, Dom, her brazen actions and reasons behind them endeared me to her cause." Dom scoffed at this and muttered something about getting soft in my old age, a comment I chose to ignore, because well, I was fucking his daughter so didn't think there was anything he could say right now to beat that fact.

"Besides, when I discovered that she had been targeted…"

"What the fuck do you mean, targeted?!" he barked interrupting me this time.

"Multiple kidnap attempts have been made, Dom." I told him, letting him know how serious this situation was.

"WHAT THE FUCK?!" he roared again, as I knew he would. Gods, but like I said, he was a predictable bastard.

"Why by the Gods…"

"It is obvious, Dom, they wish to use her as a bargaining chip to get the box, which considering what it is and who I am sure you are well aware it will effect, would be a bad thing." He growled knowing exactly what I meant by this, seeing as he stood to lose his Chosen One, should anything befall me. But what he didn't know was that he stood to lose both of the woman in his life, for Amelia was also tied to my soul and not just from being my Chosen One.

But that was my pain to bear.

My secret.

I shook these thoughts from my mind to focus on the problem at hand, that being an overbearing father.

"I can protect her here," I told him firmly, before continuing,

"I think we both know that Königssee is the better option. Besides, I can't risk trying to get her to you without another attempt being made," I said knowing that I was about to completely twist events and play them to my advantage, something I was a fucking master at.

After all, *I always got my way.*

"What attempt! Was she hurt?" he demanded.

"Check Munich news and you will see for yourself," I told him knowing what he would soon find but as usual with Dom, he had no fucking patience, something I was counting on.

"I want to hear it from you, Luc!" he snarled anxiously.

"Very well, as you wish." I said playing the age old King.

"First they hit the club," I informed him, knowing this would come as a surprise.

"Fuck! How bad?"

"Bad enough that it is barely still fucking standing!" I snapped because well, the thought of it pissed me off!

"Who?" he asked through gritted teeth.

"I have my theories and have my people working on discovering the source but what we do know is that Rogues are banding together and using the mortal society Skull and Bones as a financial front. Hundreds of mercenaries have been hired and not enough of them have died yet for my liking. Which is precisely why I will not risk them getting Amelia," I told him.

"You sound very protective there, Luc, do I have something else to fucking worry about here?" he asked coming right out and saying it!

Yes, you fucking do.

"No, you fucking don't, other than I am not particularly

fond of the idea of handing over my life in exchange for hers and risking the lives of an entire race I rule over...you fucking getting me now?!" I growled making him scoff but not reply with anything more.

"And the Rogues, how is it you haven't dealt with them yet?" Alright so this was the part of the conversation I didn't exactly relish in divulging, as neither would he if ever in my shoes, for no king as powerful as we are would be in a rush to admit a weakness in our armour. And unfortunately, this was a big fucking weakness in mine.

"They have a grade six witch." At this he hissed,

"Impossible."

"I witnessed their strength of will firsthand, Dom, I assure you the threat is real," I replied in annoyance.

"Fuck!"

"My sentiments exactly, which makes the Rogues immune to me being their Sire and exerting my will," I said, telling him something he knew already.

"Hence why you are pulling your people in," he surmised, obviously having his lackies keeping tabs on my movements still. Well, at least he hadn't yet lost his edge and grown soft in the last thirty years!

"And why I am amassing my armies, yes," I added, knowing it would give him food for thought.

"You believe this will lead to war?" he asked in surprise and I ran a frustrated hand down the back of my neck and said truthfully,

"The fuck if I know, Dom, but what would you do if you were me?"

"The fucking same. Alright, you have my loyalty," he said shocking the shit out of me!

"I do?"

"This is my wife and daughter we are talking about, of course you fucking do!" he snapped in irritation and I could imagine why. For him to grant me his loyalty meant giving me rights to the use of his army also and that most certainly tipped the scales in our favour big time.

"And what of Theo and his people?" I asked, knowing the strength in that force alone was enough to make the difference. After all, he was as strong as his father, even if not as ruthless as his twin.

"Now I know more I will set up a meeting, call in the table of Kings." Dom agreed.

"And what of…"

"Don't." Dom said cutting me off, knowing of whom I would ask about next.

"So, no changes there I take it?" I enquired sincerely.

"With a demon inside of him stronger than my own and one to battle against daily, what the fuck do you think?!" he snapped and I released a sigh.

"We did all we could, my friend," I offered wondering why the fuck I did. Although I did feel somewhat responsible seeing as he had been placed in my care.

"Yes, and maybe one day it will be enough," was Dom's reply in return, for I knew that he struggled as any father would.

"And his whereabouts?" I asked for I was curious.

"Last I heard from my source, Japan and lost in the masses as he prefers," he replied somewhat bitterly as was understandable.

"He always did," I scoffed knowing this firsthand seeing as I had been his mentor.

"Are we done?" I asked after some extended and awkward silence.

"Can you assure me she is safe there and can't be reached?" Dom asked and had he known who she was to me then he would have known how insulting this question was. For you never questioned the ability of a master over his Electus. But he didn't. Which was why I bit back the snarl of anger and instead, threw at him a bitter sting of the past,

"You tell me Dom, did you manage it with Keira?!" At this he growled low and menacing, warning me,

"Be careful, old friend, for you will not like the outcome of reminding me of such a time!"

"As is the same for you, *old friend...*" I said mocking his words with a hiss and continuing on,

"...So, I suggest not questioning my abilities again!" At this point I hung up and did so with enough control left, that I wasn't the one who ended up crushing my phone in my hand or throwing the fucking thing against the wall! But in all honestly his words had hit a nerve, because *she had been reached* and I hadn't been the one to save her, for she had saved herself, twice over!

To say this knowledge didn't sit well with me was a fucking Hell sized understatement and was the reason why last night when finding her not in my bed next to me, I had lost my fucking temper with her. Something I knew I needed to control if my plan at making this a home for her would work. Which reminded me, it was time to check on my girl.

"Ruto, get everyone back in here," I said into my phone after first calling him, for I needed to tie up a few loose ends. Minutes later and my council found themselves spread out in the different chairs in my office once more.

"So, how did it go?" Ruto was the first to enquire.

"Mainly as expected, although he has offered me his loyalty," I told them fully expecting the array of shocked expressions.

"Wow, they must be wondering why there is suddenly a blizzard happening in Hell," Clay commented making all but Hakan chuckle, as he rarely ever did. Liessa was the only missing party as I had put her on an assignment of shopping for a dress for Amelia. There was an annual ball coming up that was one I refused to postpone, despite Clay's suggesting I do and regardless of his growing concern.

But it was one I held every year for my kind and this year by letting it continue to happen would end up being a show of strength to my people. For the slight sign of weakness seen in their King was not ever an option.

"How are preparations coming along for tomorrow night?" I asked and just as Clay was about to speak once more, I held up my hand and stopped him.

"Save it Clay, it is happening. Now tell me."

"I have tripled security and at your request, I'm having your witch flown in from Norway," Clay replied quickly giving up on trying to talk me out of it. I knew of his apprehension, being my head of security, this naturally came with the territory. But seeing as there was no chance at any Rogues entering my home without my knowledge, then I didn't see the harm in continuing on with the yearly celebration. Even if its reason made me want to roll my eyes and tear my hair out for how ridiculous its cause was.

"And our people?" I went on to ask.

"They started to arrive as of last night once we put out the call but most will be here before the ball," Ruto answered this time as he was in charge of keeping track of the comings and goings of my sired. Reason enough why the mention of Rogues was one that irked him especially.

"And what of the state of the guest accommodation?" I asked, aiming my question at Percy this time who had been put in charge of making sure everyone was situated where they needed to be.

"Iith hasth all been takkken care ofth, Stthhire," he answered, with his nervous stutter adding to his lisp and catching on the word taken. I nodded and then looked at the time, seeing now that Amelia had gone too long without being checked on, but with some things left to do I had no choice but to give the order,

"I need someone to go down to check on my Chosen."

"I will do it," Caspian said first before all others and rose to his feet. I raised a brow in question to which his reply was a clipped,

"I'm your enforcer, not a fucking party planner." Then he bowed a head and left the room with the heavy pounding of his steps.

"I am almost inclined to push it upon him next year, just to see what it is he would plan if forced to," I commented making the others chuckle.

"My guess, it would be bloody and barbaric," Ruto said grinning.

"Sounds like a good night out to me," Clay remarked making me grin and reply now with quiet contemplation,

"Indeed."

Because let's face it, if there was one thing I could do with after this last week and that was breaking somebody until beaten and bloody. Which was why I said,

"Then next year, fuck the masks, gladiators will be our new theme."

Naturally, everyone in the room agreed.

A short time later Caspian entered my office, making my blood boil at the fucking sight.

"EVERYONE OUT!" I roared making everyone leave pretty damn quickly. But before the door closed behind Clay, he said before leaving,

"Err, good fucking luck mate." Then closed the door and left me to prove that there would be no such luck for him on this day!

"Tell me you did not just do what that blood on your forehead tells me you fucking did!" I all but roared.

"It had to be done," Caspian said making me growl low and dangerously. I took a deep breath and rose to my feet, demanding in a seething tone,

"Fucking kneel!" To which Caspian did without question. I then walked over to him and in my anger grabbed the wiry hair that was knotted on top of his head and tugged it back on a snarl to see for myself the evidence of the vow he had made.

"It is done," he said again and I growled down at him and bared my fangs seeing only the barest of flinches from him. Then I threw his head forward as I let go, making his head bow down, his long pointed beard now touching his chest.

"Get the fuck up and sit your ass down!" I snapped walking back to lean against my desk as he did as I commanded.

"Why?!" I snarled.

"It is the way of my people, I had no choice," he explained without regret.

"And the reason you didn't first ask my permission?" I asked with a bite of anger, very close to losing my shit seeing as I knew what he had done.

"Because you would have prevented me, and I would have had no choice but to obey your rule. This way, you couldn't stop me," he said being honest even without needing to be, for I already knew this to be the reason.

"So you thought to vow a soul of life on my Chosen One!!" I shouted.

"It is my…"

"Don't you dare fucking say it again, Caspian, for I will hurt you if you do!" At this he released a deep sigh and said,

"She protected what was mine, my demon would not have found peace without it, you know this, Luc." Caspian said, now appealing to me not as his King but as his friend. I, too, released a sigh and found myself slumping down in a chair, dragging a hand through my hair.

"You of all people remember what my demon was like before her," he said, reminding me of more testing times, for he was right, Caspian was, well sometimes a fucking rule within himself. He was a loose cannon and had been made to come to heel more times than I could fucking count before he had hunted his wife.

But still, I wouldn't let him off so easily.

"And if I had done the same to Liessa, without seeking your permission, what then?" I asked trying to maintain my cool and at least try and see if anything good could come of this.

"I would have had no choice but to accept it."

"Yes, no choice indeed as you gave me!" I snapped before he grunted a snort and said,

"Permission to speak, Sire," I rolled my eyes and snapped,

"Just fucking speak it, Caspian, before I lose my shit and make you bleed!"

"I would now die for your Queen should she need saving, which let's face it, Luc, she is a fucking disaster magnet on legs." I growled at this and warned,

"Watch your tongue, enforcer."

"Luc, she jumped out of a fucking helicopter after shooting the fucking pilot, I think the past speaks for me." I fucking hated that he was right and instead of agreeing, kept my silence for I wasn't exactly in a rush to agree with him.

"Is it really that bad knowing one of your own would lay down their life for the girl?" he asked making his point as no, it was not. But the real reason for my anger was because it was my job to protect her and up until now, well, it felt as if I had done a piss poor job at it!

"And this vow you made, what did Amelia think of it?" I asked as now I was curious, especially as he grinned in amusement.

"She said that I should stick to buying wine and chocolates when I want to say thanks." I scoffed a laugh and said,

"Of course she did."

"She also tried to give it back, told me that we were even because I helped her carry some fucking big shelf down the stairs so she wouldn't break her fucking neck," he said shaking his head as if seeing it again for himself but as for me, I instantly saw red and this time it was no longer aimed at Caspian, but now at my human.

My very breakable human.

Which is why I hissed in a dangerous tone...

"Come again?"

CHAPTER TWENTY-THREE

NOW THAT'S A DATE

The next time Amelia woke it was to the feel of me running my fingertips down her spine and up again following the line of her shoulders. I had long ago rid her of her torn bra and removed her glasses, placing them on the bedside table before I brought the covers around her so she wouldn't catch a chill. For most of what I remembered about mortals was how breakable they were and how susceptible they were at catching illnesses. Now how the fucking cold air did such a thing I did not know, but never the less, I found myself caring enough to coin the phase, 'just in case'.

But then, as I had been lying next to her sleeping form, one that had curled on its side with her back facing me, I had found that sheet travelling further and further down by the minute. Her skin was beautifully golden, and so perfectly soft that I knew being close to her and not touching her wasn't ever going to happen. Every now and then she stirred in her sleep, and half of me wished to wake her and the other half knew she could do with the rest, although she would most likely wake up hungry.

In the end, I gave in to her needs and not my own, but caressing back her hair and softly commanding her to go back to sleep, only the last time I had done that she had mumbled,

"I would, but you stroking my back feels too good to sleep through." I grinned at her back before kissing my way across her shoulder blade and giving her some of my weight as I leaned into her to brush back the hair from her neck to kiss. Her little breathy moan was all the gift I wanted, for I was already addicted to enticing these sweet sounds from her.

It was another reason that by the time I had left Caspian in my office to go and confront my troublesome little human, all I had needed to do was take one look at her and all anger fled me. Oh, I would still be reprimanding her about it, but right in that moment I had wanted nothing more than her body in my arms and my lips on her skin. Both of which won every time over starting a battle with her.

I was also beginning to understand that with Amelia, it was all about picking my times and using her weaknesses to my advantage in getting what I wanted. For example, if I had followed through with my hot headed plan of demanding her explanation to me why she would be so reckless, thus inviting potential bodily harm to herself, then she would have argued back, tried to make her point and no doubt get angry doing it.

However, now having her like this, nice and pliable in my hands and at the mercy of being naked and in my bed, then I knew my time for making my point was now. So, I suddenly flipped her over onto her back and pinned her arms above her, so she had no chance of squirming away from me.

"Err…hello there," she said in that unsure, comical little way of hers, making me grin down at those wide, questioning blue eyes and in return I no doubt resembled the hungry predator I was, looming over her.

"Mmm, my beautiful, Amelia," I hummed as I ran my nose up her jawline taking my time to breathe her in, closing my eyes as the strong scent of her hair filled my senses.

"I just adore this soft skin of yours, and these pretty blue eyes looking up at me…*from many angles.*" I said reminding her of earlier when she had been looking up at me from on her knees and seeing the expectant blush that ever so slightly warmed her skin because of it.

"This radiant yet shy smile…" I said running the pad of my thumb over the seam of her lips, lips that parted slightly, giving me the small glimpse of white from her perfectly straight teeth.

"All of these things, Amelia, and many more as to why you are utterly perfect for me, but do you know what isn't perfect for me…um, pet?" I asked, still luring her in with my tone, one she was falling under, as the soft look upon her face told me so. One I soon robbed her of the second my hands tightened on her wrists and my tone changed to hard and unyielding, as though someone had flipped a switch,

"What isn't perfect is for me to come back here and find the utter perfection I own in you, now a broken, dead and bloody mess at the bottom of the fucking cavern *after being impaled on some fucking stalagmite!*" I hissed in anger making her freeze in my hold. Then before she could get angry herself, she did a curious thing, she stretched her neck up so she could reach my face, one that was currently in her own, dominating her space. Then she ran her own nose along my rough stubble covered jaw and whispered in a soft soothing tone,

"Honey...I'm sorry."

I had just been ready to continue my reprimanding when suddenly all my anger evaporated to dust just with three words spoken. I then found my hold on her loosened, just as my gaze softened to what she would class as tender. Then I gathered her up in my arms, buried my face in her neck and as I squeezed her tight, whispered,

"Don't do it again."

Her delicate hand reached up and started combing her fingers through my hair, scratching slightly at the scalp as she replied,

"Okay, handsome."

This whole thing left me with only one thought lingering on my mind,

By the Gods, I was so fucked!

A short time later we found ourselves in the kitchen with me sat on the countertop, a beer in hand resting in between my parted legs and enjoying the show of Amelia cooking at the stove. I also had to be honest here, but if someone had ever painted this picture to me before labelling it one that would have featured in my future, then I would have punched them for the insult. As let's face it, I was far from fucking mortal normality.

Yet here I was, watching my woman stirring a pot of chilli she had made, all because she had a craving for chilli topped fries with what looked like would soon be loaded with cheese. That was if the near overflowing grater on the plate was anything to go by.

"Okay, just so you know, my chilli fries are amazing." I didn't laugh, as I knew if I didn't she would be curious enough to see what my reaction to this was and look my way. She may not have realised this, but this was something she did often. Which meant that I too found myself often holding back the reaction she wanted.

But this wasn't just so she would turn and look at me. No, it was mainly down to how she would continue to try and make me laugh until she had accomplished her goal. Something that wasn't too hard for her to achieve, as my girl was pretty fucking funny.

Unsurprisingly then, she looked back at me and said,

"Seriously, they will blow your mind." I couldn't stop my lips from twitching this time as I nodded and made an 'mmm' sound, which was all I would offer her now. This time she became more forceful, something that I will mention was a little difficult to take seriously when she was wearing what she was. After she had woken up I had given her time to shower and change, telling her I would be in the living space. The reason being was that I had taken her roughly with my fingers and didn't want to be tempted to do the same with my cock so soon in the shower, as that's what would have happened. So, after grabbing a new t-shirt and smiling to myself as I fingered her used wet panties still in my back pocket, I left her to get herself ready.

This meant that it gave me time to see the full extent of

her unpacking, grinning to myself when I did, for I knew what she was playing at. She had been on a mission to prove a point and thought that by displaying all of her stuff that I would take an aversion to this. Oh, how wrong she was! In fact, by the time she emerged and joined me in the living space, I was currently staring down at the assortment of nail varnish that she had gone so far as to spread out on the table, after it had been in use.

She then asked in a knowing tone,

"Is something the matter?" No doubt expecting me now to express my displeasure. Which is why I looked down at her feet, saw the cute girly shade of pink she had used and said,

"Not at all, it looks good on you." Then I went back to checking emails on my phone when I heard her huff. This was when I granted her my eyes and when I did, I did so laughing.

"What are you wearing?" I asked, still highly amused.

"My pyjamas, I thought they were fitting." I smirked at her, seeing the black T shirt had a cartoon Vampire on the front with bat wings and the line underneath said, 'Mornings Suck'. The pants were also black and were covered in bats and fangs in the same colour as the character on the front of her chest.

She looked fucking adorable.

And she continued looking fucking adorable, even when in the kitchen cooking and trying to convince me she had just made something only a pure genius would make.

"No, no, no, I can see you're not taking me seriously, Lucius," she said with a shake of her head.

"Is that so?" I enquired with a knowing grin, because

five, four, three, two and here it was…she was now coming at me with a large spoon in hand, cupping the other hand underneath in case any chilli dripped. Meaning that as soon as she was within reach, I removed her hand in case she got burned. Then just in that moment as she was looking up at me, over her steamy glasses, I found myself compelled to tell her that I loved her. A sentiment I never got chance to say as she stole the moment from me when she whispered secretively,

"We are talking the unicorn of chilli fries here." At this I could no longer help myself, I threw my head back and roared with laughter.

"Alright then, pet, let's have a taste." Then I took hold of her wrist and guided the spoon to my lips, so I could see for myself if there was strength behind the claim. I had to admit, there most certainly was.

"So, come on, tell me…it's great chilli isn't it…? Now come on, don't hold back," she said acting dramatic by making cute little hand gestures and I moved my beer bottle to the side. Then after a little tug on the wrist I still held, I wrapped my legs around the upper part of her body, trapping her to me whilst holding her arm stretched out to the side. After I had her where I wanted her, I used my gloved hand to tip up her chin and I lowered my neck so I could only just touch her.

After this I whispered the words she wanted to hear but for me, they were words that meant far more than what she would believe,

"The best I ever had."

Shortly after, we were sat at the dining table, eating our 'out of this world, only in the land of unicorns would you find better' (naturally her words) chilli fries and yes, cheese played a very big part in this. But as nice as her cooking was, made even better for experiencing her make it, it was the conversation that was better still.

Finally, I was able to ask her all the questions that over the years of watching her, I had been burning to know. This included everything from her upbringing, to her education, school days, etc. all the way up to working at the museum. Her love for her job was blindingly obvious, and after now getting her unpacked and soon settled, I knew it would be my biggest challenge yet.

Because I knew just from listening to her that Amelia would never be happy or contented just living her life sitting by my side. Or even, *Gods, I cannot believe these words coming from my fucking mind*, playing the little wife. She was too full of life and burning for knowledge. Waiting to experience the next item of history for her to study or one day in hopes of being the one to discover these things for herself.

It was, like most of Amelia's many attributes, an endearing and admirable one. Which meant that I knew if I was to try and dampen that spirit of hers, even just to make it safe and have her be the Chosen One most convenient for me, then it would have been like caging an exotic bird in a dark room for only myself to see. When really the world would have been a loser as well as the bird, who clearly needed to soar to new heights and bask in the sun.

My firebird.

Amelia, in turn, asked very little of my own life, which I

sometimes answered. But after steering the conversation back to her, she was a smart girl and got the hint pretty quickly. Because now wasn't the time and I could chance slipping up, saying something that she could equate to the truth I hid. I knew it couldn't be this way forever, but for right now, then it was the safest way to play it. Because she needed to trust me and only then, when I knew without a doubt she wouldn't try to run from me, that I would start explaining my past.

As for the rest of the evening, it went as followed. Amelia decided that popcorn was to be our dessert, this along with enough candy to eat into a ship's hull like acid. Or so it seemed. To say that my girl had a sweet tooth was a little too tame of a description, for I was thinking that buying a fucking company or buying shares in cane sugar was going to have to be in my future.

So, she popped the corn, the sound echoing in the vast space making her giggle and then the second she reached into the microwave drawer to pick up the steaming bag, that was when I had decided to take over that particular chore. She had laughed and shook her head as if I had done something other than potentially save her from first degree burns.

But then she was extremely clumsy and something I was only now understanding the full extent of, as she proved this fact when different coloured beans spilled over the floor when she opened the bag and, in her words, 'wasn't her fault as the bag had exploded on her'.

Then opening a bag of chips had ended up with half on the countertop, which her solution to this was to swipe an arm along so they fell back into the large bowl. Even her bottle of beer had nearly overflowed when reaching the living space. As I knew just from watching her that it had been shaken around too much. But Gods, she was utterly fascinating to watch. She was like a cute whirlwind of small destructions, as even the most basic of tasks didn't make it to fruition without incident.

Amelia naturally didn't let me pick the movie, which was a blessing, for one, I would have had no clue as to what to choose and secondly, it gave me something to tease her about. And seeing as I was counting my blessings, I could also add on the one where I got to witness her utter excitement when choosing her childhood favorite about some adventurer by the name of Jones.

"This one is the sequel, but you can watch them out of order and this one is my favorite as he has a sidekick in this one called Short Round, an 11-year-old Chinese kid," she said explaining all this to me as she put the disc into the player, one from her own collection. Then she grabbed the remotes and came and sat back down, happily arranging the bowls on the table like a buffet to kill a diabetic, as the disc loaded.

"It's called the Temple of Doom, and other than having spiders…"

"Temple of Doom…as in, Mount Doom?" I asked interrupting her and making her roll her lips inside her mouth, as she usually did when trying not to smile. This was before leaning all her weight into me and saying,

"Yes, but yours is so much prettier now." I couldn't help but laugh at her playfulness, as she had started walking her fingers up my stomach and chest. But then she came to my mouth and with speed I knew she couldn't react in time to, I captured her fingers in my mouth, holding them there with my teeth.

"Oww," she moaned making me grin around them before I let go, as was becoming our usual tease.

"Baby," I whispered softly to which her new reply now was to whisper back,

"Bully." Making me laugh again.

After this the movie started and soon had captured her attention, much to my irritation. However, I too soon got pulled into the story, and was somewhat enjoying it… other than when she had chosen to comment,

"Now why didn't the helicopter have an inflatable dingy I could have landed on?" This naturally made me growl and just before I could snap at her from cursing me with the memory again, she suddenly jumped at me, kissing me before I could open my mouth. This I found easily worked in distracting me from being pissed off and took advantage of the fact.

But by far my favorite part of the night was sitting on the couch, reclining with my feet up and a beer in hand as Amelia was nestled into my side. Granted, she had also made us both into an island surrounded by a junk food ocean, with my legs playing a major part in this, seeing as they were currently being used as a convenient place for her to put a bowl of popcorn along with a smaller bowl of sugar coated E numbers.

Gods, but considering how small she was, she certainly could consume some food. Not that I was complaining, as such food had gifted me the abundance of curves to play with at my leisure. Something I would have been doing now, had I had the freedom to do so. But this was difficult seeing as she continuously had a bowl clutched to her chest for the next thirty minutes.

However, eventually, one by one the bowls disappeared and soon she was leaning enough of her weight against me that I knew she had slipped into a sugar induced coma and was now fast asleep. Of course, what also gave this away was the fact she had stopped explaining the plot as the movie played out, doing so seconds before it actually happened for me to watch. Things like,

'Oh, this is where she is expected to eat monkey brains.' Or 'This is the part with the fireplace and its secret entrance'. Naturally, I had teased her about this too, which ironically ended with her shushing me and tell me to just 'shut up and watch the damn movie'. Something I also teased her about making her fight a grin.

But now she was asleep, I tried to look down at her to see her face but was only granted with the top of her head, as it was resting against my stomach. Her arm was draped across my waist and her fist was gripping onto my T-shirt. This was when I knew that the last few days had definitely started to catch up on her, along with her body now adapting to consuming my blood.

This was something I was hoping to increase as this, combined with my seed, would both start to repair any damaged cells in her body, along with create new, stronger ones that wouldn't degenerate like they did in mortals. It was how I intended on making her immortal. The other perks would be faster healing time, increased speed and strength, but not to the extreme where she would be like one of my own kind. No, this was more like an Olympic mortal athlete.

But all of this would take time before it started to fully take root and the more exchanges we made, the stronger the bond would become. I was simply fortunate enough that there had been only one other who had been gifted my blood and absorbed the Venom of God and that had been her mother.

Now the reasons for this had been fated for she needed this part of me inside her for the prophecy to be fulfilled. For her to be strong enough to survive what she had. But as a rule, and something I had been forced to experience firsthand, was the Venom of God that now lived inside my veins was fused with the soul of the bearer who made the sacrifice. It wasn't ever intended to be passed on, and other than attaching itself to Keira that one time, then it had only ever taken, never given.

Hence the glove I wore.

I felt my left hand, the one in question fisted at my side, whilst with my other arm I held Amelia tighter to me. This was my life now, and this was the hand I had been dealt with…*literally.*

Now all that was left for me to do was spend every day I had with her, protecting her from not only what could happen, but also…

From what already had.

The movie ended shortly after she had fallen asleep and after a death defying moment on a broken rope bridge over a river of crocodiles, all was well in Amelia's 'make believe land' once more. But as far as movies went, it wasn't bad but I did have a feeling this was mainly down to the sleeping form now in my lap. A little sleeping beauty who had unknowingly been turning me on most of the evening.

But for now, well I lifted my slumbering princess in my arms and carried her off to my bed, only realising just how out of it she was when she never made even a murmur. I decided that, although against my wishes, I would keep her in her cute but funny pyjamas so as not to disturb her. I also knew that tonight wasn't the night that I would get to sleep with my cock inside her like I had planned.

But at the very least and for my piece of mind, I located the strip of silk I had used earlier and like then, tied one end around her wrist. The other end however was for me and I wrapped it around my fist a few times.

After this, I shifted her so she was cradled to my body, with her back to my chest and our tied hands closer together. I heard her release a sweet sigh before whispering her own good night to me and I had to say, it was something that made the sweet night even sweeter,

"Now that was a date...best ever."

I tugged her close and whispered back in her ear,

"Most definitely."

I didn't know how long we had been asleep for but when I awoke it took me a moment to realise what it was that had dragged me from my sleep.

The room was like ice.

I frowned in annoyance as I tried to shake off the last spiderwebs of sleep clinging to my mind. But then I thought back to that feeling I had. That niggling in the back of my mind that something wasn't right. This was the first level of dread I felt start to seep into my conscious thoughts and as I reached out for the covers, I knew I was right to feel this way. Especially when my first concern was focused on Amelia's comfort, making me start to pull the covers up, intent on covering her. This was then when the second level of dread hit and hit me fucking hard as I realised there wasn't another body in the bed with me.

I was now alone.

I bolted upright the moment the third and final level hit me. As I had tugged hard, knowing I should have felt resistance, only when I hadn't, it made me look down in utter blind rage.

A rage that now saw a length of silk that should have kept her shackled to me.

I roared in anger, for it was clear to see…

Our ties had been cut.

CHAPTER TWENTY-FOUR

AMELIA

BLOOD AND SNOW

Burning sand.

That's all I felt scorching at my feet.

Each step an agonizing feat of strength to continue on. I don't know how long they had made me walk, or what torture they intended to inflict once we got there. Once we arrived at an unknown destination. Just how far into the desert were we to walk? Those of which I once called friends, my brothers on horseback with water at their saddles. I had long ago given up my pleas, trying to get them to understand the truth.

Trying to tell them that nothing was as it seemed.

It was all a lie.

But he would save me, wouldn't he? There was still time yet, wasn't there? Surely, he would not let me die in vain, not after all I had sacrificed for him, only now to join him in his own. For death was only the beginning, that was what he had told me when he set this plan into motion. But nothing was spoken of my brothers turning on me, calling me traitor. Was this to be my end also?

Why, God? Why this burning sand, sand that had long ago stripped the skin from my feet. I had fallen, many times, but miles ago discovered the pain of doing so far worse than that of walking. Maybe this was simply my test. A test of will, of God's mighty plan that I must still find trust in. Maybe my second life was waiting for me out there, in the haze of baked earth rising from the ground like Hell was merely on the horizon taunting me.

A test between good and evil.

But the biggest question of all, if his Lord didn't save me, like he promised, then...

Which one would I choose as they spilled my blood?

"We are here." This was the voice of two, both man and woman speaking over the other until each became an echo of the truth. I looked up in that moment to see where 'here' was and found myself looking at a dead and twisted tree in the distance. It was the only one in a sea of nothingness and there hanging from one of its thickest branches was a body swaying on a rope.

No, not swaying.

Thrashing.

"Oh, Gods no!" The second I heard my own voice, one belonging now to the panic I felt, was when I finally started to come out of this nightmare. I then started running, despite the pain, I ran and ran for I knew who it was fighting for their life at the end of that rope. But the further and faster I

ran, the further away the image of the tree was being dragged back. As if the whole scene was being plucked from existence, pulled back into the oblivion waiting to consume it whole. That was when suddenly the earth around it started to crack.

"NO!" I screamed, this time seeing the ground opening up like a giant mouth of Hell and with it the tree tilted, its roots not strong enough to keep as part of this world any longer. The desperate cries of a man as he faced the mouth of Hell was the most chilling and haunting sound I had ever heard, for it was one I knew.

It was one I loved.

Because I knew now what it was that I was laying witness to.

This was the death of Judas. The death of a mortal man who Christ forgot to save. A sacrifice chosen in the name of God only to end in renouncing a faith, making that sacrifice in vain. For nothing could save him from his fate now…

Not now the Devil had claimed him.

I screamed as the earth swallowed him up and the tree with him, before nothing more than a mound of dead earth offered up one single root remaining. A branch in the desert like the twisted hand of life desperate to survive, reaching up at the Heavens and asking it why.

Why had God forsaken one of His loyal children?

"No, no, no…Lucius…my heart," I whispered as I lowered my head, for it was done and there was nothing I could do left to save him. But then as I looked down and saw the bloody footprints in the sand they began to change. First my burnt feet became smaller, starting off as that of a man before morphing into the smaller feet of a woman.

My feet.

Then the very burning began to fade, and an icy chill stabbed at them as if suddenly they had been plunged into a bucket of snow, being forced to stay there until barely any feeling was left.

Nothing but the cold.

This was when the sand began to be swept away by a wind that started at my feet before the sands of time began to disappear into the snowy dust that now whipped at my face. This was when I finally saw the truth. For I opened my eyes again and lost the image of the past altogether. Lost the image of death that seemed to cling to me.

The death of the man I loved.

But then that wasn't right, for he hadn't yet become that man and I wasn't meant to witness his rebirth.

No one was.

I knew in that moment I hadn't really been there, not at all, but the pain I felt was real. For the second I had woken from my dream I was to realise the horror of what I was doing. I knew this when I realised my hands weren't empty as they should have been. And instead of sheets at my feet, there was nothing but blood and snow. I looked up in my panic and now what replaced the flickering image of where the tree had once been was a cloaked figure in the distance. A crimson silhouette luring me to my own death and in doing so, making me the bearer of destruction, for down in my hands was none other than…

The box.

But I had woken up too soon. I knew this when I heard the growl of anger start to shake the trees around me. It was the dead of night with only the moon beaming against the snow, lighting the way. A path that was clear of all life as if waiting for me all this time to set a foolish foot down on it. A pathway framed by the dense forest, one dark and ominous. One where glowing eyes of blood could be seen watching me from low and crouched positions to the ground. A growl, a snarl and rumble as I continued on before forcing myself to stop.

"Come to me!" A voice I knew demanded and I looked up to see the cloaked figure too far a distance away to have been the one to say it. So, I turned around and looked back, a line of bloody footprints in the snow leading the way, and a single hissed curse ahead of me was all I heard before I suddenly started running.

Running back to where I knew Lucius was searching for me.

"No!" was my only warning, from the figure in the trees and then a forceful order issued.

"Go get her!" This was when I knew that the chase was on and it was one from both ends, for I now had a pack of wild demonic wolves at my back and a Vampire King at my front. The question was,

Which would get to me first?

I held the box as tight as I could and ignored the searing pain in my feet, pushing myself despite my agony, using my fear as a weapon to drive me forward. I could now feel them closing in on me but instead of taking me down they meant to cut me off. But I could see it now, the clearing up ahead. The vast white space beyond it, like a desert of snow. It was the garden, the silent garden where no one can hear you scream. It was right up ahead, my own blood leading me back there. If I could only just make it, then maybe I had a chance.

Yes, yes, I was going to make it, despite the blur of black I could see at my sides, overtaking me. I just needed a little bit more in me, to give it everything I had!

I just made the edge, even if now I was seeing the snarling shadows surrounding me, the wolves starting to cut off my escape.

'No!' I opened my mouth, trying to force the scream out but having the garden steal it from me. This was the second I felt both my ankles being grabbed, tipping my world as I went down hard, landing on the box and hurting my chest. I reached out, now scrambling in the snow that merely crumbled in my freezing fingers for I wore nothing but what Lucius had laid me down in to sleep last night. But then that's when I saw it, that single piece of silk tied around my wrist, one knotted there. Its length, and one that had only hours before connected me to Lucius, now cut.

This is what gave me the strength needed to suddenly scream at the top of my lungs, claiming my fear back from the garden.

"LUCIUS!"

A mighty roar was my only reply, but it seemed too far away. Was it him, or would he fail to save me just as I had failed to save him in my dream?

After this I felt myself being dragged backwards, and I twisted my body around, trying to kick out at what it was, or should I say who, for the cloaked figure was now walking back into the forest dragging me behind them. So, rather than let this happen, I kicked out again, this time making contact, and I wasn't the only one crying out in pain from my torn feet.

The cloaked figure grunted at the kick and momentarily let go of me. So, I quickly started to scramble away in the snow with one hand desperately trying to gain momentum in order to get to my feet. The box tightly held with the other arm, cradling it to my chest, knowing that I would die protecting it!

However, the one who brought me here wasn't done with me yet, as I felt a body start crawling over me, trying to drag me under it. It grabbed at my clothes, my skin, pulling at me and climbing up over me trying to pry the box from underneath me.

"No!" I shouted on a grunt when the person above started to gain enough of a grasp on me that I was suddenly flipped onto my back. Now straddling my waist was the cloaked figure, glowing eyes looming down at me in the darkness of the hood. I didn't know what else to do so I reached out, grabbed a fist full of snow and then bolted up quickly and slapped a hand in the center of that darkness. Now stuffing the face full of snow. The figure, who I knew now to be a woman, started screaming, falling backwards off me before scrambling to her feet, crying out like acid had touched her face.

I frowned in confusion at the reaction and it was only when I looked down at my hand did I open my fingers to reveal the bloody snow. I looked back and saw the handful I had grasped had been from one of my bloody footprints.

"The blood of Kings is in you!" the cloaked figure hissed as one slim hand started to cradle her face, now flashing in between one of beauty and youth and the one of death. The

same one I had seen in my first dream the night before. That was when I realised,

"You're the witch!" She hissed at me but suddenly I was assaulted by reason. It must have been the connection she had used to get me to come here. One, that to achieve it, had to be open both ways, telling me now something important about her.

"You're a witch caught between life and death. That's why you want the box, because the soul you sold will be paid if you don't," I said not fully understanding how I knew all this but like I said, feeling the connection. She snarled at me again and told me,

"Blood must be paid...*to us all.*" Then she looked up at the sky quickly and the second she saw something she obviously feared, she shouted out an order in another language and ran into the forest, her red cloak quickly disappearing into the darkness.

But I couldn't think about her now, as I had something else to fear. I turned in time to see a rush of about twenty or so demonic wolves all running at me. She had given them the order to kill me and I knew there was no use in trying to outrun them, I would never survive.

Never survive the hungry beasts snarling at the thought of me. Drool dripping down, overflowing jaws full of oversized fangs and multiple rows of teeth, watering with just the thought of tearing into my flesh and ripping me limb from limb.

In that moment, instead of facing death, I looked down at the reason for it, cradled in my arms. It was a noble cause and my only hope was that Lucius was proud of me for trying to save his people. Trying to save my mother.

Trying to save him.

"Goodbye, Lu...*what the Hell?*" I uttered in disbelief as the second I placed both my hands on the box it started to vibrate in my hold, shaking as if trying to get at something. But then my mind was ripped from the box and back to the danger racing my way. Because this time it was no longer just the sound of beasts growling and snarling my way. No, now it was the sound of the sky splitting open as a roar so loud tore through the night, creating it from only one place of origin...

Hell.

This was when a demonic figure suddenly dropped from the sky just as the first wolf leapt and lunged for me. This turned out to be a mistake, its last in fact. As the second it did, it quickly found itself caught in the grasp of a Devil on Earth!

Mighty wings spread out, and it truly was a demonic sight to be seen. Leathery skin hung from two enormous horns like some Asian water buffalo, as each was over a metre in length. Long skeletal fingers looked hooked on to each section of the horn and ran down the length of the wing, bending at the many knuckle joints, creating a shape similar to a bat's wing. The end of each of these bone fingers was a razor curled talon that looked the size of my hand, as though they could do serious damage.

The rest of his body seemed bigger somehow with what bare muscle I could see tensed and ready for the fight ahead. But his entire being seemed to have a demonic presence surrounding him, like a pulsating power just waiting to be absorbed and used with the promise of blood as its payment.

He stretched out his wings as far as they would go the

second I saw the other wolves now trying to get around him. To try and get to me. But he had just blocked off the sight, creating a barrier between him and me. After this I heard the deep whine of an animal in pain and watched as Lucius raised up the wolf in his demonic hand, before snapping its neck in one sickening crunch of bone.

Lucius looked as though he had brought with him the wrath of the Gods, for the second the wolves all thought to dive onto him as one force, I screamed in panic,

"No, don't hurt him!" At this Lucius looked behind at me, over his shoulder and the burning crimson in his eyes was like staring into the pits of Hell. His handsome face was still there but warped into something truly sinister. Black around his eyes, like the demon had infected the host and was holding him prisoner until the deadly deed was done.

But then he grinned at me, the length of his fangs growing and this time when he spoke, it belonged solely to his demon,

"This is when you run, pet."

CHAPTER TWENTY-FIVE

A DEMON'S WINGS

"*This is when you run, pet.*" The moment his demon said this, he erupted into flames, and the earth beneath me started to shake with the power of his rage. The snow on the ground vibrated around me as if it too feared the wrath of a God.

But he didn't need to tell me twice and I managed to scramble to my blood soaked feet and start running as fast as my injuries would let me. I did so to the sound of murder behind me, as one by one the demonic beasts fell to the sound of their dying brethren before them. A chorus of howling pain before the very last whine of death could claim each of them.

In the end I could go no further and fell to my knees first before the rest of my body followed. My glasses were flaked in snow, surprising me that they had even survived the fight with the witch. But then, I guess in getting me, she had needed me to be able to see, which still made me question, how had she accomplished it? How had I managed to get the box for her, even with the obvious control she had held over my mind to do so? Making me now question,

How had no-one seen me?

I shook these questions from my tired mind and curled in on myself, pulling my knees up and hugging the box to my chest, creating a cocoon of flesh around it. I then opened my eyes and looked through the flakes of snow on my lenses, to find in the distance the fight was quickly coming to an end. And to be honest, it didn't look like much of a fight in the first place.

More like an eradication of one's enemies.

The demonic wolves weren't any match for Lucius, and each time I opened my eyes, I saw something new. One wolf caught in both his hands, just before he literally ripped it in half. This before he threw away each end of the now very dead wolf until the two pieces skidded to a stop in the snow, leaving a long crimson road leading to their lifeless body parts.

Then on another flicker of my eyes opening, one wolf was currently being set alight and ran into the forest howling in pain, causing it to set the trees on fire. But Lucius, unconcerned by this, just raised a hand in the air and made a fist that instantly extinguished the flames. My eyes closed again, for longer periods this time, as the next eye opening revealed more bodies on the ground, now with their fur coated with blood and matted with their spilled insides.

Again, came another wave of exhaustion as my eyes fluttered shut but still my mind was not ready to give up on consciousness and forced my heavy lids to open. However, this time he turned to face me with the very last wolf still in his demonic hold. Then when finding my near sleeping form in the snow, he merely ripped the head from the once squirming form in his hands and threw the pieces aside.

Then he took a determined step towards me.

It had to be said that it was a truly terrifying sight, no matter that I knew who he was to me. Or more importantly in that moment, *who I was to him.*

But that didn't dismiss the fact that to see what essentially looked like a version of the Devil walking towards me was a sight that stole the air from my lungs in a gasp of fright. A sight, which admittedly this time was why I closed my eyes. Because I didn't fear what he would do to me, I feared what he would think I'd done.

Now finding me lying here with the box in my arms, one I had no knowledge of even stealing this time. Well, let's just say that given my prior history, it was a sight that could have been taken as me trying to escape him yet again. And what if he just believed that the witch had been watching and waiting for me to make my move?

So naturally, I didn't want him to think this. Because I hadn't wanted to leave. Not for a single second since being here. Since being with him. Yesterday had been one of the best days of my life, our simple but sweet date night especially. Because in that single day he had proved to me that even if those moments were to be the rare ones, then they were worth spending a lifetime of unknown factors just at the promise of those alone.

That was what Lucius had given me.

A glimpse into the life he was willing to build for me. One done out of love and care for my fear of losing the old one I had built. I had tested him yesterday and yet no matter how I had pushed, he had simply continued to give.

And now he must have thought that his reward for that was my attempted escape. All I could hope for was that he would believe the truth. One that I tried to tell him when I barely had enough strength to whisper his name,

"Lucius."

I then forced my eyes to open and watched as each time I did he was closer and closer in a flicker of heavy lids. But then the last time I did, I found boots at my body and darkness overshadowing the moon, casting me into the ashes of the night. This was all from his wings that blocked out the light, and the sight above me was one that should have had me quaking in fear like before. But instead, I simply let my head fall back into the snow as the last of my strength left me, the box now safe, rolled from my frozen fingers. I could now only make out a blur of motion as Lucius picked up the box, seeing for himself how I had protected it.

If I'd had the energy in that moment, I would have asked him if he was proud, but then why should he be, he probably thought I was trying to steal it again. Gods, but all I really wished for right now was for him to have said something.

Anything to stop this inner turmoil!

But instead, I simply felt myself being scooped up from the snow and hoisted up in his arms before he rose to his full height, the box being put back in my care. Then, without a word, he turned around and started walking back towards the silent garden as if it too had the power to steal his voice. In fact, it was only when I felt the whoosh of his wings folding to his back, tucking themselves in tight, that I opened my eyes again.

"Luc...ius." I uttered his name again and this time a rumbled growl was heard before his demon spoke to me.

"Save your strength, little human, you are safe now." I did as he said and didn't try to speak again. Not that I think at this point anything would have come out, as my lips wouldn't stop quivering as I started to shake in his hold, making him hiss a curse. Then suddenly he snarled,

"It can't fucking wait!" Then he dropped to his knees, barely even jarring me. I opened my eyes to see his enormous wings open and suddenly they were pushed forward, cocooning us now in his impressive wingspan. Only then did I feel him lower me and I released a sigh as this time it wasn't on to the freezing snow but instead on to warm skin. I shuddered again at the feel and the difference in temperature, then I felt a callused hand come to my face and with little pressure it was lifted up to his face. One now bathed in darkness as most of his demonic features were lost in shadow, all except for the burning Hell in his eyes.

"You will drink...yes?" The deep grate and depth of his demon's voice speaking to me in what was a soft and tender way, was astounding, as the two combined made me suck in an astonished breath.

"My mortal, you will drink," he declared then in a more forceful tone before raising his wrist to his lips and biting into the flesh, making a sickening sound. This was when I could see the difference in his hands, one that was barely the hint of what it usually was. But it was his left hand that had drastically changed. For it now looked consumed in a metal gauntlet this time, as long gone was the leather. No, this was a black armoured glove that looked forged in Hell, tipped

with deadly talons I wanted to stay clear of, fearing by just one touch they would sheer my skin right off.

"Drink" The sound of his order dragged my eyes from the hand that was essentially a deadly weapon. I didn't speak, for fear of disappointing him, so instead nodded before he placed his wrist to my lips. His uncovered hand was that of a demon, longer than before and rough, hard skin taking the place of the manly hands of Lucius that I loved to feel on my skin.

But I knew it was still him. He had simply given way to his demon side and to be honest, it was quite exhilarating being able to witness it. Even more startling to be able to witness its kindness and caring side, for it obviously wanted to heal me before all else.

So here I was, wrapped up in the wings of a demon I belonged to and at the first taste of his blood I couldn't help but moan in pleasure. It just rippled through me, a warmth unlike any other. A rumbling sound started from Lucius' demon and I realised that he too was experiencing the same pleasure I was.

In fact, I worried that I would take too much as the warmth and feeling started to come back into my body, so I started to pull away. But then that pleasing rumble turned into a snarl of disapproval and his metal hand suddenly came up to touch me, making me flinch back from it. He stopped it from coming any closer, pausing with it in midair and for a moment, the burning red in his eyes disappeared meaning he had closed his eyes.

"I won't hurt you, little one," his demon told me in obvious strain and with wide eyes, I nodded after first pushing my glasses up my nose, ones that were blurring the

edges of my vision from dirt. He too nodded again before reaching out, this time without me flinching away from him. He then cupped the back of my head with the demonic glove being as gentle as if it hadn't even been there and then he nodded down at his wrist before telling me,

"You're not done. Now drink."

"But you will need..." I started to whisper, stopping when he gave me a pointed look and growled more forcefully this time,

"Drink, girl" So I latched my lips around his dripping wound and did as he said for me to do, which was drink him down until he deemed it was enough. This took a while, but he was right, once he pried his bloody wrist from my lips, I felt amazing. The pain in my feet was gone and the cold that wracked my body was nothing but a mere chill. Then he licked at his own wrist and I watched as his skin started to knit back together now that his head was angled enough to let in a small beam of moonlight.

After this he gathered me up close, amazing me that he could be so careful with his taloned tip fingers. His wings uncurled from around us at the same time he rose to his feet, lifting me once more in his arms. Then he walked down the length of the garden, and this time he did so with my arms around him and my head buried in his neck.

The neck of my Demon.

The Demon that saved me.

The Demon I loved.

CHAPTER TWENTY-SIX

WASHING AWAY MY DEMONS

L ucius carried me back inside, which turned out to be through a maze of tunnels and hallways, after first being faced with a narrow turret of steps to contend with. This turned out to be the only way into the garden, which made me shudder just thinking about me making this journey without even knowing it.

I took one look at the small space and reached up with a hand and tapped him on the cheek to get his attention.

"I could walk," I offered in a quiet voice, to which his demon scoffed, a deep grunt made at the back of his throat, that sounded more like a pissed off bull. So, I retracted the offer with a small,

"Or maybe not." However, his answer to the steps had been a rumbled demand for me to hold onto him at the horns as he shifted me around to facing him. But then he could see the trepidation in my eyes as I was unsure if I really should or not.

"Go on, little one, now do as you are told," his Demon said, his voice trying to take on a more gentle tone, making me do as he asked. I was even surprised to find them so smooth, and I gripped on in between where his wing fingers were curled around at different points. I decided to avoid them in case they moved, and it freaked me out as I didn't think screaming in fright right now was going to help in keeping this beast tame.

But once he felt me gripping on he then lifted me further up his body, holding me tight to him after first taking the box from my lap. Then, with only one hand he held me there, with me now clinging onto his front and my legs wrapped firmly around his waist. Meaning that now he was free to walk us both down the narrow steps. I had to admit it felt like such an intimate position, that I couldn't help but bury my head in his neck, my lips peppering little kisses there that made his chest rumble, like he was tiger purring.

So, with my legs squeezing him tight and his one hand on my ass, I clung on until we reached the bottom where before I could even ask what now, I was tapped on the leg as a silent command to let go. Which I did expecting to find the ground beneath my feet. But instead found my legs quickly swept to the side so I was once again being carried as I had been before.

I had to admit, that I would have loved to have seen what we had looked like together. Me in the arms of Lucius' Demon, with my arms still clinging on around his neck and held tight to his chest like I was the most precious thing to him in the world.

Like I was his to protect.

It wasn't long until we were soon at the three arched

entrance and instead of bothering with any opening or bridge, he simply walked to the center arch and to the small ledge beyond it. Then with only a deep and guttural demand,

"Hold on," he stepped from the ledge falling a little way so he was clear to release his wings. I wasn't scared of heights but even that made me cry out in fright. But then he started lifting us thanks to the large and effective drag of his wings, capturing the air beneath them. He flew us back up and over the ridge of stone that had the tunnel running through it that led straight into his home.

A home that quickly came into view before he started to fly us down, now aiming for where the carved stone bathroom was. He landed with a soft thud of heavy boots against the stone, before folding his wings back so he could fit us both inside.

Once inside he lowered me down, but not to my feet, as I would have thought, seeing as there was nowhere else he could take me. Or so I believed, as I ended up being lowered into the hot springs bath that was a constant stream of hot water that smelled like natural minerals. This made me hiss as the heat licked at my skin making it itch.

"You will get used to it," he rumbled and I nodded before his arms slipped free from my body. Then he turned to leave and in that moment the vulnerability of the night hit me. Meaning I suddenly called out,

"Don't go...*please."* I then looked over my shoulder at him to see him now frozen in the doorway, his back tensed with his wings tightly pulled in, doing so in what I swear was a flinch.

Finally, he said,

"I need a moment, Amelia." His voice was tense and

strained, for this time it was Lucius managing to push through. That was when I knew what he meant. He needed time to come back from his demon side. Which was when I said shyly,

"I don't mind." At this there was a rumbling sound that got louder and if I had to equate it to anything I would have said it sounded this time like a demonic purr.

"I can't get too comfortable here." This time it was a strained mix of the two voices that spoke as one, making me swallow harder knowing what it was that he was saying. If he let his demon continue to take charge then Lucius was in danger of losing all control and never getting it back. Gods, but I had heard rumors once that this had actually happened to my father and it was said that my mother saved him. How she did this I was unsure, but the way Pip had told the story she had made it sound like it was achieved by reminding my father of his humanity. Of course, the story also said that to achieve this she first had to go to Hell to do it.

So, for my mum, the saying 'to Hell and back' was a literal meaning when it came to doing anything for my dad and oh boy, did he know it!

"I understand," I told him softly and then turned my head away, not wanting to watch my brutal saviour walking away from me. Not when I didn't know when it was that I would ever see him like this again.

But then I felt his presence still dominating the room and just before I turned to check, I felt a hand reach for my chin. My face was turned towards him and I found him bending on one knee so he could reach my level. Then he tipped my head back even further, with his demonic features much clearer now. It showed the same handsome face of Lucius, only one made to look more deadly. More sinister and dangerous. But even now, with eyes burning through the darkness that swirled under his skin, he still managed to look tenderly down at me.

I felt his taloned thumb come to my lips, but only the callused pad caressed down them, pulling them open slightly. I wanted to kiss him so badly in that moment, but I didn't know if he would let me. Now he seemed to be holding himself back. And I knew I was right when he said,

"Such sweet temptation." Then he skimmed the back of his talon down my neck, continuing down until running it over my breast. One free of a bra but still covered by the cotton of my t-shirt. I sucked in a quick breath at the feel of it flick over my nipple dangerously making it hard and erect. He was staring down at me and I watched as the lust burning in the eyes, those of a demon, seemed to ignite. I knew he wanted me and Hell, I wanted him, even like this!

But just before I was about to make that step towards telling him. He released a heavy grumbled sigh before looking back into my eyes and cupping my cheek.

Then he said,

"I thank you for the gift you bestow." He rose back to his feet and just before he left, I had to know,

"What gift?" I quickly asked him. To which he told me on a soft rumble,

"The gift of you." Then he bowed his head to me before he was gone, this time having no choice but to watch as he walked away, leaving me with a single tear to fall.

A tear for my brutally sweet Demon.

I don't know how long it was before I jolted awake next, but I found myself still in the bath and also dressed, with my pyjamas clinging to me. I had done nothing in here, like clean my body or my hair. I had simply watched my Demon saviour leave and then silently cried asking myself why.

The gift of me.

That was why.

Lucius had said some beautiful things to me in the past but I was startled with the knowledge that the most beautiful of all would come from his Demon.

But now, I felt my body being shifted forward and Lucius' gentle voice was at my back as he said,

"Time to let me in, pet." So, I shifted forward with his help and then once he too was sat in the bath, he guided me by the shoulders until my back was flush with his chest. Then he playfully tugged at my wet top and teased,

"Bathing whilst dressed, how very old fashioned of you." I would have chuckled had my mind not been weighted down by all the emotions I clearly didn't know how to process.

"Hey…" Lucius called now turning me to face him and the second he looked down at my face he knew something wasn't right.

"Sweetheart…" Yep and this was all it took! Just hearing this sweet endearment was all that was needed before I opened the gates and let my own Demons out.

"I am so sorry!" I shouted and threw my arms around him as the tears started to flow.

"Amelia, why…why are you sorry, sweetheart?" he asked, his tone worried and above all sincere.

"I swear I didn't try and steal it this time, I don't even

know how it happened! One minute we were watching Indy kick ass in that temple and then I was in bed with you. I don't even know how I got it, or where from! And then I was on the rooftop garden from my dream…but I swear, *I swear to you, Lucius,* I wasn't trying to run, I wasn't trying to run from you…*I promise you!"* I said in a rush and he just silently let me until it was clear I had said enough. Then he pulled the back of my head to his chest and held me there before he told me tenderly,

"I know that, sweetheart. None of this was your fault, *I know this…"* He said this last part in a whispered promise before telling me,

"But I have to confess, that hearing it from you warms my heart." I then pulled back and he let me look up at him before he used both thumbs to wipe away my irrational tears. One hand in particular now back to being covered in leather.

"I love you," I told him making him take a moment to close his eyes before he demanded in a strained voice,

"Say it again." So, I crawled further up his bare chest, kissing my way up his skin from where he had been holding my head and said more firmly this time,

"I love you."

"Again," was yet again his firm command.

"I love you," I said this time with a smile in my tone as I reached his neck, kissing my way to his jaw.

"Again," he gritted out and this time I reached up over his lips when I whispered,

"I love you, Vampire."

Then he crushed his mouth to mine with a possessive hand at the back of my head, holding me captured to his lips. Our kiss was one of pure desperation this time, as the only time we broke our connection was when my top was dragged up over my head. This before being tossed back in the water with a slap. At the same time my hands were busy freeing my legs and once they were, I sat astride Lucius with the aid of his hands gripping my hips. This meant that we both lowered me down after I first took hold of his hard length in my hand, lining him up at my entrance.

"You're fucking mine!" he growled, swiftly impaling me down on his cock. The reaction to this was simultaneous as we both sounded out our pleasure at the connection. His on a hissed curse and mine letting my head fall back to groan at the ceiling. Then I started to move my hips, something his hands on my ass encouraged with each lift as I took him inside me over and over again. My cries of pleasure growing louder and louder the more my orgasm built. Because like this, he was so deep, oh so deliciously deep it was almost too hard to take. But even this thought ended in driving my lust to maddening depths, as I wanted to be used by him. The thought of belonging to him, his plaything, his lover, his pretty doll he called Goddess, all of it I fucking loved! And because he knew it, knew this dirty side to my lust, he added to it by nodding down to my breasts before demanding,

"Offer yourself to me," he all but snarled and again the order only managed to sink me further into his sinful domination of my body. Enough that I did so without making him even wait a second for it. Now reaching down to cup my breast with both hands and like he said, I offered it to his waiting teeth.

I felt the sting instantly as he started biting it, rolling it in between his teeth and just before it got too much to bear he would soothe the sting with a roll of his tongue. This before sucking me in deep. This combination continued as did my riding on his cock, which unsurprisingly meant it wasn't long before I was throwing my head back and coming over his shaft. My core contracting around him as I lived and breathed through the waves of pleasure that assaulted me.

Gods, it was nothing short of glorious!

But then Lucius hadn't yet finished with me and cared little for the mess we were making in his bathroom as small waves crashed over the end of the bath, splashing onto the floor. No, now with my body near spent of energy, I was left with nothing but pleasure and the need to hold on. Lucius then tore his mouth from my nipple before snagging me at the back of my neck, to yank me hard to his lips, first for a demanding kiss and then for something more. He then fisted my hair and tugged my head to one side roughly, telling me on a growl,

"I fucking love this soul I own!" Then his fangs emerged, no longer slow and in a show of strength but one of desperation for his next meal...*me*. His head disappeared into my neck as he buried his fangs there, and I was crying out at the rush of sexual energy the act forced me to endure. He sucked harder and harder all the while still pumping his cock into me, but before long, even this it wasn't enough, for he still wanted more.

I knew this when he grabbed my ass with both hands and stood, walking me now through the water towards the wall at the far end. Then he pushed us both through the waterfall until we were both against the wall. And now being firmly trapped between his solid frame and against the smooth rock at my back he was free to power into me with greater speed. This time he removed his fangs from my neck and pushed my breast up as far as it would go so he could get his feast from somewhere else. He then sank his fangs around my nipple, and started sucking harder at what blood he could get.

The rain of water over his shoulder, along with the feel of his cock stroking my every nerve that mattered and powerful pain at my nipple, Gods, but it was intoxicating! To the point I nearly feared what was coming, for I knew it would be almost too much to bear. It felt as if it had the power to tear me apart and break me beyond repair.

But then his roar came in the form of a demand,

"You will come! Come for me...COME FOR YOUR MASTER!" his demonic bellowing was enough to allow myself to get past my fears and let go completely. I did this to the deafening sound of his own powerful release and this time when I screamed my own, I did it with his name coming from my lips,

"LUCIUS!" And at this I came and came and continued on and on, until I didn't think it would ever stop. It was like a continuous motion and the only thing keeping it going was Lucius and his control over me and my body. It was only when all motion stopped and I felt myself relax in his hold to the point I would have drowned had he not been holding me, for I had no strength.

This was when we both knew that he had taken too much from me, but I didn't care. Not after what I had just experienced. The fucking Heaven of it all! And not when I felt his hand smooth back my hair after first bringing us back through the waterfall.

"Gods, I love you, Amelia," he whispered down to me and then without even having the strength to open my eyes, I

felt his wrist for the second time tonight being pressed to my lips,

"Now drink, my love." I did as I was told, but to be honest, I had little choice when I felt his thumb pull down at my chin making my mouth open so he could fill it with his lifeblood dripping straight past my lips. I drank him down, swallowing as he fed me his blood, doing so now to make me stronger. And all the while praising me for being his good girl. For drinking down his blood like he wanted me to.

And suddenly through the haze, that was when it hit me. What the witch had meant.

Why my blood had affected her.

Because it wasn't just my blood was it?

No, it was the…

Blood of Kings.

CHAPTER TWENTY-SEVEN

BLOOD OF KINGS

A little time later and I was being placed down on the sofa wrapped in a fluffy black bathrobe by Lucius. He originally wanted to put me in bed. But after a little shake of my head, telling him without words that I wasn't ready for that, he understood. Especially as I knew what was coming. He didn't say it, but I knew just from the hard lines of his jaw that he was about to tell me something he didn't want to.

So, I beat him to it, making it easier on him.

"It's okay, I know you have to go." His gaze softened and he lowered to one knee before me, reminding me of his demon earlier. Both of which were a powerful sight to behold, for a powerful being like Lucius, well he didn't kneel for just anyone.

"Tell me that you want me to stay and I will," he said fervently bringing his forehead to mine, holding himself there for long seconds.

"You need to go and be king," I whispered back knowing it was true. His people needed to know what had just happened. Orders needed to be given and demands needed to be made.

After all, Lucius was King, and I knew this. A role that, unlike many foolishly believed, wasn't an easy one. Your freedom came secondary to your people and your needs were often left behind in the shadows of others. I had seen this too many times before when growing up. But I had also learned from it the strength that a good soulmate could provide. Even in just a knowing nod granted from my mum, that said so much. It said, 'go on and be king, we will still be here, loving you as you are.' Which helped soothe the soul of any guilt that I knew my dad had, more often than not, felt to his core.

So right now, it was what Lucius needed. And after all, he had put me before all others by giving me what I needed first...*his care.* That in itself I knew was huge, so this was the very least that I could do in return. Even though I knew that with only a word from me and he would have stayed.

So, I let him rise to his feet without a word of protest and I watched as he was about to pick up the damn box from the table. One that he intended to take back to wherever it had been before I had unknowingly stolen it. This was when I stopped him.

"I would like to examine it again, if you don't mind." He raised a brow at me in question, so I told him,

"The witch, she said something, and I know it's probably nothing, but I just wanted to be sure I hadn't missed anything." Lucius looked unsure at first, making me ask,

"Can anyone get to me in here?" And it was a valid

question as the witch had been powerful enough to make me take the damn box to her and right under Lucius' nose, which I know must have been a blow to his ego.

"No, I have taken precautions against it happening again, as for anyone getting in here, it is impossible," he said sounding certain and rightly so, annoyed at it being able to happen at all.

"Then it should be okay...right?"

"Alright, I will leave it for the moment, but only for you to examine...*yes, Amelia?*" I nodded knowing what he was secretly saying, behave and don't get into trouble. And really could I blame him?

"I won't be long and have stationed my people at all exits that surround this part of the castle, they won't enter unless you permit them to...okay?" he told me in a serious tone.

"Okay, so scream if I'm in trouble and then shout, 'welcome in'...got it," I teased.

"Amelia." He hummed my name in soft reprimand and I said,

"Aww come on, if I don't make jokes then I will cry and if memory serves me right, I already did the girly crying thing already." At this Lucius gave me a gentle smile before coming back to me, granting me a kiss goodbye on the top of my head.

"Go on, honey, I will be fine, I promise. Now go and be your kick ass king self." Now at this he really grinned, and he tipped my head back so I was looking up at him. Then he caressed the backs of his fingers down my cheek and told me,

"You will make a fierce and glorious queen, Amelia..." Then his hand trailed away, and I was left to watch his back as he walked away. Then I watched as he released his wings, this time with his angel on glorious display. For now the demonic skin stretched between taloned fingers was replaced by the burnt sunset colours of the phoenix coating every one of his feathers.

But just before launching himself up to into the air he looked back over at me and finished that sentence, shocking me now to my core with…

"My queen…when I soon make you my wife."

I don't know how long it was I sat there for, still staring at the place he had been standing when he told me that he intended to soon make me his wife, but it felt like an age ago. Had he been serious? I mean, in a relationship it surely wasn't a usual thing for the man to joke about that type of thing…*was it?*

"Oh, Gods, Fae, what are you even thinking!" I said scolding myself aloud. For starters, this was Lucius we were talking about, so I think it was safe to say that all normal relationship rules went up in a puff of smoke and sucked out the window.

But marry me?

Did this mean what he had said at the side of the road had been real?

"Okay, time to focus here Fae, starting with the box that is constantly trying to get you killed, kidnapped or most definitely injured," I said talking to myself as I often did when I was alone.

So, with this in mind, I picked up the box and like I

always did, ran through all the obvious text carved there and all the text that whoever had made it had tried to keep hidden. It was like a network of information you couldn't really see but knew was there. All of it interlocking and telling a story, but only when read in the right order and well in this case, there was what looked like a million ways to tell it!

Or more like in our case, a warning needing to be told.

It spoke of what lay inside having the power to destroy all Vampire life, that much had been clear enough to read. But with that also came a million questions. Like what did it mean, was there some kind of weapon inside or was it like the ark in Indiana Jones that basically killed everyone who looked at it?

(Conveniently, so Indy didn't have to)

But most importantly, what was it that the witch had spoken of, about blood. She had said that blood had to be paid to all of us and I wondered now if she had been referring to Lucius. Maybe to the blood he gifted when making one of his turned. Did she believe his blood was owed? Owed to who, to all he had turned?

But wait, that wasn't right, for what had been the actual words she had used...

That blood will be owed to us all.

Not all of us. So, what if she hadn't been referring to Lucius at all, but what if she had been referring to the box or more like what the box could give them.

Had we all gotten this wrong?

What if the box didn't take the life of Vampires but in fact was the only other power on Earth that could gift it as Lucius did? Gods, but that would mean that anyone who had the box also had the power to build an army of rogue vampires!

But then what was the proof, other than the twisted words of a desperate witch? A witch who had reacted that way to my blood. Now why had she done that? And what had she called it?

"The blood of Kings." I repeated on a whisper as a sudden and crazy thought came to mind and before I could stop myself, I snatched the box and ran to the kitchen.

"Oh, this is bad, this is bad…" I muttered as I wrenched open the drawer and was now faced with a blade in every size. So, I tried not to think of Lucius' warning for me to be good and grabbed a large kitchen knife, holding it steady.

"Not a good idea, Fae…most definitely *not a good idea,"* I said before closing my eyes and suddenly slicing into my palm, gritting my teeth against the pain as air was sucked through them. This before I could chicken out or convince myself further on just how bad of an idea this was.

"The Blood of Kings," I said again, and then without pause I grabbed the box, coating it in my blood and holding on as it started to shake in my hold as it had done earlier.

So, this time I said again, only more forcefully,

"Open for the Blood of Kings!"

And this time…

It opened.

To be continued…

ABOUT THE AUTHOR

Stephanie Hudson has dreamed of being a writer ever since her obsession with reading books at an early age. What first became a quest to overcome the boundaries set against her in the form of dyslexia has turned into a life's dream. She first started writing in the form of poetry and soon found a taste for horror and romance. Afterlife is her first book in the series of twelve, with the story of Keira and Draven becoming ever more complicated in a world that sets them miles apart.

When not writing, Stephanie enjoys spending time with her loving family and friends, chatting for hours with her biggest fan, her sister Cathy who is utterly obsessed with one gorgeous Dominic Draven. And of course, spending as much time with her supportive partner and personal muse, Blake who is there for her no matter what.

Author's words.

My love and devotion is to all my wonderful fans that

keep me going into the wee hours of the night but foremost to my wonderful daughter Ava...who yes, is named after a cool, kick-ass, Demonic bird and my sons, Jack, who is a little hero and Baby Halen, who yes, keeps me up at night but it's okay because he is named after a Guitar legend!

Keep updated with all new release news & more on my website
www.afterlifesaga.com
Never miss out, sign up to the
mailing list at the website.

Also, please feel free to join myself and other Dravenites on my Facebook group
Afterlife Saga Official Fan
Interact with me and other fans. Can't wait to see you there!

 facebook.com/AfterlifeSaga
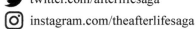 twitter.com/afterlifesaga
instagram.com/theafterlifesaga

ACKNOWLEDGEMENTS

Well first and foremost my love goes out to all the people who deserve the most thanks and are the wonderful people that keep me going day to day. But most importantly they are the ones that allow me to continue living out my dreams and keep writing my stories for the world to hopefully enjoy… These people are of course YOU! Words will never be able to express the full amount of love I have for you guys. Your support is never ending. Your trust in me and the story is never failing. But more than that, your love for me and all who you consider your 'Afterlife family' is to be commended, treasured and admired. Thank you just doesn't seem enough, so one day I hope to meet you all and buy you all a drink! ;)

To my family… To my amazing mother, who has believed in me from the very beginning and doesn't believe that something great should be hidden from the world. I would like to thank you for all the hard work you put into my books and the endless hours spent caring about my words and making sure it is the best it can be for everyone to enjoy. You make Afterlife shine. To my wonderful crazy father who is and always has been my hero in life. Your strength astonishes me, even to this day and the love and care you hold for your family is a gift you give to the Hudson name. And last but not least, to the man that I consider my soul mate. The man who taught me about real love and makes me not only want to be a better person but makes me feel I am too. The amount of support you have given me since we met has been incredible and the greatest feeling was finding out you wanted to spend the rest of your life with me when you asked me to marry you.

All my love to my dear husband and my own personal Draven… Mr Blake Hudson.

Another personal thank you goes to my dear friend Caroline Fairbairn and her wonderful family that have embraced my brand of crazy into their lives and given it a hug when most needed.

For their friendship I will forever be eternally grateful.

I would also like to mention Claire Boyle my wonderful PA, who without a doubt, keeps me sane and constantly smiling through all the chaos which is my life ;) And a loving mention goes to Lisa Jane for always giving me a giggle and scaring me to death with all her count down pictures lol ;)

Thank you for all your hard work and devotion to the saga and myself. And always going that extra mile, pushing Afterlife into the spotlight you think it deserves. Basically helping me achieve my secret goal of world domination one day…evil laugh time… Mwahaha! Joking of course ;)

As before, a big shout has to go to all my wonderful fans who make it their mission to spread the Afterlife word and always go the extra mile. I love you all x

ALSO BY STEPHANIE HUDSON

Afterlife Saga

A Brooding King, A Girl running from her past. What happens when the two collide?

Book 1 - Afterlife

Book 2 - The Two Kings

Book 3 - The Triple Goddess

Book 4 - The Quarter Moon

Book 5 - The Pentagram Child /Part 1

Book 6 - The Pentagram Child /Part 2

Book 7 - The Cult of the Hexad

Book 8 - Sacrifice of the Septimus /Part 1

Book 9 - Sacrifice of the Septimus /Part 2

Book 10 -Blood of the Infinity War

Book 11 -Happy Ever Afterlife /Part 1

Book 12 -Happy Ever Afterlife / Part 2

Transfusion Saga

What happens when an ordinary human girl comes face to face with the cruel Vampire King who dismissed her seven years ago?

Afterlife Chronicles: (Young Adult Series)

Stephanie Hudson and Blake Hudson

OTHER WORKS
BY
HUDSON INDIE INK

Paranormal Romance/Urban Fantasy

Sloane Murphy

Xen Randell

C. L. Monaghan

Sci-fi/Fantasy

Brandon Ellis

Devin Hanson

Crime/Action

Blake Hudson

Mike Gomes

Contemporary Romance

Gemma Weir

Elodie Colt

Ann B. Harrison

CPSIA information can be obtained
at www.ICGtesting.com
Printed in the USA
BVHW032038111121
621198BV00011B/101